Cul De Sac

Donald DeHarde Jr.

PublishAmerica
Baltimore

First printing

ISBN: 1-4241-4816-2
PUBLISHED BY PUBLISHAMERICA, LLLP
www.publishamerica.com
Baltimore

Printed in the United States of America

This book is dedicated to
my wife, Karen,
and daughter, Gabrielle.

Also, to my mother, Cindy,
who, sadly, never lived to see my dream become a reality.

Karen,

Great name! All
Karens have great taste

Donald D.

Chapter 1

Miranda Grant held her breath as her husband pulled up to their new house, number two Sherwood Circle. For the first three years of their married life, they had rented. Her husband Oren had recently been promoted and, after his student loans were paid off, they started house hunting. Miranda was surprised when he suggested they look in St. Bernard, a suburb fifteen minutes outside of New Orleans. She was certain he would want a place closer to the hotel. The Breakers Inn was a small motel near the lake and Oren had just been promoted to Assistant General Manager, making more money than he ever had. The truth was, both he and Miranda were scared to death. When they signed their thirty year mortgage, they were more in debt that either of them had ever been. She let out a long sigh as he turned off the car and went around to open the door for her, ready to start their next big adventure, together.

"Do I carry you over the threshold?"

"You better."

Oren bent over and scooped his wife up in his arms. He carried her through the door and put her down in the living room. She put her hands on her hips and looked around the room. They were standing in what was going to be the dining room. Miranda liked to entertain and her only request was that they got a house with a formal dining room. The room was supposed to be the living room, but the house had an extension on it for that purpose. Oren's only request was that they have a separate place for the computer so it wouldn't be in the living room anymore. The computer and desk were going in the third bedroom.

"Do you still like it?"

Miranda walked into the kitchen and back into the dining room.

"It'll do."

"It'll do?"

He picked her up and swung her around. When he put her down, she walked to the window.

"Where's the stuff? I thought your father and brother were right behind us."

"They were."

He walked up behind her, reached around and started caressing her breast.

"You now, since they're not here yet..."

She turned around and unzipped his pants. Slipping her hand inside, he was already rock hard and straining against his underwear. He looked up at her, his eyebrows raised.

"What's that?"

She started kissing him and pulled him down to the ground. Unbuttoning her shirt, he covered her breast with kisses. Miranda moaned slightly. As their passion grew, they were interrupted by the large moving van pulling into the driveway.

"Perfect timing."

Oren got up and made sure his zipper was up. Miranda buttoned her shirt and followed her husband outside.

The draped across the street parted.

"Mom, it looks like someone is moving in across the street."

Cora Mayhelm walked up to her daughter and smacked her on the back of the head.

"Don't be so nosey."

"But, Mom..."

"Go get your brothers and sister for lunch."

Her daughter gone into the back of the house, Cora turned her attention back to the window. The house across the street had been for sale for months. The people who bought it looked like a young couple. They didn't appear to have any kids. Kids were good for the neighborhood. Cora and her husband had four. The York's had two boys. Jo Ann next door had a young son. Genie Van Matthews had two children, one grown. The circle was full of children. Cora suspected that may have been one of the reasons the young couple moved in. The young woman across the street noticed Cora watching so she quickly shut the drapes.

"It looks like the welcoming committee has arrived."

"What are you talking about?"

"Someone across the street was watching us."

"I guess someone new moving in is big news in this neighborhood."

Oren's father got out of the moving van and looked around.

"Oren, your mother is going to hate that she missed this."

"We wanted to wait until we got everything set up before we showed it to anyone."

"Even your mother?"

"Yes."

"Dad, where's Charles with my car?"

Before he could answer, Oren's brother Charles pulled up in Miranda's car.

"Do I get a tour before we start all the hard work?"

"Of course."

Miranda ran up to her brother-in-law and took his arm. Oren was already inside turning on the lights and water. He had paid the deposits a few days ago and wanted to be sure everything was in order. He took a phone out of the moving van and plugged it in. So far, everything was in working order. The next day, the new furniture was coming. Everything he and Miranda had had been handed down to them when they first got married. They kept the bed and the kitchen table and chairs. Oren had bought a new living room set, bar stools to match the bar in the den and a formal dining room set and china cabinet. Miranda had insisted on new mattresses. All that would be coming tomorrow.

"Dad, we have everything clearly marked. The den is through the kitchen. Down the hall are the bedrooms. The computer and stuff goes in the small bedroom on the left. Miscellaneous stuff goes in the garage and good china goes in here."

Between the four of them, they had the truck unloaded with an hour. By the time Oren and Charlie had returned from returning the moving van, the pizza Oren had ordered for lunch had arrived. Starved from work, the men ate quickly. Not wanting to use the whole day, Oren's father and brother left as soon as they finished eating. Miranda put her hands on her hips and looked around at the mess they now had to deal with.

"I guess I'll start in the kitchen."

"I'll do the bathroom."

"Oren, that's the smallest room."

"I'll do both."

He winked at her and ran into the back of the house. Miranda laughed and started putting pots, pans and dishes away.

Genie Van Matthews reread the termination notice from the electric company. She had three days to pay the entire sum or her power was getting cut off. Her husband had walked out on her seven years ago and left her with nothing. Her youngest son Jeremy was thirteen years old. Her other son was a lawyer in the city and she thought of asking him for help but couldn't bring herself to do it. There were other single mothers who made it on their own and she was determined to be one of them. The one thing she was thankful for is that her ex-husband paid for Jeremy to go to private school. He had insisted on it. She was proud of the fact that Jeremy was on the honor roll at Mary, Mother of God. However, she could feel his embarrassment whenever she came to school functions. She didn't do anything to bring this on but knew most of his school friends came from affluent families. Genie's problem was, with only a high school education, her witnessing job barely covered the bills. Determined not to cry, she fought back the tears as Jeremy came through the door.

"Mom?"

"Hey."

"What's for dinner?"

"What's for dinner? I work all day and that's all I get?"

"Sorry."

"Well, dinner is in the microwave. I have to work tonight."

"You're working a double?"

"I'll be back after you go to bed, so I'll see you in the morning. You had better be asleep when I get home."

"Yes ma'am."

She kissed him on the forehead and walked out the door. After she was gone, Jeremy hunted around for something to snack on. Instead of cookies, he found the notice Genie had left on the counter. In a panic, he called his older brother. He would know what to do.

Gretchen York got out of van laden with bags. She struggled with the door, calling out for her two sons to follow her. As she entered the house, her husband, Ben, came in from the back bedroom.

"Do you need some help?"

"No, thank you, Benjamin. I've got it."

She put the groceries down and began to sort through them.

"I thought I'd make lasagna for the new people next door."

"Gretchen, they moved in like ten minutes ago. Besides, isn't that like a 1950s June Cleaver thing to do?"

"Look around darling. I'm a stay-at-home mom with two kids living in the suburbs. I am June Cleaver."

"June Cleaver has nothing on your lasagna."

She stopped what she was doing, suddenly unsure of herself.

"Do you really think it's too pushy, going over there with food?

"I think it's a very nice thing to do. Besides, their gas probably isn't on yet and they'll appreciate something hot. Remember how long it took for our gas to be turned on?"

She nodded and smiled.

"I'd better get to work then."

She started to preheat the oven when she heard a yell from the back of the house. She looked at Ben and raised an eyebrow.

"Do you want me to get that?"

"Do I want you to?"

Her expression gave him his answer.

"I'll take care of it."

He kissed her and went to the back of the house to see which son had killed the other.

Doris Shepherd closed her blinds. The new couple hadn't come out since they had gone inside over an hour ago. Dammit! She hadn't gotten a good look at them. Of course, the morons next door were blocking the view with their second car. Should she go to the end of the walkway to see if she could get a better view? Better not. Today was not a good day. An agoraphobic, Doris hadn't left the protection of her immediate surrounding in over ten years. On a good day, she could go into her back yard and sit on the swing where the backyard fence protected her. She thanked God her mailbox was in her front door. If it was a nice day and she was feeling really good, she would walk to the end of the walkway, never further. There were days when she hated herself for being how she was and told herself she was being silly. One time, she tried to go past the driveway and got herself so worked up, she burst into tears. She hadn't tried that since. She shrugged her shoulders and went back to her lunch.

"Crisis averted."

"What was the drama?"

"Boys being boys."

The York's had two small boys. Benjamin Jr. was seven. Timothy was five. Gretchen had wanted at least one girl, but it didn't work out. Complications from Tim's birth had lead to an emergency hysterectomy. At only twenty nine years old, a hysterectomy seemed like the end of the world. But that was five years ago and Gretchen wouldn't trade anything for her boys.

"Could you get me a strainer? Stir the noodles, too."

"Yes, ma'am."

"That's right, do what I say."

Smiling to herself, she drained the meat.

"Can you believe we have the entire house set up in three hours?"

"Just don't look in the garage."

Oren and Miranda were reveling in their efficiency.

"The new furniture comes tomorrow and then we'll have everything done."

Oren stifled a yawn.

"Are you tired? Let's go take a nap and go get something to eat later."

"You don't want to cook on the new stove?"

"I'm not doing anything until this house is completely set up."

"You were doing something earlier."

Oren smirked at his wife. She smiled and pushed him away.

"That was an impulse that has since passed. You'll have to wait until the new mattress gets here tomorrow."

"You're killing me."

"Not yet. Wait for the new furniture."

Oren followed his wife into their new bedroom. They barely got undressed before they collapsed on the bed, exhausted.

Cora and Cameron Mayhelm's four kids were never all at home at the same time. Colleen was always off with her friends. Their twin boys, Christopher and Christian, were thirteen and went to school with Jeremy Van Matthews. The three boys were inseparable, especially during the summer months when they lived in the Mayhelm's pool. Their youngest daughter Candice was a surprise. She was six and played with the York boys a lot. There always seemed to be kids in and out of the Mayhelm's house and Cora liked it that way. She would have had ten more if they could have afforded it. Cameron was happy with the ones they had and did well to support them. He owned his own garage and made enough money for Cora to be able to stay at home with the kids. He loved his whole family and secretly hoped one of his sons would follow in his footsteps. He prided himself on being a fair mechanic and tried to pass those values on to his children. On this rare Saturday afternoon, all the Mayhelms were having lunch together.

"Mom, do the new people have any kids?"

"They didn't seem to."

Christopher shrugged and went back to eating his lunch.

Miranda walked onto the back patio with a glass of wine and put her head on her husband's shoulder.

"Are you scared?"

"Yeah, it's a big step, owning a house."

Miranda nodded. Oren sipped his wine.

"Are you happy?"

Miranda got up and started pacing.

"Happy, scared, excited, I can't help but smile."

"I see your nap helped."

"Hey, you said we would have dinner."

"Grab your purse, let's go."

That night, things were winding down on Sherwood Circle. Gretchen York slid into bed next to her husband. He put his arms around her; taking her close and making her feel safe. She loved being in his arms, the way his aftershave smelt on him, the way his semi-hard flesh pressed into the back of her thigh. The sound of her husband's breathing lulled her off to sleep.

Cora turned off the television and walked into the kitchen, surprised to find her oldest daughter staring into an open refrigerator.

"Colleen, I didn't hear you walk past the living room."

"That's because you were sleeping on the sofa, snoring like a lumberjack."

"I was not."

Colleen laughed at her mother's defensiveness.

"Anyway, I was still hungry and hoped there was some ice cream left."

"I think your brothers ate it. But if you look behind the icemaker…"

Colleen rooted around and found a pint of Godiva ice cream it was her mother's favorite and cost almost five dollars a pint

"Care to share, Lady Godiva?"

"We don't have to get naked, do we?"

Cora laughed at her daughter's joke and went to get two bowls.

Genie opened the door to Jeremy's room and was satisfied he was in bed. She slipped off her shoes and ran a bath. She almost made enough tonight to cover the electric bill. The blisters on her feet were proof of how busy she had been. She undressed and sat in the hot water, relaxing every muscle as she sunk lower and lower. She needed to get the money for Jeremy's lunches this week but would worry about that later. She had to be at work tomorrow for five and was thankful that Sunday was her busy day.

Chapter 2

The next morning, Oren jumped out of bed, startled by the doorbell. They had overslept and were awaken by the furniture store. He shook Miranda awake.

"Miranda, wake up! The furniture is here."

Miranda jumped up and slid into the jeans that were beside the bed. She ran a brush through her hair before joining Oren outside. He was already directing the movers where to put the new furniture. Being professionals, it took them less than an hour to unload everything. Once they were done, Oren switched mattresses and Miranda began putting away the good china.

"It's ashamed we don't use this more."

Oren came in from the bedroom.

"What?"

"I said it's ashamed we don't use this more."

"We'll use it tonight. Our first dinner in our first house."

"I think that would be nice."

"I thought you said the furniture came yesterday."

Ben York looked up from his book.

"Whose?"

"The new people next door. I just saw a furniture van pull away. I thought they had everything yesterday."

"I guess they didn't."

"Well, it's almost time for church so I'm bringing over the lasagna I made."

Gretchen took the lasagna she had been warming and walked next door. She rang the bell at number two and waited.

"Look at her, god she makes me sick."

Jo Ann Mott looked out her window as Gretchen was leaving her house.

"I think it's a nice thing to do, bringing the new people food. I might make a cake."

Jo Ann turned to her mother, Mary.

"Don't you dare. Gretchen thinks she's so perfect. It would be just like her to do something like that."

Jo Ann Mott had grown up on Sherwood Circle. She and her young son had moved back in with her mother after her marriage ended. Her son, Chad, was almost eight and was a constant thorn in his mother's side. Diagnosed as hyperactive, he lived on daily medication. Last year, he had started a fire in the bathroom at school. Jo Ann thought he needed a psychiatrist but couldn't afford it. Mary thought her grandson was acting out as a way of getting attention. The loss of his father as a male figure in his life wasn't helping him. Jo Ann worked two jobs to support them all and all her free time was spent taking care of her aging mother. Her life was a far cry from the affluent, housewife lifestyles of Cora and Gretchen. She had heard Cameron comment that her *white trash* family brought down the property values of the otherwise picture perfect suburban existence. She longed to get her own apartment, even if it meant moving into the city. She couldn't stand being wedged between the pictures perfect Mayhelms and the crazy old lady that lived by herself.

"But..."

"No cakes, mother!"

Jo Ann sighed and looked at her watch. It was almost time to take her anti-depression medication.

"Who do you think that could be?"

"You did tip the movers, didn't you?"

"Yes."

Oren moved to the front door with Miranda hot on his heels. He opened the door and smiled at Gretchen York.

"Hello. May I help you?"

"I'm Gretchen York from next door. I just wanted to come by and introduce myself."

Oren took the food and stepped aside.

"Would you like to come in Mrs. York?"

"Gretchen, please. Actually, I'm almost ready to leave for church."

Oren finally remembered his manners.

"By the way, I'm Oren Grant. This is my wife Miranda."

The ladies shook hands while Oren put the food on the table.

"Gretchen, are you sure you can't stay for something to drink?"

"I'll take a rain check if it's okay. I shudder to think of the trouble my husband and kids are getting into. We have two boys."

Miranda smiled and led her back to the door.

"Well, stop by anytime for that drink and next time, bring your husband."

Miranda waved her out the door. Shutting the door, she turned to Oren and rolled her eyes.

"Oh my god. Can you believe that? Bringing food over, what is this 1957? And I see she put it in a real lasagna pan so I'll have to go over there and return it. I can imagine what the inside of her house looks like, like Martha Stewart threw up in there."

"She has two kids. I doubt her house is spotless."

The doorbell rang again.

"She's back. She probably knitted potholders with our initials on them so we won't burn ourselves on the hot pan."

Oren laughed. He couldn't imagine why his wife had taken such an immediate dislike to their new neighbor, but she was still funny. When Miranda opened the door, it wasn't Gretchen York standing there, but Christopher Mayhelm.

"Yes sir, can I help you?"

"Ma'am, my name is Christopher Mayhelm. I live across the street. I came by because I used to cut the grass for the people that used to live here and was wondering if you did that yourself or if you were looking for someone to do it."

"Well, as a matter of fact Chris, my husband hates manual labor. How much do you charge and how often do you come by?"

"Twenty bucks, once a week."

"It's a deal."

"Thank you, I'll see you next week."

"Bye, Chris."

Miranda shut the door and called out to Oren who was already slicing up the lasagna.

"I got you a grass cutter."

"Who?"

"Some little guy who lives across the street. He used to do it for the people that lived here before."

"Works for me."

He came out of the kitchen, stuffing his face.

"Say what you want. This shit is good."

"Would you get out of here with that!"

"This is the dining room."

"Move it!"

The Sunday lunch rush at The Breakers was crazy. With the seafood buffet on the weekends, it was their busiest time and Genie Van Matthews was a pro at it. She floated from table to table, never flinching if she had more people or had to pick up the slack of a new girl. She was practically working two sections at the present time. She went to her next table and was infuriated at the fact that the guy wouldn't even put his paper down to look her in the face. He probably thought he was too good to give her the common courtesy of looking at her when he ordered.

"Good afternoon sir, would you like to start with something to drink?"

The guy put his paper down and smirked at her. It was her ex-husband Geoffrey. She rolled her eyes and sighed.

"Geoffrey, I'm too busy for this."

"What? I just want lunch, just like everyone else."

"And you came here?"

"The food sucks but I hear the service is pretty good."

"What do you want to drink?"

"Sweet tea."

Without a word, Genie left the table and went to the back, furious.

"Benjamin Daniel!"

"I'm right here, Momma."

"I'm yelling for your father, darling."

Gretchen hated being late for church. The York's were one of the founding families of Mary, Mother of God parish. Ben and his sister had gone to school there from preschool to twelfth grade and now her two boys went there. There was never any doubt that the York boys would be at Mary's. It was tradition.

"What's all the yelling for?"

"We're late."

"No we're not. Look, Cora and Cameron haven't even left yet. As if on cue, all the Mayhelms came out of the house and piled into the minivan. They pulled into the parking lot behind one another. Discretely, they tried to find seats together, a feat nearly impossible with six kids. Once they were all seated, Gretchen gave her boys a stern look, warning them to behave.

Cameron watched as Colleen whispered something in her mother's ear and then got up to sit by a boy he didn't know.

"What was that all about?"

"I'll explain later."

Cameron looked over to where his daughter was sitting and saw her holding hands with a boy he knew nothing about. The choir leader announced the opening hymn and everyone stood up.

Genie was pacing frantically in the back break room when her boss found her.

"Your tables are waiting for you."

"I'll be there in a minute."

She took a drag off the cigarette she had clutched between her fingers.

"I never knew you smoked."

"Very little, when I'm stressed."

"Is it a customer? You've handled busy Sundays before."

"It is a customer. My ex-husband is here and I can't deal with him."

"Which table?"

"Twenty four."

"Relax. I'll handle it."

Parker Winslow went back into the dining room.

As the closing prayers were finishing, Father Thomas Bradley stood up and addressed the congregation.

"Friends, it is with a heavy heart that I address you today. Next week will be my last week here at Mary, Mother of God's. I'm retiring."

There were gasps from the crowd. Father Tom had been with the parish since the beginning. Cora took Cameron's hand. It was Father Tom she had turned to when she and Cameron were having marital problems a few years ago.

"I've baptized many of you, married more of you and buried some of your family members. This decision wasn't an easy one for me. My replacement will be Father David West. He's the young guy you may have seen hovering around me for the past few weeks. I will miss all of you and will keep all of you in my thoughts and prayers."

The closing hymn was announced and Father Tom exited the church. Everyone started to file out. Cameron noticed his wife was visibly shaken.

"How about going to The Breakers for lunch?"

"That sounds nice."

Cameron took his wife's hand and they walked out together.

"Uncle Allen!"

Allen Boudreaux bent over and hugged his two nephews. He was married to Ben's sister, Hope. Ben walked up and shook his brother-in-law's hand.

"Allen, where's my sister?"

"Over there with Bea, planning a going away party for Father Tom."

"That was quick."

"You know Bea de la Roche."

Ben looked over and saw Hope had gotten Gretchen into the planning. Bea was giving instructions with great fervor. You would think she was discussing her views on abortion or the moon landing. He smiled and turned back to Allen.

"How's the house hunting going?"

"Slow."

"The house next door to me is going up for sale."

"I thought Gretchen said a new family had moved in yesterday."

"The other side, number six."

Allen nodded.

"I'll talk to Hope about it."

Allen had no desire to live next to his brother-in-law but figured it wouldn't hurt to take a look. It was probably out of their price range anyway, but would pacify Hope for a while.

Miranda was coming out of the house when the woman at number three came out screaming. Moments earlier, Miranda had almost been run over by a small boy on a bike.

"Chad! Chad Michael!"

When it was apparent that the boy wasn't going to stop, the woman shook her head and lit a cigarette. She noticed the new girl across the street watching her.

"Don't ever have kids."

"What?"

Miranda, embarrassed at being caught watching, walked across the street.

"What did you just say?"

"I said don't ever have kids. They're a pain in the ass."

"Point taken. I don't have any kids yet. Is he your only one?"

"Yeah. Chad. He's eight going on twenty-two."

Miranda smiled. The woman obviously had her hands full. She didn't see a wedding ring and assumed the woman was a single mother.

"I'm Miranda Grant. My husband Oren and I just moved in across the street."

"I know. I saw the welcome wagon bearing gifts this morning."

"That was our new furniture."

"No. I mean Mary Sunshine from next door."

"She brought lasagna."

"It's probably pretty good. She has nothing else to do all day but cook. She doesn't work and her kids are in school."

Jo Ann flicked her cigarette into the grass and introduced herself.

"Jo Ann Mott."

She extended her hand. Miranda shook it.

"Nice to meet you, Jo Ann."

"Oh no, that won't do. That won't do at all."

Doris huffed as she closed her curtains. The new girl in number two was making friends with the trash from next door. That wouldn't do. She had to call someone, but whom? She had lived in her house for over twenty years but hardly knew her neighbors. She could call Cora, but knew she was at church. Should she walk out front and introduce herself? Better not. She was too busy today to venture out. Too many things to do. Yea, she was just too busy.

"Sir, are you ready to order yet?

Geoffrey looked up from his menu.

"Where's Genie?

"She's at lunch. I'm working her tables now. My name is Nova and I'll be happy to get you whatever you need."

"Sweet tea."

"I'll be right back."

Nova went back into the kitchen where Genie was watching.

"Thanks Nova."

"No big deal."

Nova went about getting what she needed. Parker took Genie aside.

"Do you think he wants to see the kids?"

"Which kids, Park? The one who's wedding he missed or the thirteen year old that can't stand hearing about him?"

"Was it that bad?"

"I have to be civil so he'll keep paying Jeremy's tuition."

She ran her hands through her hair and smiled when the Mayhelms came through the door. Cora waved to Genie. Genie waved back and went to get their menus. She led them to the back of the restaurant. She knew what they all drank and went to fix their drinks. Geoffrey stopped her when she passed his table.

"I thought you were at lunch."

"I'm back. And I wasn't at lunch, I was on a break. I'm leaving as soon as I finish with Cameron and Cora."

"I was hoping we could talk."

"I told you before, I'm busy."

She walked away without waiting for his response.

"Do you want to come inside for some tea or something?"

"If it's no trouble."

"Take advantage. It's probably as neighborly as I'll ever get."

Miranda laughed and followed her inside. Once in the house, Miranda looked around. The house was clean but not very neat. Miranda could smell the cigarette smoke in the air, something she despised in her own house. Smoking didn't bother her, but she didn't like when the smell seeped into everything.

"Excuse the mess. I was yelling at Chad about picking up when he ran off."

Jo Ann poured two glasses of tea and motioned for Miranda to sit down.

"Do you smoke?"

"No."

"Do you mind if I do?"

"Jo Ann, it's your house. Go right ahead."

"I know, but I don't want to be rude."

Miranda shook her head and Jo Ann lit up. Jo Ann's mother, Mary, came in from the back of the house.

"What was all that yelling about?"

"Your grandson. I told him to pick up the damn video games and he took off for god knows where."

"He's probably over at Kathleen's."

Mary's other daughter, Kathleen, lived two streets over. She had a husband and three kids. They lived the kind of life Mary wished for Jo Ann, but things didn't work out. Within her first year of marriage, Mary noticed the bruises on Jo Ann. Questioning her led nowhere. Mary's thoughts were interrupted by the phone. Jo Ann grabbed the phone.

"Hello."

"I think I have something here that belongs to you."

It was her sister, Kathleen.

"Send him over here so I can tan his butt."

"He's eating. I'll send him over when he's done."

"Kathleen, I have food here. I am not broke!"

"Jo Ann, he came over and we were having lunch. What was I supposed to do?"

"Never mind, just send him home when he's done."

Jo Ann hung up the phone and went to find something to eat for her and her mother.

Later that afternoon, Miranda and Oren were sitting in the living room when the doorbell rang. Oren got up as Miranda rolled her eyes.

"I thought the suburbs were supposed to be quiet."

Oren shook his head and went to get the door. Standing in the doorway was his best friend from work, Gage Trenton and his wife, Serena.

"Come on in you guys."

At the sound of Serena Trenton's voice, Miranda's blood began to boil. Two years ago, Miranda had gotten pregnant by accident. Despite the financial burden they weren't ready for and the rift it caused in their relationship, Miranda and Oren decided to keep the baby. During an argument while the two women were alone, Serena pushed Miranda down a flight of stairs and she lost the baby. Miranda resenting Serena, the two women kept the secret between them. Even Oren thought his wife fell down and was found by their good friend. Unwillingly, Miranda joined her husband in the dining room.

"Miranda, this place looks fantastic."

"Thank you."

"We brought you this as a house warming present."

Miranda took the box and opened it. She had to admit, despite the fact that she was a baby killer, Serena had good taste.

"Oren told us what the bathroom motifs were, so we got you some towels, bath towels, hand towels, facecloths, you know, stuff like that."

Miranda put the box down and hugged Serena and Gage. She was playing the part of the perfect suburban hostess to the tee.

"Oren, go open that bottle of champagne while I give them the grand tour."

She led them down the hall to the bedrooms. When they got back to the dining room, Oren was waiting with four champagne glasses. Oren passed them around and Serena made a toast.

"Here's to the Grants. May your new home be filled with children."

Before she realized what she had said, Serena felt Miranda's eyes cut her in two. Oren felt the tension and tried to lighten the mood.

"That's what we're hoping."

He clinked glasses and put his arm around his wife.

"I hope you guys can stay for dinner."

Gage looked at his wife, then nodded to Miranda.

"I made lasagna."

Oren followed his wife into the kitchen to applaud her hostess skills. He found her hacking the food into chunks and putting it on plates.

"Can you fucking believe what she just said?"

"About children?"

"How heartless can one person possible be?"

"She probably just wasn't thinking. I'm sure it was an accident."

"Like the accident I had? When I lost the baby?"

"Do you want me to ask her to leave?"

"No, I'll be fine."

She grabbed two of the plates and went into the dining room. Oren sighed and followed her.

"So, Scott, what are your plans for the summer?"

Colleen wanted to die. Her father was giving the guy she was interested in the third degree. Scott was handling himself well.

"Just work for now, sir. I work in the deli at Sav-U-More."

"Colleen just got a job there as a cashier."

Colleen clarified the situation.

"My parents said if I got a job this summer, I wouldn't have to go to summer camp."

"You used to love summer camp."

"When I was twelve."

She turned back to Scott.

"My brothers and sister are going to camp for six weeks."

"Which camp?"

"Country Acres."

"I went there."

"Went where?"

Cora returned to the table and saved her daughter.

"Mom, Scott went to the same summer camp the kids are going to."

Cora loved hearing her daughter refer to her siblings as, "the kids." She would be eighteen at the end of the summer and was acting so grown up.

"You know, Scott, you and Colleen were probably there at the same time."

"Maybe."

As Genie was passing out the drinks, Cora and Cameron exchanged glances.

"You know, Scott, with you and Colleen both working this summer, I hope you'll stop by and visit this summer. Mr. Mayhelm almost has the pool ready."

"Thanks, Miss Cora, I'd like that a lot."

Genie bent down and gave Cameron his drink and he raised his eyebrows at her. Genie, remembering what it was like when her son was that age, smiled at Cameron and patted his arm.

"Miranda, you went through too much trouble."

Serena noticed they were eating on what looked like good china.

"Nonsense, Oren and I were just saying we need to use these dishes more often. Our first impromptu dinner party in our new house seemed like the perfect occasion."

"Speaking of occasions, you should have a housewarming party. Get to know the new neighbors. Oren, didn't you say your mother hasn't seen the house yet?"

"She hasn't."

"I think a party is a great idea. I could invite my brother. You know it's been so long since I've seen him. We were so close, I miss him."

Miranda smiled to herself, trying her best not to look at Serena. Two years earlier, right after Miranda lost the baby, Serena's brother was murdered. If Serena was going to hit below the belt about babies, Miranda was going to hit lower about brothers. She smiled as she ate, ignoring Oren's eyes boring into her.

Chapter 3

The next morning, having taken the weekend off to move in, Oren and Miranda returned to work. They were both getting into their cars when Jo Ann came out of her house to get the paper.

"Jo Ann, did Chad ever show up last night?"

"Yea, the little shit was at my sister's house."

"See you later."

Miranda waved and Oren looked at her strangely.

"New friend?"

"Maybe."

"The nerve."

Ben was finishing his coffee and looked up at his wife.

"What's that?"

"I bring food over and she's over there talking to Jo Ann! She needs to be careful who she associates with if she wants to fit in around here."

"Give her a break. Jo Ann isn't that bad."

"You know for someone who was brought up the way you were, you are a horrible judge of character."

"I didn't realize being psychic was a curse of the well to do."

She was going to be late. For the past fifteen minutes, Genie searched for the electric bill that was past due. It wasn't where she had left it, in her bedroom, or any of the usual places. She gave up and finished getting ready for work. Jeremy would be getting up in an hour. He could get himself ready and off to Cora's. All the kids walked to school together. Genie took one more look around before getting in her car and heading to work.

"Mom, have you seen my gym uniform?"

"Mom, I don't want peanut butter for lunch again."

"Mom, Sister Joan says if I don't get a haircut by the end of this week, she's going to cut it for me."

Cora moved around her kitchen with the skill of a traffic cop. Monday mornings brought their usual chaos and today was no exception.

"Colleen, gym uniform, in the dryer. Candice, fine, take two dollars out of my purse for lunch. Christopher, chill out, we're getting your hair cut tomorrow."

"Hey, if Candice gets to buy lunch, I want to."

"Candice, get money out for your brother too."

Cameron came into the kitchen, surprised by the fact that his wife hadn't had a nervous breakdown yet. He went over and kissed her good morning. She had every intention of kissing him back but was distracted by one of her sons spilling his juice.

"Dammit!"

"Christian, watch your mouth!"

She handed him a paper towel as the doorbell rang.

"That would be Jeremy. Cameron, could you let him in?"

Cameron smiled at his wife and went to get the door. Cora called out to him.

"Jeremy, do you want cereal?"

"Mom, all I could find was ten dollars."

Cora looked down at her daughter.

"Candice, you're not even in your uniform yet? Why are you worried about lunch money when you're not even dressed?"

She pushed her daughter back into her room and took out a bowl for Jeremy's cereal.

"You, eat."

Cameron laughed.

"You want ten more?"

"Bring it on. This is the best exercise I get."

"Try and have a good day."

"You too, sweetie."

Amazingly, fifteen minutes later, the house was quiet again. Cora went to change before starting the breakfast dishes. She despised being in her robe and pajamas all day. She always tried to wear matching separates, shoes and socks and always tried to fix her hair, at least in a decent ponytail. At least this way, she didn't look like a frumpy old housewife.

When she finally got a break, Genie called the electric company. She needed to request another copy of her bill. After going through the hoops of the electronic phone system, she finally got to talk to a real person.

"Yes ma'am, I need another copy of my bill. I'm sending it off and I can't find it."

"What's the address ma'am?"

"Number eight, Sherwood Circle. St. Bernard."

"After a moment, the lady came back on the line."

"Mrs. Van Matthews, that bill has been paid."

"What?"

"Yes ma'am. The bill was paid online Saturday by Patrick Van Matthews."

"Thank you."

Genie hung up the phone and thought for a moment. How could her son Patrick know about the overdue bill and the termination notice? Someone must have told him. Jeremy. Jeremy must have found the bill, panicked, and called his older brother. She hung up the phone and dialed her son's office.

"McKenzie Van Matthews."

"Patrick Van Matthews's office please."

She waited while she was transferred and finally her oldest son picked up his line. Patrick was a partner in a small law firm in the city. He had gotten through college and law school on scholarships. Two years into law school, he met and married his wife Melissa, a secretary at the Hotel Bentley. After six years of marriage, Genie was still waiting for grandchildren. When Pat announced he was leaving his big firm to start his own practice with a law school friend of his, Genie figured she would have to wait longer than expected to be a grandmother. Pat's career was obviously his main focus.

"Patrick Van Matthews."

"Pat, it's your mother."

He knew exactly why she was calling. His little brother called him Saturday in a panic, afraid their lights would be cut off. He immediately went to his computer and paid the bill online.

"What's up?"

"Did Jeremy call you about our light bill?"

"Yes he did."

"I wish he wouldn't have done that."

"He was scared. I wish you would have called me sooner."

"I didn't want to ask you for anything."

"You're my mother. I owe you at least that much."

"Well, I got the money. I want you to come and pick it up."

"No. If you have it, send it to them and get a start on next month. How did you get the money so quickly by the way?"

"I robbed a bank."

"Very funny. Listen, I don't want you working doubles at the restaurant. You're going to kill yourself, Mom."

"Let me worry about that."

Patrick smiled and started to end the conversation when Genie interrupted.

"While I have you on the phone, I might as well tell you. Your father is in town."

"I don't have a father, not since he walked out on you and Jeremy."

"I'm just warning you. He may try to see you."

"Thanks for the warning."

Genie wrapped up the conversation and went back to work.

"Your sister is dating a jackass."

The bell for homeroom rang and Jeremy and Christopher took their seats.

"He's not that bad."

"Scott Winslow, right?"

"Yes."

"He's the guy who kicked my ass last year for touching his car, which I didn't do."

"That was him?"

"That was him."

"Well, he had lunch with us yesterday and he seemed nice."

Jeremy rolled his eyes at his friend.

"Yea, well don't touch his car."

That afternoon, Gretchen herded Tim and Ben Jr. into the car and headed for her sister-in-law's house. They were going shopping for decorations for Father Tom's going away party. Ben, resigned to the fact that he was alone for dinner, went to take a shower. He had left work early, looking forward to spending the evening with his family, but figured he would enjoy the peace and quiet just as much.

Jo Ann parked her car and used every ounce of energy she had left to pull herself out. She had just finished her shift at Barrister's Department Store and needed a nap before her next job. Overnight, she cleaned offices from eleven to seven a.m. Thankfully, her mother would start dinner and help Chad with his homework. She hated relying on Mary so much, but didn't know what she would do without her. She wanted to get out of her mother's house but admitted to herself that it was highly unlikely. She walked into the house and called out to Chad. When he didn't answer, she went into her mother's room.

"Have you seen Chad?"

"No I haven't. I assumed he was in his room."

"You don't know?"

Jo Ann went to Chad's room and immediately worried when it was empty.

"Do you think he went to Kathleen's again?"

"Let me call."

Jo Ann dialed her sister's number, trying to calm her nerves and clear her mind of all the bad possibilities.

Miranda unloaded Gretchen's lasagna pan from the dishwasher and walked next door to return it. She knocked on the door and waited. When she didn't get an answer. She knocked again. Finally, Ben answered the door wrapped only in a towel.

"Can I help you?"

Miranda was dumfounded. She couldn't get her thoughts together, her mind taken in by the *Playgirl* centerfold standing in front of her. The water from the shower made his perfectly chiseled chest and stomach glisten. His chest was bare and broad, but Miranda couldn't help but notice the blonde trail of hair leading from his belly button to the forbidden place hidden by his towel. Finally, she found the words.

"I'm Miranda Grant from next door. I'm returning your wife's lasagna pan."

"Nice to meet you, Miranda. I'm Ben York."

She shook his hand and almost died at the sight of the muscles in his arm flexing.

"Give this to Gretchen and tell her we enjoyed it."

"I'll pass on the message."

"I didn't mean to interrupt your shower."

"No. I got off of work early and was just enjoying the time alone."

"I did too, got off work early I mean."

"What do you do?"

"I'm the head chef at Mariners."

"Well, you should be cooking for us then."

"It's a date."

Miranda turned and walked home, cursing herself for being happily married.

"No, Jo Ann, he's not here."

"If he shows up, call me."

"Is anything wrong?"

"He didn't come home from school today."

"Maybe he's still there."

"It's after four."

"Well, call me when he gets in."

"I will."

Jo Ann hung up the phone and ran to her car. She had to drive to the school, just to see if he was there. Maybe he had missed the bus. She got in her car in such a hurry; she didn't notice Miranda waving to her from across the street.

Oren walked into the Breakers for a late lunch. He had to stay late at the hotel today because the general manager was out of town. This was the first time today he was able to stop and eat. He was sitting waiting when he noticed one of his favorite waitresses leaving.

"Going home, Genie?"

"Finally, yeah."

"Have a good day."

"You, too, enjoy your dinner."

"Lunch."

"Lunch?"

"I had a ton of work today and am now finally getting to eat."

"Is the hotel busy?"

"No. I took some days off to move. My wife and I just bought our first house."

Genie tilted her head. She knew she recognized the car parked in front of number two.

"Did you just move to Sherwood Circle?"

"Yes."

"I'm at number eight, three doors down from you, or five, depending which way you walk around the circle."

Oren smiled at her.

"Small world."

"No kidding."

"Well, I'll see you around neighbor."

Oren paid for his food and headed back to the hotel.

Jo Ann pulled in front of the school and ran into the office, hoping the secretary was still there. Thankfully, an older woman sat behind a computer.

"Can I help you, ma'am?

"I'm looking for my son, Chad Mott."

After a few keystrokes and the shuffling of paper, the woman looked up at Jo Ann.

"Mrs. Mott, he was checked out today at one fifteen."

"What? Chad Mott?"

"Yes, ma'am."

"But that's impossible. The only two people authorized to check him out are I and my mother and I've been at work all day."

The secretary went to the filing cabinet and rooted around. She pulled out a piece of paper.

"I thought that was unusual, so I researched it. Here."

She handed the paper to Jo Ann. It was a form authorizing Chad's father to check him out of school.

"See here, it was updated February of this year."

"I didn't sign this."

"I double checked the signatures Mrs. Mott. They matched."

"Thank you."

Stunned, Jo Ann walked back to her car. Forgery was one of her ex-husband's many talents. Why would Louie take Chad out of school? He hadn't seen him in months, let alone shown any interest in his education. She tried to tell herself there was an explanation, but her gut told her something was wrong. She got in her car and drove home, trying to calm herself down.

Chapter 4

Bea de la Roche held back her emotions as Father Tom began to load these things into his truck. He began moving out of the rectory earlier that day, making room for the new priest. Bea had been the church secretary for almost ten years, nearly half the time Fr. Tom had been at Mary, Mother of God.

"Bea, call Tessa Martin and let her know I will do her wedding as planned."

"Yes, Father."

Bea flipped open the Rolodex and began looking for the number she needed. Father David West came into the rectory carrying the first of his boxes. At twenty-six, Bea considered him too young to take on the responsibilities of a whole parish. The way he was dressed made him look more like a camp counselor than a priest. Bea was so used to the habits and styling of the old fashioned priest she was used to working for, she figured getting used to this new young man was going to take some time.

"Oh, Father West, I didn't know you wore a beard."

"No, I just haven't shaved in a few days. I wish you would call me Father David."

"We'll see."

Bea returned her attention back to the phone.

"Mother!"

Jo Ann called out to her mother and ran into the kitchen for the phone. Mary came running in from the back.

"Where is he? Did you find him?"

"Louis checked him out of school."

"I thought only you or I could do that."

"He forged my authorization."

"How did he do that?"

"Forgery was always one of his better talents."

Jo Ann picked up the phone and started dialing.

"Who are you calling?"

"Louis."

After a few rings, a woman answered the phone. She sounded stoned and Jo Ann knew immediately who it was. She only hoped Chad wasn't over there if her ex-husband's new wife was getting stoned.

"Brandy, it's Jo Ann Mott. I need to talk to Louie."

"Well, if that son of a bitch ever decides to come back home, I'll pass the message."

"What do you mean?"

"Lou hasn't been home in three days. His probation officer called and said he missed a meeting. Typical asshole."

"Do you have any idea where he might have gone?"

"What do you care? You didn't care when you were married to him."

Jo Ann sighed. She could only imagine the lies Louis had told this dumb girl.

"Brandy, he has Chad. He checked Chad out of school today and apparently disappeared."

"Don't panic and don't call the cops yet."

Brandy began to panic. The cops would definitely come to the apartment looking for Louie and she had enough coke in the place for a week-long party. Jo Ann knew exactly what was going through her head.

"I'm going to check out some of his old stomping grounds. I'll call you after I call them."

"Good, let me know."

Jo Ann hung up and Brandy began searching for a suitable hiding spot. She stopped to look at herself in the mirror and knew she had to clean herself up first.

"I don't think she likes me very much."

David sat his boxes down next to the bed in his new room. Tom knew exactly who he was talking about.

"Who Bea? Relax. She's just some little old church bitty. She does know her job though, so try to stay on her good side."

"She does know that retiring was your job and that I was assigned here by my boss."

"She does. Relax; you'll get a much better reception at the party Sunday."

"I can imagine. It's your retirement party, Tom. I'm going to look like this young ringer they brought in to replace you."

"Listen David, this parish is full of good people. They'll get to know you and embrace you as family. You'll see. Relax."

"You say that a lot."

"I know, it's my new mantra."

"What did she say? Does she know where Louis is?"

Jo Ann turned to her mother.

"No she doesn't. I'm going to look for them."

"Now? Jo Ann call the police first."

"No, I need to get to some of Louie's old hang outs before it gets dark."

Jo Ann grabbed her keys and ran out the door. Mary closed her eyes and said a silent prayer for her daughter and grandson.

Cora sat by the television and busied herself sewing. Colleen looked at her mother and shook her head.

"Mom, only old ladies sew."

"Yea, well middle aged mothers sew their sons' names into their clothes when they go off to camp."

"You are hardly middle aged."

Cora smiled.

"Listen, your father will be home soon. Would you mind setting the table and stirring the rice on the stove?"

Colleen did as she was asked. While she was setting the table, Cora kept the conversation rolling.

"That was nice meeting Scott yesterday."

"I'm glad you finally got to meet him."

"Does he go to Mary's, too?"

"Yes."

"Is he a senior, too?"

"Yes. Why so many questions?"

"I just wanted to know how serious you two are. You're going to be seeing a lot more of each other at work and school."

Oh god, was this the talk? Colleen thought she was too old for this, but her mother had never had the girls' only talk with her. They chatted briefly when she was eleven and got her period, but had never talked about sex together. Colleen decided to steer the conversation away.

"School is almost over and we'll never see each other at work. I'm a cashier. He's in the deli. They're at opposite ends of the store."

"Just asking."

There was a knock on the door and Colleen was relieved her mother's attention was diverted. Cora went to answer the door and smiled at her new neighbor.

"Hi, I'm Miranda Grant from across the street. I just wanted to drop off this invitation. My husband and I are throwing a little party to get to know the neighbors this Saturday."

"Well, you can get to know me now. I'm Cora Mayhelm. I wanted to come over sooner, but I've been busy. I have four kids."

"I think I hired one of your sons to cut my grass. Chris I think."

"Which one?"

"Excuse me?"

"Which Chris? Twins. Christian and Christopher."

"Doesn't that get confusing?"

"Not to me. Although my mother in law brings it up whenever she can, usually at family gatherings."

Miranda smiled.

"I guess I'll have to find some other way to tell them apart."

"Good luck, especially since they work together when they cut the grass."

"Goodness. Well, I hope we'll see you on Saturday."

"We'll be there."

Miranda smiled and went next door to Jo Ann's house. She knocked on the door and Mary opened it immediately, hoping it was Louis with Chad.

"Hi, Mary, is Jo Ann home?"

"No honey, she's out."

"I just wanted to drop off this invitation for a party we're having Saturday night. We hope the three of you can make it. Chad's invited, too."

"I'll talk to her abut it when she gets back."

Miranda could tell something was bothering the older lady.

"Mary, is something wrong?"

"Jo Ann went out looking for Chad. His father checked him out of school today and disappeared."

"Did you call the police?"

"Not yet. Jo Ann went looking for him first."

"Well, let me know if there's anything I can do."

"I will, thanks."

Miranda left awkwardly. She felt horrible delivering a party invitation when her new friend's son was missing.

Jo Ann sped to the third bar on her list. Her mind kept returning to a movie she had seen once. A man kidnapped his son, drugged him and set his hotel room on fire. The little boy was Chad's age and was scarred for life; having had third degree burns over ninety percent of his body. Jo Ann couldn't understand how anyone could do that to their child. After all, the movie was based on a true story.

Genie pulled up to her house behind a car she didn't recognize. She went into her house and found Geoffrey helping himself to coffee.

"How did you get in here?"

"I still have the key. This is still my house."

"This is your mother's house. You lost all rights when you walked out on us."

"Can I get you some coffee?"

"Geoffrey, you need to leave. Jeremy will be home any minute and I'm sure he won't be pleased to see you."

Genie sorted through the mail and picked up the invitation to the Grant's party.

"What's this?"

"One of your neighbors dropped that off."

"And you answered the door?"

"Yes."

"And you gave the impression you still live here?"

"Yes."

"Dammit Geoffrey!"

She threw down the invitation and walked past him. He stopped her by grabbing her arm. He pulled her close to him and started kissing her deeply. Her legs weakened as a passion she had forgotten started to burn inside her. Finally she remembered who he was and tried to pushed him off, slapping him.

"No."

"Leave her alone!"

Genie turned to see Jeremy standing in the kitchen doorway.

"Jeremy, you're father and I were just talking."

"Good to see you, bud."

"Don't call me that. Don't ever call me that."

Genie had noticed Jeremy's ands were closed in tight fists. Was her thirteen year old planning to hit his father? She couldn't be sure he wasn't. She went to him and steered him to his room.

"Let me show him out and then we'll do dinner."

Once he was out of the room, Genie gave up and collapsed in a chair.

"What do you want, Geoffrey."

"I want to see you. I want to talk, alone."

She gave up.

"Fine."

"Terrific. Meet me for dinner at my hotel."

"Drinks."

"No dinner?"

"Remember our first date? Dinner gets me pregnant."

"Drinks then. Nine o'clock?"

"Which hotel?"

"The Bentley in the city."

"You're lucky I'm off tomorrow."

"I'll meet you downstairs."

Jo Ann walked into her house and immediately went over to the phone. She lit a cigarette and dialed nine one one.

"Did you find him?"

Jo Ann looked at her mother with tears in her eyes.

"No."

Finally, the operator picked up.

"Hello, I'd like to report a missing child."

Jo Ann could barely hold back the tears as she gave the woman her information. She hung up the phone.

"That didn't take very long."

"They're sending the cops over to fill out a report. I'd better call Brandy."

She picked up the phone again and dialed Louie's wife.

"Brandy, it's Jo Ann. Look, I just called the police. No, I couldn't find him."

In a moment of desperation, Jo Ann pleaded with her ex-husband's new wife.

"Brandy, are you sure you don't know where they may have gone. Yea, I checked all those places. Please call me if you hear from them."

She hung up the phone and, unable to say anything, turned to Mary. She collapsed, crying, into her mother's arms.

"You know, Hope, you and Allen should look into the house next door to us."

Gretchen was gathering her things to go home. The two women had finished the decorations for Father Bradley's retirement party.

"It's three bedrooms, one and a half bathrooms. It has a huge back yard."

"I'll see what Allen says."

"It's a good neighborhood for a family."

Gretchen knew exactly what to say to her sister-in-law. She knew Hope was anxious to start a family.

"Anyway, Bea wants us at the hall an hour before Mass starts."

"Sounds good to me."

"Ben! Tim! Let's go!"

The two boys followed their mother out to the car and climbed into the back seat. She had her own reasons for wanting family living next door, built in babysitters.

Oren pulled into his driveway exhausted. He went into his house and looked for Miranda.

"What's with the police car outside?"

"Oh god."

"What's up?"

"Mary told me Jo Ann's son is missing."

"Oh my god."

"I'm going to see if she needs anything."

"Do you think that's a good idea? She may need to be alone right now."

"She may need a friend. From what she tells me, she has none in the circle. Everyone thinks she's trash."

"Well, she doesn't take care of her yard."

"Oren, we don't even know her, how can you make that judgment? Besides, she still doesn't deserve to have her child missing."

Miranda ran out the front door.

Gretchen parted her curtains.

"I wonder what Jo Ann's kid did now."

"What?"

Ben looked up from doing the dishes.

"There's a cop car across the street. Her little juvenile delinquent probably broke into someone's house or something. There goes the new girl from next door running across the street. They sure are chummy."

"I don't know. We did get invited to their house this weekend for a housewarming party."

"That'll be nice. I'll go tomorrow and pick something up."

"Speaking of this weekend, how did the decorations come out?"

"Pretty good. I talked to Hope abut the house next door."

"That's odd, I talked to Allen about it last week at church."

"Did he seem interested?"

"I couldn't tell. I wouldn't want to seem too anxious. The house isn't even listed yet."

"No, but it will be."

Gretchen walked over to Ben and kissed him.

"Sorry about dinner. The boys and I had fast food."

"That's fine. I pretty much worked all evening."

"All work and no play makes Ben a dull boy."

"Not dull, horny."

Gretchen smiled seductively at her husband.

"Let me give the boys a bath and I'll meet you in bed in an hour."

"Sounds good to me."

Genie was walking out the door when she called out to Jeremy.

"Jeremy, I'll be back in a while. Miss Cora is home if you need anything."

"Where are you going?"

"Out."

"With him?"

"Yes, if you must know."

Jeremy shook his head and started to walk away.

"I give up on you."

The thirteen year old's attitude infuriated his mother.

"Hey. Listen young man, I am a grown woman and can make my own decisions without any backtalk. Do you understand?"

"Yes."

"Yes, what?"

"Yes, ma'am."

Jeremy went back to his room feeling defeated. Her son's attitude bothered Genie. Was she making a mistake?

"Here's his latest school picture."

Jo Ann handed Chad's picture to the police. Miranda, wanting to be there for her friend but not wanting to get in the way, busied herself making coffee. She carried the tray into the living room and sat next to Jo Ann.

"Ms. Mott, is this your ex-husband's latest address?"

"The most recent one I know of, yes."

"I need you to sign this. It's a release for a wiretap to be out on your phone. We'll monitor it from the station."

He slid the paper over to her. Jo Ann signed it and slid it back.

Jo Ann had been in a trance-like state since she had gotten back from the bars. She knew the police were talking to her but had no idea what they were saying.

"Ms. Mott, do you understand?"

"Yes."

She had no idea what she was agreeing to. The police got up and returned moments later with the phone equipment. Once it was installed, Mary walked the police to their car. Miranda suddenly felt out of place.

"Jo Ann, I'm going to go home. Call me if there's any news."

"I will. Thanks for coming by."

After Miranda left, Jo Ann went to her room and took a sleeping pill. Despite the horror that had become her life in the last few hours, within minutes, she was sleeping soundly.

"Hello."

Patrick Van Matthews hurried to catch the phone on the second ring. His wife Melissa had gone to bed earlier with a headache and he didn't want to work her.

"Pat, it's me."

Patrick, surprised to hear his little brother's voice so late, smiled to himself.

"You should be in bed."

"It's not even ten."

"It's a school night."

"I always stay by myself when Mom's working late."

"Is she working late tonight? I asked her not to do that."

"That's why I called. She went out to meet our father."

"She told me he was in town."

"Did she tell you that I caught them kissing this afternoon?"

The thought infuriated Patrick but he knew he had to tread lightly as not to hurt his brother's feelings. Jeremy had obviously called for something.

"The thing is…"

"Yes?"

"I've been thinking and I want to see him. I'm afraid to see him alone and was hoping you would go with me to see him."

"Oh, Jeremy, I don't know…"

"Please, Pat. I know what he did to us was awful, but I feel so bad for the way I treated him."

"Are you sure?"

"Yes."

"Well, tell Mom to have him call me."

"I don't want Mom to know I'm seeing him."

Patrick sighed. He hoped his little brother knew what he was doing.

"Do you know where he's staying?"

"The Bentley, I think."

"I'll take care of it. I'll call you when the arrangements are made."

"Thanks, Pat."

Jeremy hung up the phone and went to bed.

Genie walked into the Streetcar Bar in the lobby of the Hotel Bentley and looked for Geoffrey. She saw him in the corner and went to sit at his table.

"I'm glad you decided to come."

"I said I would."

"You look fantastic."

"Thank you."

The waiter came by to take their drink orders.

"I'll take a rum and Coke."

The waiter nodded and walked away.

"Geoffrey, I can't stay long. Jeremy is home alone."

"Is that such a good idea?"

"Cora Mayhelm is looking in on him."

The waiter returned with her drink.

"Now what did you want to talk to me about?"

"I've missed you."

"You wouldn't have known it from our end. You've hardly been in your sons' lives, except for missing Patrick's wedding and not paying Jeremy's tuition."

"Yea, well your big time lawyer fixed that problem."

"I'm sorry about that."

After a moment of silence, Geoffrey continued.

"Look, I don't expect you to welcome me back with open arms…"

"Good thing."

"...but I want us to be a family again."

"Are you serious? Geoffrey, I could never trust you again, ever. You walked out on us and left me with nothing. If the house wasn't already paid off, your son and I would be living in our car."

"Don't be ridiculous, you could have stayed with Patrick."

"Are you listening to yourself?"

Genie stood up.

"I'm leaving Geoffrey. Know this, I will talk to the guys about seeing you, I would never keep you from a relationship with them. As for you and I, it's never going to happen again."

He watched as genie walked out of the bar. Geoffrey couldn't help but notice what a nice ass his ex-wife had.

With her boys finally tucked in and herself showered and relaxed, Gretchen slipped off her nightgown and slid into bed next to her husband. Already aroused, she brushed her bare breasts against his back. She reached around and began to stroke him gently, feeling him stiffen with her touch. Ben stirred, but didn't wake up. Gretchen kept at it for a few more minutes, but decided it was a lost cause. She had no idea what could have put him in such a deep sleep, but turned over and went to bed, unsatisfied.

Chapter 5

Doris Shepherd made one last pass through her house, checking the locks and turning off the lights. She noticed the invitation from her new neighbors and reread it. The young girl had seemed nice enough, but there was no way she was leaving the house to go to a party. If she went, she thought to herself, at least she would be able to find out what happened at Jo Ann's house this evening and why the police had been there. Never mind. She would just call the florist tomorrow and send a welcome bouquet to the new neighbors. She turned off the lamp and went to bed.

The next day at lunch, Jeremy called his brother's office. Most of the other kids at Mary's had cell phones, but Jeremy couldn't sell his mother on that idea. He put two quarters in the pay phone and dialed. Christian Mayhelm came up behind him.

"Jeremy I have an extra sandwich if you want one."

"Thanks Chris, I'll be right there."

As Chris was walking away, Pat answered the phone.

"Patrick Van Matthews."

"It's me."

"I was wondering who was calling my private line from a number I didn't recognize."

"I'm on the pay phone at school. Look, I know you said you would call me, but I was wondering if…"

"If I had talked to him yet."

"Yes."

"Everything is set up for lunch on Saturday."

"What did he say when he found out I wanted to see him?"

"He seemed excited."

"Good. What should we tell Mom?"

"Are you still against telling the truth?"

"Yes. I'm going to tell her you're taking me out for my birthday."

"Won't she wonder why she's not going out with us?"

"Think about it. I'm turning fourteen. Maybe I need to talk to my older brother about guy stuff. You know the first time I say the words wet dream, her hair will turn gray and she'll throw me out the door."

Patrick laughed at his brother's joke. He secretly wondered how much Jeremy knew about stuff like that. He was at an age when a young guy needed a male role model he could talk to about certain things. He attempted to joke back.

"Hey, how do you know about things like that?"

Jeremy rolled his eyes over the phone.

"God, I'll see you on Saturday. I got to eat."

Smiling, Patrick hung up the phone and returned to work.

"Miranda, someone wants to meet the cook."

Miranda left the kitchen and took off her baseball cap, running a brush through her hair. She put on her white dress chef's coat and made herself suitable for meeting clients. She walked outside and was escorted to the table. She smiled when she saw Ben York.

"Well, Ben, it looks like I'll be cooking for you after all."

Ben introduced her around the table and everyone complimented the food. Miranda beamed with pride, but remembered she had issues to take care of in the kitchen.

"Thank you gentlemen. If you'll excuse me..."

She nodded, smiled, and headed to the back. Ben went after her and stopped her.

"Miranda, I wanted you to know that Gretchen and I are going to be at the party Saturday night."

"Fantastic. And the boys?"

"We're sending them off to my sister's."

They stood smiling at one another for a moment, the issue in the kitchen forgotten. Ben attempted small talk.

"That was some drama with the cops last night, huh?"

"I know, isn't it awful?"

"What happened?"

"Chad is missing, Jo Ann's son."

Ben couldn't believe his ears. He and Gretchen had been so quick to assume the worst.

"That's horrible. Do they have any idea what happened?"

"His father did it. Apparently he checked Chad out of school yesterday and they haven't been heard from since."

"I thought you had to wait forty eight hours to file a missing person's report."

"Not if it's a minor."

Ben nodded. Miranda got called into the kitchen.

"Ben, I have to go. It was great seeing you. See you Saturday."

She ran into the back and Ben rejoined his business associates.

Jo Ann finally woke up, remembering the nightmare of the day before. She walked into the kitchen and dialed her ex-husband's phone number. After several rings, she gave up and hung up the phone. Mary came in from the laundry room.

"How did you sleep? Did that pill help?"

"How did you know I took a sleeping pill?"

"Who do you think left it on your night stand?"

Jo Ann sighed.

"Any news?"

"Brandy called earlier and said she was going to work but that she still hadn't heard from Louie."

"I just tried to call her. Any word from the police?"

"They called to say the wire tap was working."

Jo Ann nodded and picked up the invitation from Miranda.

"What's this?"

Miranda dropped that off yesterday while you were at the school. They're having a little party to get to know the neighbors Saturday night."

"Oh."

Jo Ann sat down and lit a cigarette.

"That's nice."

Cora turned off the television and went into the kitchen. She hated being a housewife that watched soap operas, but *Gulf States International* was her one guilty pleasure. She cleared off the kitchen table and prepared for the madness. Afternoons could be just as crazy as mornings. Candice needed help with her homework. The boys needed to be made to do theirs. Thankfully, Colleen could be depended on to finish hers without any drama. She usually did hers at night after she got off from the store. Then it happened, the storm hit. The kids came in the house, everyone calling out to her at the same time. Cora raised an eyebrow to her daughter when she saw Scott follow her into the house.

"Scott, are you off of work today, too?"

"Yes, ma'am?"

"Well, come on in and get something to drink."

"We're going to take it in my room. We have a lot of homework to do."

"Colleen, you know the rules. Keep the door open."

"Yes, ma'am."

Cora watched them go down the hall and turned her attention to her sons.

"Christopher, Jeremy didn't come home with you?"

"Miss Genie was off of work today so he went home."

"Okay."

Jeremy hated lying to his mother but hoped she would buy the birthday story.

"Mom, Pat is taking me out for my birthday on Saturday."

"That's nice. Do you think he would mind if you stayed the night there?"

"Why? Are you trying to get rid of me?"

"No. I just have a party to go to Saturday and you can't stay by yourself."

"Mother, I'm almost fourteen. Besides, Miss Cora could look on me."

"That won't work because Cora and Cameron will be at the party."

"I'll ask Pat about staying over."

Jeremy smiled to himself. That was almost too easy.

Gretchen York looked out her window waiting for the carpool to drop the boys off. The phone rang and she picked it up immediately.

"Why did you pick up the phone so fast? Is something wrong?"

"The boys aren't home from school yet. Oh wait, here they are."

Ben Jr. and Tim jumped out the minivan and ran into the house. Gretchen turned her attention back to her husband.

"What's up?"

"I found out why the police were at Jo Ann's last night."

"What happened?"

"Jo Ann's ex-husband ran off with Chad. He's missing."

"Good Lord."

Miranda looked over at her two boys and thanked God they were okay.

"Miranda told me."

"When did you see her?"

"We went to Mariners for lunch. That's where she works."

"Did you tell her we'll be at the party Saturday night?"

"Yes."

Gretchen sighed.

"The party Saturday and the reception for church on Sunday. This weekend is going to kill me."

"I have total faith in you."

Gretchen laughed.

"You'll be home for dinner?"

"I'm leaving the office in a few minutes."

Ben hung up with his wife and went to finish his work.

Cameron walked into his house, surprised to see his wife still helping with homework.

"Is everything okay?"

"This is ridiculous. They have less than a month of school left and they still have all this homework. By the way, Scott is staying for dinner."

"Where is he?"

"They're in Colleen's room studying for a history final."

"The door is open?"

"Of course."

Cameron sat down behind his wife and began to massage her shoulders.

"Can you believe she's graduating high school next week?"

"Hardly."

"One down, three to go."

"One down? Do you think because she's finished high school, we're done raising her? Once she goes off to college, it starts all over, except this time the problems are grown up."

Cameron got up and walked down the hall.

"Where are you going?"

"To be sure that door is open."

Cora laughed at her husband and started dinner.

Chapter 6

Three days later, there was still no sign of Chad or word from his father. Mary cleared the dinner dishes and noticed Jo Ann hadn't touched her food.

"Jo Ann, you need to at least try to eat something."

"I'm not hungry."

"Brandy still hasn't heard anything?"

"She said she would let us know if he called."

"What the hell is he doing with that boy? It's not like he's holding him for ransom, we don't have anything."

"I have no idea. He's beat him before. Maybe he's graduated to molesting him, or even worse."

Before Mary could respond, the phone rang. Jo Ann ran to pick it up. Mary couldn't hear the conversation but could see the terror in her daughter's eyes.

"Okay, thank you. We'll be right down.":

Jo Ann hung up the phone and turned to her mother, horrified.

"The police have a body in the morgue, a little boy Chad's age. They want me to come identify the body, to see if it's him."

Before Mary could even process what her daughter had said, Jo Ann ran past her to the car. Mary followed after her and jumped in the passenger seat just as Jo Ann was taking off.

Ten minutes later, Jo Ann and Mary were in the coroner's office, neither one of them able to sit down or stop pacing. A Mexican woman came in and introduced herself.

"Ms. Mott, I'm Juanita Gandolfo, coroner."

Jo Ann shook her hand. Juanita hated this part of the job. Identifying dead relatives was one thing. A woman identifying her dead eight year old was quite another. Jo Ann spoke up.

"I guess the best thing to do is to get this over with."

Juanita nodded and went to the drawer. The little boy's body had been found that morning in a field behind a convenience store in town. There were no identifying marks or reports of a missing child to help figure out who he was. The only report the had to go on was Chad's and Juanita doubted that he and the dead boy were the same age. Juanita opened the drawer and slid the body out, covered in a sheet.

"He was found this morning."

Juanita didn't tell them that he had been found naked and had been raped. The tears coming from Jo Ann's eyes told her she didn't have to say anything more. Jo Ann grabbed Mary's hand and nodded to Juanita, who pulled back the sheet to the boy's chest, fully exposing his upper body. Jo Ann collapsed into her mother's arms, weeping. Tears of joy ran down Mary's face as she shook her head at the doctor.

"That's not him."

Mary could hardly get the words out.

"Excuse me?"

"That's not Chad. That's not my grandson."

By then, Jo Ann had begun to compose herself.

"Ms. Mott, can you be one hundred percent sure this isn't your son?"

"My son has a scar on his chest from a surgery he had as a child."

She pointed to the place on his chest where the scar would have been. Juanita nodded and covered the body back up. She slid the body back into the drawer and closed the door.

"I need both of you to sign these forms."

She handed the paperwork to Jo Ann and escorted the two women out of the room. Jo Ann dried her eyes.

"That means he's still out there. It's been three days."

Juanita nodded. She had heard the story from the police commissioner. She only hoped this woman would find her son. More importantly, she hoped they would find the family of the poor little boy in drawer twelve.

Father David was almost finished unpacking his stuff. He had settled in comfortably and was becoming accustomed to his duties as a parish pastor. He was starting to look forward to the party Sunday afternoon. Despite the fact that it was Tom's retirement party, David was looking forward to meeting some new people. He walked downstairs into the rectory's office to where Bea was sitting.

"Bea, is there anything left to do for the party Sunday? Anything I can help with?"

"No Father West, I have everything taken care of."

David smiled at her. He hoped Father Bradford was right and that Bea would warm up to him eventually.

"If anything comes up, just let me know."

"Yes sir."

She hardly looked up from her computer. David knew he was an outsider but hoped the rest of the congregation would be more welcoming.

The ride home had been filled with silence. Mary had no idea what to say to her daughter. She had glanced over several times and noticed tears running down Jo Ann's cheeks. When they got home, Jo Ann went straight inside. Mary was getting out of the car when Miranda, who had just gotten home, came across the street.

"Mary, any word?"

"We just got back from the coroner."

"God, no."

"It wasn't him. But Miranda, you can't imagine what it's like to see a child's body covered in a sheet like that."

"I hope we'll never have to know."

Mary tried to lighten the conversation.

"How's everything going for the party Saturday night?"

"Almost done. I hope by then we can turn it into a real celebration."

"In this neighborhood, who would care? Everyone thinks we're trash."

"They would care. Mary if they only knew the situation…"

"Well, be careful. You and your husband may be considered trash by association."

"Fuck what they think. Mary, you and Jo Ann have been so nice to me since we moved in. I pray every night for you, that this ordeal will be over soon."

"Thank you. You're right. Don't let what people may think keep you from coming around. We like you. I'm sure we'd like your husband if we ever met him."

"I'll bring him over soon. Let Jo Ann know I'm home if she needs anything."

Miranda gave the old lady's arm a squeeze and walked back to her house. Once she was inside, she could hear the shower running. She slipped off her clothes and joined Oren.

"You scared the shit out of me."

"That wasn't the reaction I was going for."

She kissed his neck and slowly worked her way down his chest to his stomach. Oren moaned slightly as his wife took him into her mouth. The hot water created a steam that enveloped the two of them and he finished with a force that almost made his knees buckle. They got out of the shower and he dried her off, taking her into the bedroom to return the favor.

That night, Cora climbed into bed next to Cameron.

"Let me ask you something. Do you think Colleen and Scott are having sex?"

"I certainly hope not."

"Don't be so naïve, Cameron. I remember what I was like when I was a senior in high school."

"Have you talked to her about making a responsible decision?"

"I think she would make the responsible decision on her own."

"You can't trust teenagers to do that, especially when it comes to sex."

"Do you want me to talk to her?"

"If you don't talk to her, I'm talking to him."

"You have your own sons to talk to."

"I don't even want to think about that."

Cameron kissed Cora, rolled over, and went to sleep.

Chapter 7

It was Saturday afternoon and Jeremy was getting ready for lunch with his father. His brother Patrick was picking him up and they were all meeting at Mariners for one o'clock. He paced around the room, making Genie nervous.

"Would you stop that?"

"What?"

"Pacing. You're driving me crazy."

"Sorry."

Before Genie could ask if anything was wrong, Patrick honked his horn from outside. Jeremy picked up his overnight bag and ran out the door. Genie looked around and realized she had the whole day and night to herself. She kicked off her shoes and ran herself a hot bath, thankful that Park had let her have the day off.

Oren collapsed into a chair and looked around the house. It was finally spotless and party worthy. Miranda was busy in the kitchen.

"Do you need some help?"

"No, you just finish cleaning."

"I'm done."

"Everything?"

Oren rolled his eyes. His wife was such a perfectionist.

"Everything."

"Then help me finish the food."

Oren sighed, got up, and went into the kitchen.

"Colleen, there's money for pizza on the table. Do not let Candice stay up past nine and the boys need to be in bed by eleven. I heard the boys whispering about some movie called *Boarding School Massacre...* "

"What?!"

Christopher couldn't believe they had been found out.

"Yes, because they had, what was the term you used Christian James, half naked hotties."

Her other son's reaction was the same as his brothers.

"What!?"

"Yea, well think again. No R rated slasher flicks with half-naked women. I don't care what Miss Genie lets you watch."

Cora knew there was no way Genie would let Jeremy watch anything like that but she knew that was the boys' next line of defense.

The maitre'd led Patrick and Jeremy to the table where their father was waiting. Patrick still had his qualms about this lunch but wanted to support his brother. They sat down as the waiter came to take their drink orders.

"I'll have a gin and tonic."

"Me, too."

Patrick looked at his brother.

"Try again."

"Coke."

The waiter left with their orders. Geoffrey started the conversation.

"Thank you guys for coming to see me."

Jeremy tried to smile at his father. Patrick busied himself with the menu.

"Jeremy, after the other day, I'd assumed you'd kill me before you'd have lunch with me."

Jeremy blushed, embarrassed.

"I'm sorry about that."

Geoffrey waved him away as the waiter returned with their drinks.

"You had every right to be angry."

"I had no right to yell at you the way I did. There's just one thing I have to know. Why did you leave us? Don't give me some mid life crisis excuse because that's bullshit. You abandoned your family. I mean, Patrick was off on his own and I was hardly a baby, but what you did to Mom. You left her in such a position, I mean, she was struggling to make ends meet."

"I don't have a good excuse. Jeremy, I got married when I was eighteen years old. I hadn't had a chance to live and I always felt I had missed out on something. There were so many things I always wanted to do."

"You don't get to do everything you want, that's what being an adult means. You make sacrifices when you have a family."

Geoffrey sat back and raised an eyebrow to his youngest son.

"I can't believe how mature you are for your age."

"I have to be."

The waiter came back to take their orders. Patrick, who had been silent the whole time, finally spoke up.

"Look, what are your plans? Are you moving back to St. Bernard? Are you going to live in the hotel? What are your intentions with our mother?"

"Well yes, I am moving back to St. Bernard and I am living in the hotel until I can find a place to rent. As for your mother, I tried to make a fresh start with her, but she wanted none of it. I wanted to salvage my relationship with my sons."

Pat looked away as he sipped his drink.

"Or is it too late?"

Before his brother could answer, Jeremy spoke up.

"No, it's not too late."

"Hope thanks for taking the boys."

Hope Boudreaux was picking up her nephews so Ben and Gretchen could go to the party next door. Gretchen was ecstatic. She loved the boys but hadn't had a night away from them in forever.

"Any news about the house next door?"

"I saw the real estate agent come by a few days ago, but they didn't put a sign up yet."

"I think I have Allen talked into it."

"Hope, this is a lifetime investment. It should be something Allen wants too, not something he has to be talked into."

"I know, but sometimes he needs a nudge."

"Tell me about it."

Ben and Tim came running out with their overnight bags. They kissed Gretchen goodbye and practically knocked one another down trying to get to Hope's car. Gretchen smiled and shook her head.

"Have fun."

"You missed my wedding."

Lunch had fallen into an embarrassed silence. Pat was set on making his father pay.

He wasn't about to have the quick change of heart his younger brother had. Geoffrey was caught completely off guard.

"I know, I was in Aruba."

"Making love on some coral reef?"

"You're out of line young man. I don't care what kind of big time partner you are now or how you feel about me, but I am still your father. You have no right to talk to me like that and I hardly think that kind of remark is appropriate in present company!"

Jeremy kept his head bent down, unable to believe what his brother had just said. Patrick was almost ready to apologize when he thought about what his father had just said.

"You heard about me leaving the firm?"

"Gutsy, leaving a big firm and starting your own practice. When I heard the news, I was so proud. I guess I would have been just as proud if I had made your wedding."

"How did you know?"

"I've kept up with you, both of you. I know all about Jeremy making the state swim team and all about your new wife. I hear she works for one of the finest families in New Orleans."

"The Bentleys."

"Beautiful hotels."

"Yes they are."

"Melissa, right?"

"Yes."

Patrick flagged down the waiter and ordered another drink. He was about to take a big step and needed the alcohol. When the drink came, he took a sip and spoke.

"You know, it doesn't make sense, you living in a hotel like this."

Another sip.

"You could stay with Melissa and I until you find a place of your own."

Geoffrey couldn't believe his son's change of attitude. He smiled at Patrick.

"It may take awhile. I think I'll let you discuss it with your wife first."

Geoffrey winked at Patrick and sipped his drink. Jeremy just sat back and watched his father and brother, smiling.

Later that night, the Grant's party was in full swing. Miranda couldn't believe her eyes when she opened the door and Jo Ann was waiting to be let in.

"Jo Ann, come in. Has there been any news?"

"No. My mother stayed home. She said she would come get me if the police called. I'll probably go home early so she can come over for a while."

"Of course."

Miranda let Jo Ann in through the kitchen and into the den. The party had spilled out into the backyard where Oren had set up citronella candles.

"You know everyone here, I think. Let me introduce you to some of our other friends. Gage and Serena Trenton, this is Jo Ann Mott, a new friend of mine from across the street."

Jo Ann shook hands with the Trenton's as Miranda watched, unbelieving. This is the woman the whole neighborhood thought of as trash and here she was hobnobbing with one of the wealthiest couples in the country. Serena's father owned the Bentley hotel chain and Gage's grandfather had started a company that provided linens to half the nation's hotels, cruise lines, and at least one airline. From across the room, Gretchen York whispered to her husband.

"I can't believe she's here. Her son is missing and she's here partying."

"What you should be doing, Gretchen, is going over there and asking if there's been any news. Show some neighborly compassion for Christ's sake."

"You didn't show too much neighborly compassion when she backed into our mail box last year."

Ben, not wanting to fight with his wife, ignored her comment and walked off without saying a word. Gretchen walked over to Jo Ann.

Cora noticed Miranda looking around the room and walked up to her with a fresh drink.

"Looks like you could use this."

"Thanks."

"Cora Mayhelm, from across the street."

"Yes, the sons who are going to cut my grass."

Cora nodded.

"I'm sorry, Cora, I'm horrible with names."

"No big deal."

Miranda took the drink from Cora.

"Were you looking for someone?"

"The older lady from number five…"

"Doris."

"Yes, everyone from the neighborhood is here except for her."

"She won't be here."

"Why not?"

"Honey, she hasn't left her house in over ten years. She's agoraphobic."

"How awful. You mean, she never goes out?"

"She gets one of the boys to bring out her trash. Yea, we used to know her from church years ago. Then one day, she just stopped going. She has my number and she'll call me if she needs things, groceries and stuff."

"Is she married?"

"Her husband died years ago."

"I wonder what made her that way?"

"I don't know, but I guarantee you, there's a story there."

Cora excused herself and went to find her husband.

Damn! She saw her! Jo Ann tried to find an escape route when she saw Gretchen York walking over. She took a swig of her drink and braced herself.

"They fixed this place up nice, didn't they. Do you remember the shape it was in when the last family moved out?"

"Kind of like my house, right?"

Gretchen stopped, embarrassed.

"Jo Ann, I know we haven't exactly been friends…"

"No. Not since you called the cops on my dog."

"…but I heard about Chad and I just wanted to know if there had been any news. I saw the cop cars in front of your house the other night…"

"And you assumed Chad had gotten himself into trouble. Well, Gretchen, it's worse than that. My ex-husband kidnapped him. There's been no news."

"I'm sorry. Have there been…"

"I need to get back home. Excuse me."

Jo Ann went looking for Miranda. She was leaving and wanted to say goodbye.

"You know my daughter-in-law works for your father."

Genie was chatting with Serena Trenton.

"Who's that?"

"Your father. The man married to your mother."

Serena looked at her awkwardly, not knowing how to take the joke, if it was one. Genie started laughing.

"I'm kidding. I'm kidding. No. Melissa Van Matthews."

"Yes. Our new assistant manager, she's his secretary."

"Yes. Adam something or other."

"Adam Benton. You know, when is that girl going to make you a grandma? I keep asking her and asking her."

"I think she and my son are really focusing on their careers right now. Don't worry, I keep giving them subtle hints."

"Well, let her know everyone in the office adores her."

Serena smiled and went to the bar. Genie followed her with her eyes until a young man outside smoking distracted her. Genie walked up to Oren.

"Who is that good looking guy outside?"

"Can't you tell? That's my younger brother Charles."

"I see the resemblance. Introduce us."

"Are you serious?"

"Yes. Jeremy is staying at his brother's house tonight and it's been a really long time for me."

"What?"

"Never mind. I'll do it myself."

Genie walked outside toward Oren's brother.

Allen Boudreaux came into his apartment to find his nephews watching television. He went into the bedroom where his wife Hope was folding clothes.

"I didn't hear you come in."

"I guess not with the cartoons blaring."

"I told them…"

Hope walked out and returned a minute later.

"You know Allen, I called around and found the realtor who's handling the house next to my brother's."

"You really are excited about this aren't you?"

"I was just thinking that it would be really nice to live close to family, especially now."

"What do you mean, especially now?"

Hope grinned at her husband.

"What are you hiding?"

She went over to the dresser and picked up a stick with two blue lines on it. She handed it to him.

"I did it once with a cheap store brand but I wanted to be sure. So I bought an expensive one and did it again."

Allen's mouth dropped. They had been trying for a baby for months, but decided to hold off until they got settled in their new house.

"And just to be sure, I'm going to see Dr. Hunter next week."

"Oh god."

"Are you excited? I know we decided to wait."

"Excited? Hell yes!"

He grabbed his wife and kissed her joyfully. Then he ran to the phone.

"Who are you calling?"

"My parents."

Hope went back to folding clothes, smiling to herself the whole time.

"Can I bum a cigarette?"

"Sure."

Charles Grant fished in his pockets and pulled out his pack of cigarettes. Genie took one and accepted a light from him. He was gorgeous. He couldn't be more than twenty three at the most. His tan skin and blond hair made him look like the ultimate surfer. He looked nothing like Oren.

"You look nothing like your brother."

"I keep tanned and in shape at work. Otherwise, I'd look as pale and sickly as he does. That's what comes from sitting behind a desk."

"What do you do?"

"Construction."

A manly man, Genie almost fainted.

"Do you want something to drink?"

"Sure."

Charles escorted Genie to the bar. He slipped his arm around her waist and felt the beginnings of a hard on. This woman had the tightest body he had felt in a long time. Sure, she was older, but he didn't care.

Cameron glanced out the window and saw a car he thought he recognized parked in his driveway. He went over to Cora.

"You did tell Colleen that Scott couldn't be there when we weren't there, right?"

"I think so."

"Well, either you didn't tell her, or she's disobeying us because his car is parked outside."

"Do you want me to take care of it?"

"Let's put it this way, if I go over there and see something I don't want to see, I'm liable to kill that boy, and your daughter."

"I'm on it."

Cora finished her drink and walked across the street, stumbling as she went. She had lost count after her fourth drink. She got to her house and saw Colleen and Scott sitting on the front porch, perfectly innocent.

"Colleen, who's watching the kids?"

"They're all asleep."

Cora couldn't believe what she had heard.

"Is it after ten already?"

"Mother, it's almost eleven."

"Right. Scott, I think you'd better head on home. Colleen has to work tomorrow."

Scott got the hint and said good night. As he drove off, Colleen looked at her mother.

"I don't have to work tomorrow."

"Well, you still have to go to church."

Cora opened the door and followed Colleen inside. She went into her bedroom to change her shoes. Once she was in there, the room started spinning. She couldn't believe she had drunk so much. She laid down on the bed and was passed out in less than two minutes.

"You're Cameron, right?"

Oren introduced himself to his new neighbor. He couldn't believe the party had lasted this long and he still hadn't met everyone.

"Right."

"I think you worked on my car last year. Good work."

"I try."

"My wife hired your sons to cut our grass."

"Remind me to thank her. That's less allowance I have to pay them."

Both men laughed as Cameron looked around for Cora.

"Speaking of wives, have you met mine?"

"Earlier tonight, yes."

"Have you seen her?"

"No."

"You'll have to excuse me Oren, I think she may be across the street."

Cameron went to find Miranda to thank her for a wonderful evening and said goodnight to Genie. He went to his house and found Cora asleep on the bed. He picked her up and almost wretched at the smell of her breath. His wife was passed out drunk. He laid her on her side of the bed and wondered what was wrong. Cora rarely drank.

Soon enough, the party was winding down. Ben slipped his arm around his wife and the two of them went to say good night to their hosts.

"Are you Catholic?"

Miranda was put off by the question and wondered if Gretchen the Lasagna Lady had ulterior motives.

"Yes we are."

"Well, you should come to noon mass tomorrow. After, there's a party for Father Bradford. He's retiring."

"I can't. Sundays are our biggest day at the restaurant with the champagne brunch and everything."

"We'll have to check it out one Sunday when we don't have the kids."

"We always have the kids."

Ben bent over and whispered into Gretchen's ear.

"Not tonight."

Gretchen turned to her husband, embarrassed.

"You are horrible."

Oren defended him.

"Nah, you two have fun."

The York's left the party. Miranda went into the kitchen and found Serena cleaning up.

"Serena, I can do that."

"I don't mind."

"But it's so late…"

Serena got the hint and put down the sponge. Just then, the husbands came in.

"What did I tell you Miranda? Have a party. You should see all the cool presents you have out there."

"I know Gage, I unwrapped them."

"Well Miranda, the dishes are in the dishwasher, the counters are clean, and I took the trash out the back."

"Thank you so much."

"We've one our way. Oren, was that the waitress from the restaurant I met earlier?"

"She lives at number eight."

"Who was the guy she was with? I thought she was divorced?"

"Probably my brother."

Miranda thought about the York's.

"It looks like everyone is getting laid tonight."

"On that note, we're leaving."

Oren walked Gage and Serena out. He came back inside.

"You were certainly nice to Serena tonight."

"I didn't have the energy to be rude to her."

"I guess not everyone is getting laid tonight."

Miranda went over and kissed her husband lightly.

"Sorry honey, but I'm exhausted. Do you mind?"

"Not at all. I'm going to take a shower and hit the bed."

"I'll see you there."

Genie handed Charlie a drink. She sat next to him, unable to take her eyes off of him. They had left the party awhile ago and he had walked her home. Once there, she invited him in for a drink. He accepted and the two of them had been getting to know one another.

"There is no way you have a fourteen year old son."

"And a thirty year old."

Genie sensed she was pushing him away and kissed him hard on the mouth. She felt alive, almost twenty years younger, as her tongue darted in and out of his mouth. She unbuttoned his shirt to reveal a perfectly chiseled body. She got up and led him to the bedroom. Unable to believe himself, he protested.

"I usually don't do this on a first date."

"I always do this. The problem is, I haven't been on a date in thirty years."

Charles laughed and went to make love to a woman old enough to be his mother.

Chapter 8

The next morning, Gretchen met Hope in front of Mary, Mother of God to collect her kids.

"Thanks Hope. How were they?"

"Fine."

Hope was beaming and Gretchen couldn't understand why. She certainly didn't feel that way after a full night of her kids.

"Is something going on? You're in a very good mood. You must have finished your night the way Ben and I finished ours."

"Actually…"

Before Hope could spread the good news to her sister-in-law, they were interrupted.

"I'm glad you ladies are here. We have a lot of work to do."

Bea de la Roche took each one of them by the arm and dragged them to the school cafeteria where the party was going to be.

"Agnes already has the food set up and Bernice is moving the tables and chairs."

"Bea, she's like ninety."

"Well, she's supervising. All we're waiting for is the decorations."

Hope and Gretchen sighed and made their way to the cafeteria. Once inside, Bea took over like a cop running a well oiled machine. By the time Mass was ready to start, everything was done.

"Now ladies, after Communion, everyone meet back here so we can make any last minute adjustments."

The ladies walked across the parking lot to the church. Hope lagged behind, giving herself and Gretchen some privacy.

"Gretchen, I'm pregnant."

Gretchen stopped in her tracks. She turned to her sister-in-law open mouthed.

"When did you find out?"

"Yesterday. According to my period, I'm about three weeks. I'm going to the doctor next week to be sure."

"Who's your doctor?"

"Dr. Hunter."

"He was great taking care of Tim. Does Allen know?"

"I told him last night."

"Hope, I am so happy for you. You really need the house next door now."

"We're going to look at it this week."

"Fantastic. I can help with the nursery, the shower..."

Gretchen seemed more excited than Allen had been. She always claimed she was okay with two kids. Hope knew she wanted more, and wondered how Gretchen really felt about her having a new baby.

Genie rolled over and looked at the clock. She panicked when she saw what time it was. She rolled over and shook Charles.

"Charlie! Charlie, wake up!"

"Huh?"

"You have to leave before my son gets home."

Charlie stirred awake then remembered where he was. He kicked off the covers and pulled up his underwear. Genie hurried out the bedroom, saw Jeremy watching television and did an about-face. She hurriedly pushed Charles back into the bedroom. This is what she had been reduced to, sneaking around with a man half her age and hiding him from her son. She walked back into the living room and talked to Jeremy.

"How was yesterday? Did you have fun at Pat and Melissa's?"

"It was alright."

Jeremy got up and headed for the door.

"I'm going to see what Chris and Chris are doing."

Without thinking, she called out to him.

"They're probably at church."

Damn! At least if he was at their house knocking on their door, she would have time to get Charlie out of the house quickly. She suddenly had an idea.

"Jeremy, we're out of sugar. Go see if Miss Doris has some. We need about two cups."

Jeremy huffed and did as he was told. As soon as he was out the door, Genie ran to her bedroom and scooted Charlie out the back door. Genie thanked God he was still parked in front of Miranda and Oren's house. At least there were no strange cars to pique her son's attention.

"Can I call you sometimes?"

"Better let me call you."

Genie gave him a quick kiss and pushed him out. She closed the door and could feel her heart pounding. She felt eighteen again and smiled as she remembered Charlie's toned body and skill as a lover. She almost felt bad for what she had done but remembered the way he smelt, the way his body felt pressed against hers, filling her every desire, she decided to forgive herself.

"Gretchen, where were you? I told everyone to be here after Communion!"

"Sorry, Bea, I just wanted to hear Father Tom's last prayer."

"Well, I would have liked to heard it too, but there's work to be done."

Gretchen rolled her eyes and looked for her mother-in-law. She knew Muriel York wouldn't be expected to work, but she knew the grandee dame of Mary's would definitely make an appearance. She went over to where Hope was standing and greeted parishioners as they arrived from Mass. She waved to Cora and Cameron as they walked through the doors, followed by their children and Scott Winslow. Cora kept her sunglasses on, due to the major hangover she had.

"Some party last night, huh?"

"Gretchen, I have no idea how much I drank."

"It was a lot."

"That's what Cam told me. I woke up this morning still dressed."

Cora looked around the room.

"How did you get involved in this fiesta?"

"Fiasco is more like it. Darling, I'm a York. You know I have to be down with all the church stuff."

"Well there's Father Tom. I'm going to say goodbye before a crowd gathers around him like Jesus himself."

"Well, say goodbye for me, too. I doubt if Bea is going to let me from behind this table."

Cora laughed and went to see the priest she had regarded as part of her family since before her children were born.

"Colleen, so what are we doing after our last final tomorrow?"

"I don't know. I do know I want to celebrate. Why don't you come swimming tomorrow?"

"Your parents would have a fit if they knew I was there alone with you."

"Who's going to tell them? The kids won't be home till after three and my mother is visiting friends in Baton Rouge. She won't be home till late. She even told my dad he was on his own for dinner."

"What time is your last final?"

"Civics is over at eleven."

"That sucks. I only have one left, French at nine thirty."

"Will you wait for me?"

"Sure."

"How did all your other exams do? Are you still graduating with honors?"

"Yea, what about you?"

"Freshman year saved me. I had a 4.0 all year. After that, I started to slide downhill, but enough to graduate with honors."

"Great. I'm going for some cake, do you want some?"

"Sure."

Scott walked to the cake table where Bea was handing out cake to the masses. To watch her, you'd think she was feeding the five thousand.

Gretchen York smiled at her mother-in-law as she walked toward her from across the room, followed by her own entourage of church ladies, her own twelve disciples.

"Gretchen, I'm so glad to see you helping out."

"Of course, Muriel."

"You know the York's have always been involved here at Mary's."

"Well, you know I've always been proud to be one."

Gretchen smiled at Muriel. She wondered if Hope had told her about the baby yet.

"I understand that Allen and Hope are going to be looking at the house next to you and Benjamin."

"We hope so."

"That'll be good. It's always nice to be near family."

Muriel smiled primly.

"Well, I need to see if Bea needs any help. By the way, have you met the new priest?"

"Father West? No I haven't."

"He seems a bit too nervous to me."

She walked away. Gretchen immediately felt sorry for the new priest. If Muriel York didn't like you, that could certainly lead to problems down the line. She was probably on her way to voice her concerns to Bea and the girls.

"Cameron, how much did I have to drink last night?"

"Too much. How are you feeling?"

"Like this cup of coffee is my best friend."

Cameron smiled at his wife.

"How are you doing with all this goodbye stuff?"

"I went to see Father Tom and said what I had to say. I will miss him though."

"I think the new priest will be just as nice. There he is."

"Should we go introduce ourselves?"

"Better take those sunglasses first. You don't want to be too obviously hung over."

"Trust me, once he sees these eyes, he'll figure it out."

"Sorry, I'm late."

Genie ran into the restaurant and almost knocked Parker down.

"No problem, babe."

Genie put her things away, smiling from ear to ear.

"Did you get laid?"

"What?"

"You're unusually late and you're smiling from ear to ear."

"Come here."

She took him by the arm and pulled him into the back.

"God Park, I had a one night stand with a totally hot guy I had just met at a party."

"You dirty slut!"

"Don't say that."

"Does he have a brother?"

"Yes, but his brother is my new neighbor."

"Oh my goodness."

"The worst part was that I had to sneak him out the back door. I felt like I was eighteen again."

"Where was Jeremy?"

"I sent him on an errand."

"You are so bad."

"I know. It was fantastic."

She was giddy as a teenager. She skipped around the kitchen, grabbed a tray and went out to meet her tables. Nova came into the kitchen and smiled at Park.

"Someone got laid."

"Patrick, I never did ask you how lunch went with your father."

Melissa was setting out lunch for her husband. Patrick wanted to discuss having Geoffrey stay with them, by the didn't know how to go about it. He figured now was as good a time as any.

"Actually, it went pretty good."

"Is everything patched up or do you think it'll take a bit longer? Seven years is a long time."

"I know. We're headed in the right direction."

"What are his plans?"

"He's staying in St. Bernard."

"In the hotel?"

"I wanted to talk to you about that. I think it's crazy for him to stay in a hotel while he's looking for a place. I asked if he would want to stay here."

"Absolutely not."

"Melissa, you're not even going to think about it?"

"I know how these things work. He stays with us indefinitely, even though it's supposed to be 'for a little while.' The next thing we know, he's here for months and we lose our privacy. What did he say?"

"He actually turned me down. He said I should talk to you about it first."

"That was decent of him."

They ate for the next few minutes in silence.

"Look Liss, don't be mad at me. I guess I got caught up in the whole reunion atmosphere."

He took her hand and smiled into her eyes.

"You're forgiven."

"I'll talk to him later today."

"Just don't make me look like the bad guy."

"Don't worry. I think he'll understand."

Genie walked up to Geoffrey's table. For some reason, she didn't feel the animosity she had felt for him earlier. She couldn't figure out why.

"Coffee, Geoffrey?"

"Thanks."

She returned with it in a minute.

"Listen, thanks for letting Jeremy see me yesterday. I'm glad to see you were true to your word about not keeping me from having a relationship with the boys."

"Jeremy told me he was having lunch with his brother yesterday for his birthday."

"They both had lunch with me."

"Why would he lie?"

"He probably thinks you hate me and feels bad for calling me. He called me to have lunch."

"I never meant to make him feel that way."

"Maybe he got the idea when he walked in on you slapping me across the face."

"Well, if you didn't have your tongue down my throat."

"I don't recall you complaining."

"Not at first, no. We've been over this."

"I know. Listen, talk to him. Make sure he knows he doesn't have to sneak around to see me."

"I will. You want breakfast or anything?"

"What are you offering?"

He winked at her.

"Coffee is fine."

Genie shook her head as she walked away. Why was she being so nice to him? Oh yeah, because she had gotten laid. Thank you Charlie.

Chapter 9

The next morning, Jo Ann walked into her house as the phone was ringing. She hurried to answer it as Mary came in from the laundry room. Her heart stopped when she heard Chad's voice on the other line.

"Mom?"

"Chad?"

Tears filled her eyes. Mary waited for confirmation that it was him.

"Chad, is Daddy with you?"

"He went out to get us something to eat. He told me I shouldn't call and bother you, but I wanted to call you and let you know I was having fun."

"Fun?"

"We're going to Disneyland. Dad said it was okay with you if I missed a few days of school."

Jo Ann's mind raced. She knew that the call tracer would trace the call but she wanted to be sure the police knew Chad was alive. She knew to keep him on the phone as long as possible, but not too long. If Louie found out he had called her, he would take Chad off again to God knows where. She turned to Mary.

"Mom, go next door to Cora's and call the police. Let them know Chad is on the phone so they can trace the call."

Mary ran out the door. Jo Ann tried to stay calm.

"Chad, where are you, honey?"

"Some hotel."

"Do you know the name?"

"It's written here on this pad. I can't say it."

"Spell it for me."

"T-U-M-B-L-E-W-E-E-D."

"Good boy. Is there a city? Chad, do you know what city you're in?"

"There's a phone book here."

"See if the city is on it."

"P-H-O-E-N-I-X."

"Good boy."

Jo Ann knew she had to act like she had agreed to everything or it would scare Chad.

"Are you having a good time with Daddy?"

"You're not going to tell him I called you, are you?"

"I won't tell. You better keep this call our little secret."

"I will."

"I love you, Chad."

"Me, too."

Mary came in and gave a thumb up. Cora was right behind her.

"Mom?"

"What is it?"

"How much longer do you think it'll take us to get to Disneyland?"

"Not much longer. You be a good boy and I'll see you when you get home."

"Bye."

Cora hung up slowly, tears running down her face.

"Mom, what did the cops say?"

"They already had the location pinpointed. Tumbleweed Motel in some little town outside of Phoenix."

"Chad told me that. I need to call them. Louie went out for something to eat, but it's early in the day. They'll probably be moving on."

"Commissioner Graham told me the Arizona State Police are already on it."

Jo Ann picked up the phone, lighting a cigarette as she did.

"Who are you calling?"

"The police."

"They told me they would call us once he was in custody."

Jo Ann laughed.

"That's something every mother wants to hear about her son."

Cora, previously silent, finally spoke up.

"Jo Ann, is there anything you need me to do?"

"Actually, Cora, if you can get me Transcoastal's number. I guess I'll have to get to Phoenix."

Jo Ann wanted to call her job but didn't want to tie up her phone line. Her boss knew the situation so she figured getting time off wouldn't be a problem. Since the ordeal began a week ago, she hadn't missed a day at either of her jobs. Some days, being busy at work was the only thing that kept her from crying. Cora handed Jo Ann the number for Transcoastal Airlines.

"Cora, thanks for everything."

"I'm glad I was home. I'm leaving to spend the day in Baton Rouge. Did you need me to help with anything else?"

"No, thank you."

Cora went home. She couldn't believe that Jo Ann had been going through this all week and nobody in the neighborhood had any idea.

The doorbell rang and woke Miranda from a deep sleep. She stumbled to the door, cursing whoever was on the other side. When she opened the door, she smiled. A man was standing there with a beautiful floral centerpiece.

"Miranda Grant?"

"Yes."

"Sign here please."

Miranda placed the flowers on the dining room table. After tipping the man, she went to read the card.

"Welcome to the neighborhood. Doris Shepherd, number five."

Miranda remembered Cora talking about the old lady that never left her house. She smiled to herself, grateful that she had to work the evening shift, and went to get dressed. Cora thought there might be a story to the goings on at number five. Miranda was going to find out.

Jo Ann was watching the clock. In a few minutes, she would have to risk tying up the phone to call work and say she wouldn't be in. It had been almost an hour since Chad had called and both Mary and Jo Ann were getting nervous at the lack of an update. Jo Ann lit another cigarette and the phone rang. She grabbed it on the first ring.

"Hello."

"Mrs. Mott, this is Peter Graham."

"Yes Commissioner."

"The good news is, we've located your son."

"Is there bad news?"

Mary began praying silently. She expected to hear Jo Ann talking to Chad by now. Something was wrong.

"The Arizona State police tell me your ex-husband is holding your son hostage in the motel room, at gunpoint."

Jo Ann cried out and took Mary's hand.

"They're in a stand off situation right now. Mr. Mott refuses to let the boy go."

"A stand off? Like in some cheesy cop movie?"

Jo Ann regretted the words as soon as she had said them. She didn't want to insult the police trying to help her.

"I'm sorry."

"No offense. Actually, it's pretty serious. Do you have any idea what kind of mental state your ex-husband might be in?"

"No. I haven't talked to Louie in months."

"I see. Do you think he might be dangerous?"

"Yes. He's been in jail more than once for assault. He was on probation when he kidnapped Chad."

Jo Ann began to panic.

"I need to get out there. Can I get out there?"

"I've already booked seats on the next flight. I'm going with you since the case started in our jurisdiction."

"Of course. When do we leave?

"Two hours. Transcoastal flight eight eighty two. Can you meet me at the airport?"

"I'll meet you at the ticket counter."

Jo Ann hung up the phone and called her bosses.

"Mom, I'm leaving for Phoenix. That asshole is holding Chad hostage."

"I'm coming with you."

"No. I need you to stay here in case there's any word while I'm en route."

Mary nodded. Jo Ann packed a small overnight bag and headed for the airport. Miranda saw her from her window, but, by the time she got to the door, Jo Ann was gone. Miranda only hoped it was good news about Chad.

Doris sat at her kitchen table, sipping her second cup of coffee. She was surprised by the knock on the door. The delivery guy from the grocery store wasn't due for another two hours. She got up and smiled when she saw her new neighbor standing in her doorway.

"Mrs. Grant, how nice of you to stop by."

"Mrs. Shepherd…"

"Call me Doris."

"Doris. I just wanted to come by and thank you for the flowers. They're beautiful."

"When did they arrive?"

"This morning."

"Damn. I was hoping they would get there in time for your party."

"No, they came about an hour ago."

Doris smiled at her.

"Would you like to come in? I was just having coffee."

"If you're sure it's no bother."

"None at all."

Doris opened her door wider and let her new neighbor in.

"Commissioner Graham…"

"Peter."

"Peter, I wanted to thank you for everything your office has done. One minute I'm coming home to make dinner between jobs and the next minute, my son is missing."

"You have two jobs?"

"I work at Barrister's during the day. At night I work for a company cleaning offices."

"When do you sleep?"

"Whenever I can, which isn't much. Thank god my mother helps Chad with his homework. She used to be a teacher. She retired years ago but she's still sharp as a tack. Don't tell her I said that."

"I won't."

The seven fifty seven banked to the right and Jo Ann almost spilt her drink. She hated to admit it, but she enjoyed talking to Peter. It took her mind off what was waiting for her in Arizona.

"How long were you married, Jo Ann?"

"Too damn long. Five years."

"You have your son to show for it."

"My son and three cracked ribs, four broken noses, dozens of back eyes, hundreds of bruises and two permanent scars."

"It must have been horrible."

"He was abusive to begin with, but once he got into drugs, it got worse. I even looked the other way when he started having an affair."

Jo Ann sipped her drink.

"What about you, Peter, are you married?"

"I'm a widower."

"I'm sorry. Any children?"

"My son, Paul, is thirteen."

Jo Ann nodded, staring off into space.

"What are you thinking?"

"You asked me earlier if I thought Louis might be dangerous. You know, I think he might be."

Colleen was relieved when she didn't see her mother's car in the driveway. Although she had assured Scott that Cora wouldn't be home, she still wasn't one hundred percent sure. Scott followed her into the house and went into the kitchen.

"Scott, get me a Diet Coke."

The phone rang and she picked it up, putting her finger to her lips to keep Scott quiet. It was Cameron.

"Hey, baby."

"Hey, Dad."

"How did your final exams go?"

"Pretty good."

"Well, relax and enjoy the rest of your day. Your brothers and sisters will be home after three and I'll be home after that. I was thinking of ordering Chinese for dinner."

"I'll take care of it and have it waiting for you when you get home. Did Mom say when she was coming back?"

"Not until later tonight."

"Dad, I've got to go. Kelleye is here and we're going swimming."

"Have fun."

Colleen hung up the phone and turned to Scott.

"We have the whole pool to ourselves until three."

"I'll go change."

Scott went to the bathroom while Colleen searched for where she had hidden her bikini. She had bought a very skimpy one at Barrister's earlier in the week and kept it hidden from her mother. She pulled the bag out from behind the washer machine where it was hidden and slipped it on. She grabbed two warm towels from the dryer and went to find Scott. When he came out of the bathroom, Colleen couldn't help but be disappointed. She had been dying to check out his body, but he had a shirt on. As captain of the baseball team, she knew he was in great shape, but she wanted to see for herself. She was rewarded when they got to the deck surrounding the pool and Scott peeled his shirt off. Just as she had suspected, he had the perfect body. At eighteen, he had just started to get hair on his chest and it totally turned Colleen on. Now it was her turn to do the same for him. She dropped her towel, revealing her tiny suit, her breast almost spilling over the top. Scott stared at her.

"You look great."

"I think this bathing suit is a bit severe."

He nodded, not wanting to admit he was already semi-hard where it counted. He hoped she wouldn't be able to tell through his bathing suit.

"A little bit, but it still looks great on you."

She laid down on her stomach, undoing her straps to avoid tan lines.

"Will you put lotion on my back?"

Colleen knew exactly what she was doing and Scott nearly exploded right in his bathing suit. He slathered lotion on her back and went to lie next to her, causing himself a dilemma. One: does he lay on his back, letting his eighteen year old flag fly or two: lay on his stomach and crush it like canned pineapple? He remedied the situation by diving in the pool, splashing Colleen.

"I thought you were going to lay out with me?"

"I'm going to swim laps until you come in."

"Fine by me."

She flipped herself over, enjoying the warmth that celebrated her last day of high school.

Mary ran to the phone and answered it on the second ring.

"Hello?"

"May I speak to Mrs. Mott?"

"This is Mary Bishop, her mother. Can I help you?"

Mary knew it was the police calling about Chad.

"Miss Bishop, this is Carter Daniels, Arizona State Police. We have your grandson in custody."

Mary let out a sigh of relief.

"Is he alright?"

"Yes, but there were some complications."

"What happened?"

"Mr. Mott is dead."

Mary couldn't believe what she was hearing.

"Was there a shoot out? I know that sounds like I've seen one too many movies, but was there one?"

"After about two hours, we thought we had an agreement reached. Then, we heard a gunshot and stormed the room. We found Mr. Mott dead on the floor and your grandson on the bed, crying. Mr. Mott apparently shot himself in the head."

"In front of Chad?"

"Yes, ma'am."

"Does Jo Ann know?

"No. Her plane lands within the hour and we'll take her to her son and tell her everything."

"Thank you, Mr. Daniels."

Mary hung up the phone, unable to believe what she had just heard. What kind of person kills themselves in front of their eight year old son? Mary picked the phone up and called Jo Ann's sister, Kathleen.

Colleen jumped into the pool and started chasing Scott around. He turned to her and pulled her close to him. They had been dating exclusively for five months, but hadn't gone all the way yet. Colleen was a virgin and was pretty sure Scott wasn't. What she didn't know was that Scott was still a virgin, too. With his jock status and natural sex appeal, everyone assumed he could have had any girl he wanted. He could have. His outward confidence hid the fact that he was just as nervous as anyone would be. He kissed Colleen hard on the mouth, his hands fondling her breast. He felt him through his suit and panicked. She had never felt a guy that close before. She kind of liked it. What she liked even more was the way her nipples felt as they hardened against her bathing suit. After a few minutes of making out, Scott made his move. He began to pull Colleen's bathing suit around her knees. Against her better judgment, she pushed him away. She knew they had been going out awhile and that he had been very patient with her. She knew she had to do something or she was going to lose him. What she had just felt confirmed the fact that he could have any girl he wanted.

"Scott, not here. Not in the pool."

"Why not?"

"I want my first time to be romantic. I want to be seduced. What was your first time like?"

"Colleen, this is my first time. The only sex I've ever had has been with me."

She pretended to be horrified.

"I didn't think you did that."

Scott turned red immediately.

"Well…I do."

He turned away embarrassed. Colleen came up behind him and ran her hands up and down his chest. She couldn't believe what she was about to do, but the fact that Scott admitted that he jerked off made her want him more. Suddenly, he seemed so innocent and vulnerable.

"You know, I saw this in a movie once…"

Se slipped her hand into his suit to his still hard penis. He moaned as she began to tug on him gently. She and her friend Kelleye had watched a porno once when they were sixteen and, since then, she had never seen a naked man before. Scott turned around to kiss her and, with his suit around his knees, she got a full view. She couldn't take her eyes off of him. He was gorgeous. She kissed him back, never losing the firm grip she had on him. Scott felt his stomach muscles tighten as the anticipated moment approached. She felt him twitch in her hands he finished what had started with the suntan lotion. Exhausted and sweating, Scott collapsed against the side of the pool.

"What movie did you say that was from?"

Colleen giggled and ran her hand down his length once more before pulling up his bathing suit.

Peter and Jo Ann deplaned and met the state trooper waiting for them.

"Commissioner Graham?"

"Yes, sir."

"Chad is in our custody. There were, however, some complications."

He glanced uneasily at Jo Ann. Peter introduced her, letting him know she had a right to know anything.

"Mr. Mott is dead. He killed himself in front of the boy. When we heard the gunshot, we stormed the motel room and found the body."

"Where was Chad?"

"On the bed, crying. We took him to the station and he cleaned up."

The thought made Jo Ann's stomach turn. Cleaned up? Had Chad been close enough to get bloody?

"Right now, he's being interviewed by the police psychiatrist."

Jo Ann could only imagine the therapy Chad would need. Seeing his father blow his head off had to screw a little boy up. Jo Ann instinctively held on to Peter for support as they followed the trooper to the car.

Genie had gotten off of work early and was waiting for Jeremy when he got home.

"What are you doing home?"

"Well, it's nice to see you too."

"I meant, I thought you would still be working."

"I'm not."

Genie went about the kitchen, preparing dinner.

"So I saw your father this morning."

Jeremy panicked, he had been caught.

"He said he loved having lunch with you the other day."

"I have to go..."

"Jeremy, why did you lie to me? I think it's great that you're seeing your father again."

"Why do you care? You pushed him away when he tried to get back together..."

"Did he tell you that?"

"Do you know he's living in a hotel, mother? He has no place to go."

"He never mentioned that."

"You probably never gave him a chance, not that you would care anyway!"

Before Genie could reprimand him, Jeremy ran out the front door. Genie prayed that he had only misinterpreted things and not that Geoffrey was dragging her name through the mud. She picked up the phone.

The tension on the drive to the police station was unbearable. Jo Ann sat in the back with Peter, her mind racing. Would Chad need therapy? How could she afford it?

Once at the station, the three of them were escorted to a one way mirror. Through the window, Jo Ann could see Chad watching television. A woman came through the door and introduced herself.

"Mrs. Mott? I'm Lorna Hall, staff psychiatrist. We've been observing Chad since he was brought in."

"How is he?"

"He hasn't spoken much. I'd like him to see a colleague of mine in New Orleans. I'll set everything up."

"Can I see him now?"

"Of course."

Jo Ann went into the room and held back her tears as Chad ran into her arms. She noticed blue ink on his hands and turned to Lorna and Carter.

"What's this?"

Carter took her aside.

"We needed to take his fingerprints."

"What the hell for?"

Carter lowered his voice.

"We had to eliminate the possibility that Chad didn't shoot his father, himself."

"He's eight years old!"

"He was also the only one in the room with his father."

Jo Ann couldn't believe what she was hearing.

"We need to go."

She pulled Chad out of the room and went to the car., followed by Carter and Peter. They drove off to the airport.

The flight wasn't in the air ten minutes before Chad was asleep. Jo Ann rang for the flight attendant and ordered vodka. Once it arrived, she sipped it and caught Peter watching her.

"I suppose you think I'm a horrible mother?"

"Jo Ann, you're a mother who has been through a horrible experience. I don't blame you."

"I would feel better if you joined me."

"I'm on duty."

She nodded.

"Listen, Jo Ann, would you like to have dinner with me tomorrow?"

"When you're off duty."

"Yes."

"Sure, I'd love to."

Peter smiled and put his seat back.

"Am I boring you?"

"No. I just want to end the conversation on a good note. Wake me when we land."

"Alright."

Jo Ann smiled and sipped her drink.

Mary and Kathleen were waiting for them when they got home. Mary ran and embraced her grandson, tears streaming down her face.

"I think we need to celebrate. Kathleen, can you join us for dinner?"

"Sure."

"Chad, how about the Breakers?"

"That's fine."

Mary and Jo Ann exchanged worried glances.

Chapter 10

That Saturday night, Colleen waited impatiently for Scott to arrive. She had waited for her Senior Prom all year and tonight was the night. She came out of her room when she saw the limo pulling up. Cora pushed her back down the hall.

"Don't you know you have to make an entrance? Make him wait a few minutes."

Colleen laughed and went back into her bedroom. Cameron let Scott inside where everyone was waiting to take pictures. Scott tried his best to make conversation with Colleen's brothers and sister.

"So, when do you guys leave for camp?"

"Next week."

"Are you excited?"

"Excited to be getting out of this place."

Scott smiled. He was about to try his luck with Candice when Colleen came down the hall. His mouth dropped when he saw how much cleavage the royal blue gown showed. Against her mother's better judgment, Colleen had put a slit in it that went all the way to her upper thigh. Both kids looked gorgeous and happy as they posed for pictures. They had both graduated with honors three days ago and now was the time to celebrate.

"Mom, don't forget I'm staying at Kelleye's tonight."

"I won't."

"I'll be back tomorrow."

Colleen kissed Cameron good night and followed Scott out the door. They climbed in the limo and relaxed.

"Where did you get this?"

"My dad arranged for it through work. It's ours for the whole night."

"Well, where are we off to first?"

"Dinner at Mariners."

"Sounds good to me."

Colleen crossed her legs, her dress falling to reveal her upper thigh. Scott

caught a glimpse of it and smiled at her, running his hand up her leg.
"You ,sir, need a cold shower."

"Where are you going tonight?"
"Peter's taking me to Mariners."
"You never did tell me how the first date went. I hope I get more details about tonight."
Jo Ann was finishing her make up when Mary came into the room.
"There's nothing to tell. We like each other. We enjoy spending time together. It's not like we're getting married or anything."
"He would definitely be an improvement."
Mary didn't see her grandson storm off and slam his door shut. Jo Ann ran past her mother to her son's room.
"Mother, the doctor told us not to bad mouth Louie in front of him!"
"Sorry."
There was a knock on the door while Jo Ann was trying to talk to Chad.
"Go let him in. I'll take care of this."
Mary knocked on her grandson's door, apologizing.

Jo Ann came in from the back of the house and opened the door. She was dressed in a red pants suit.
"You look fantastic."
"Thank you, sir."
"Where's your mother. I always thought it was good manners to meet my date's parents. I mean, I've already met her, but this is different."
"Better circumstances."
"Yes."
"Well, she's dealing with a Chad issue. Do you want me to go get her?"
"No. I'll see her later. Shall we go?"
He held out his arm and Jo Ann took it. She had never been treated this way before, like a lady. She smiled at Peter as they walked to the car.

Later that night, Miranda got called to the front of the house for a phone call. She knew it wasn't Oren because he always called directly to the kitchen. She was on the phone when she saw two of her neighbors. Colleen and her date were sitting in a corner by themselves she looked a lot older than seventeen: beautiful, but not appropriate for her age. Miranda tried to remember what she had worn to her prom and figured she probably looked the same way. Jo Ann was sitting with a man Miranda recognized as the officer working on Chad's case. Jo Ann saw her and waved from across the room. Miranda gave her a thumbs up and hurried to the kitchen. She came out a few moments later and called to one of the waiters.

"Paul, take these desserts over to table seventeen. Young couple, girl in blue gown. And take this champagne over to table twenty five, red pants suit."

The waiter ran off and Miranda went back into the kitchen.

"I talked to the guy Lorna Hall recommended and Chad has an appointment on Monday."

"Good."

Jo Ann and Peter were enjoying themselves when the waiter came over with the champagne.

"We didn't order this."

"Compliments of the chef."

"Tell her, I will call her later."

"You know the chef?"

Peter raised an eyebrow.

"Miranda Grant, from across the street. You met her."

Peter had been trying to forget the night Jo Ann reported her son missing. He was having a good time and didn't want to think of bad things past…He nodded and poured champagne for himself and Jo Ann. Jo Ann began to tear up.

"Jo Ann, what's wrong?"

"It's just that…it's been so long since I've been to a nice restaurant, with a nice man. I have been made to feel like trash for so long, by my husband, my neighbors…"

"Miranda doesn't think so."

"She's a great girl. It's just that, things like this don't happen to me. I got pregnant right out of high school, married the loser and let him beat the shit out of me. I moved back home with my mother and struggle with two jobs to support us, which I barely do."

"You know what I think? I think you're fantastic."

Peter reached across the table and took her hand. Jo Ann smiled through her tears.

After dancing for hours, Scott and Colleen decided to call it quits. They left the Magnolia Room of the Hotel Bentley hand in hand, heading toward the valet stand. Instead, Scott pulled her toward the elevators.

"What's going on?"

"Nothing."

"You're up to something."

God, she hoped so. Colleen secretly hoped Scott had planned something romantic for the night. She had planned to spend the night with him one way or another, hence the lie to her parents. She wanted to be with him and hoped that he had taken the seduction jokes to heart. They got in the elevator and rode to the top floor.

"Did you get a room here?"

"Maybe."

"How?"

"I'm over eighteen."

They got off the elevator and passed a bellman the bellman winked at Scott, confirming what was prearranged. Scott got to the door and pulled out a key.

"You dirty boy."

He opened the door and held it open for her. The dark room was illuminated with dozens of candles. Rose petals were scattered on the bed, like something out of a movie, like something out of Colleen's most romantic fantasies. She walked in, unable to speak. Scott took her by the hand and led her inside.

"Colleen, I don't want to do anything you're not ready for, but I love you and want to be with you. I wanted to make tonight as romantic as you've ever dreamed."

Colleen looked around at the candles and flowers.

"But no pressure?"

Scott smiled.

"Maybe a little."

Colleen smiled back.

"Dance with me."

Scott took her close to her and the two of them danced to music only the two of them could hear.

"Well, you know my life history. What about yours?"

Jo Ann and Peter were walking in the park, eating ice cream cones for dessert.

"My wife was a flight attendant on Pacific Pride flight twelve."

"Oh god."

Ten years before, terrorist had blown up Pacific Pride flight twelve, a full seven forty seven en route to Tokyo.

"Paul was three years old."

"That must have been horrible for you, raising him alone."

"He's had a lot of nannies, especially when he was little. Now mostly, it's just the two of us, two swinging bachelors."

"I can imagine the trouble the two of you get into."

Peter smiled.

"Did you ever want to get remarried?"

"Hell yeah. I wanted more children, but now I'm getting old."

"You can't be more than thirty five."

"Thirty four."

"You're awful young to be the Commissioner."

"I'm one of the youngest in the state."

Peter felt awkward about his professional achievements. It was true he had advanced quickly and was one of the youngest police commissioners in the state. He was proud, but he didn't want to flaunt it. He turned the conversation back over to Jo Ann.

"What about you, Jo Ann, ever consider getting married again?"

"Oh god. The first one was so horrible. I guess if the right guy came along. Of course, Chad would be my first priority. If the guy didn't like him or get along with him, then it would be over."

"Of course, with Paul, it's a lot easier because he's older. If he doesn't like someone, I knock the shit out of him and say 'deal with it'."

"Don't be so sure. When you meet someone you really care about, he may turn psycho on you."

"I suppose."

Before she could say another word, Peter took Jo Ann's face in his hands and guided it toward his. Their lips met and, for the briefest moment, Jo Ann thought she was going to faint.

Colleen's heart was racing. She was enjoying every moment of the romantic surprise Scott had set up. As they held one another close, Colleen could sense Scott was just as excited as she was, although it wasn't his heart she felt pressing against her thigh. She decided to make the first move. She pushed him back slightly and searched for the pin in her hair. She had seen it done in movies a million times and thought it was the sexiest thing she had ever seen. She had been practicing all day. She had all her hair pulled up with one pin and pulled it out, shaking her head, and letting her hair cascade down her shoulders. She gave Scott her best bedroom eyes, another thing she had been practicing all afternoon, and led him to bed. She turned around and pulled her hair up. Without a word, Scott knew what to do and unzipped her dress. By the time she turned around, Scott had his tie off and was unbuttoning his shirt.

"No. Let me undress you."

She undid his buttons one at a time and, once his shirt was off, began to kiss his chest. Scott wanted to give Colleen the full romantic experience and actually picked her up and carried her to the bed. He felt kind of silly doing it but changed his mind once he saw himself in the mirror. He, bare chested, arms flexed. She, long blonde hair, long blue gown, her breast pressing against his perfect chest. Eat your heart out Fabio.

Colleen ran her hands up and down Scott's back, loving the way his muscular body flexed under her touch. Unprepared for the pain as he entered her for the first time, she cried out as her fingernails dug into his back.

"Are you okay?"

"Yes."

"Do you want me to stop?"

"No."

Breathing heavily, Colleen kissed Scott hard on the mouth. His mind raced a mile a minute. Was he hurting her? Was she enjoying it? Was he? He was so preoccupied with her that, once he cleared his mind, he realized he was definitely enjoying it. The sensation, the feeling of being inside her, was better than anything he had ever imagined. The feeling was a million times better than anything he had felt by himself and he wondered if he would ever jerk off again. He felt his stomach muscles tighten and clutched the sheets, knowing he was almost finished. He moaned loudly, his entire body shaking as Scott had, what he considered, his first *real* orgasm. He lay down next to her, trying to catch his breath. She tried to get closer to her, but he pushed her away.

"What's wrong?"

"I'll be right back."

Scott went to the bathroom and came back a minute later, having gotten rid of the condom he had used. Colleen watched him walk naked across the room back toward the bed, her body wanting more of him, her body wanting every inch of him. He crawled back into bed and took her in his arms, holding her and listening to her breath until they both fell asleep.

"Peter, do you want to come in for coffee?"

Peter raised an eyebrow at Jo Ann.

"Is this one of those weird date things when you're really asking me for sex and if I say I don't want coffee, you think I'm not interested? Am I supposed to know that coffee equals sex?"

"First of all, coffee doesn't equal sex. If I wanted sex, I would ask for sex."

Peter raised his eyebrows again.

"And I don't have sex on the second date. Coffee means decaf and maybe some cake I bought at the store. That is, if my mother hasn't fed it to her damn bridge club. It could also mean something to drink."

"Well, since I'm off duty, I'll take you up on that offer."

Peter got out and opened the door for her. They walked hand in hand to the front door where they kissed once more time.

"The way you kiss, you can come over for coffee anytime."

She opened the door and was surprised to see Chad watching television.

"Shouldn't you be in bed young man? Where's grandma?"

"In the bathroom."

"Chad, you need to get to bed right now."

Suddenly, Peter felt like he was intruding.

"You know, Jo Ann, on second thought, I'm just going to head on home."

Oh no. Chad had scared him off. Jo Ann had to do something quick.

"I'll walk you out."

She walked him back to his car. He kissed her once more, promising to call her the next day. She stood there smiling as he drove away. She didn't notice Miranda pulling up across the street. As Jo Ann walked back toward her door, she heard her name being called.

"Jo Ann! Jo Ann!"

Miranda walked across the street.

"You're in big trouble. You've got a lot of explaining to do!"

"Mom, can Eric come sleep over?"

"Now?"

Cora couldn't believe her ears.

"Christian, it's past ten o'clock."

"I know but he says he has to get away from his sister. She's sick as a dog and germing up the whole house."

Cora's mind raced. Eric Moore was Kelleye Moore's brother. Kelleye was supposed to be at the prom tonight. Colleen was spending the night at her house. Something was up.

"Let me talk to Miss Grace."

Chris handed the phone to his mother and in a few moments, she was talking to Grace Moore.

"Cora, I'm sorry about this. The boys planned it behind my back."

"That's no problem Grace. If you can bring him over, I'll bring him back tomorrow morning. I can't leave now because Candice is already asleep and Colleen is at the prom."

"Sure, we're on our way. Are you sure it's no trouble?"

"A house full of boys on a Saturday night? It'll be a nightmare, but I don't mind. How's Kelleye? Eric says she's sick."

"Horrible. I couldn't get an appointment until Monday morning. Earlier today, she had a temperature of one hundred three."

"Is she bummed about missing the prom?"

"I don't think she was going anyway. You know my daughter, Miss Social."

"Well Colleen will be over later to fill her in on all the details."

"What?"

Exactly.

"Colleen told me she was staying at Kelleye's tonight."

"Kelleye never mentioned it. She's definitely not up to visitors."

"They never had plans?"

"Not that I know of, Cora. Sorry."

"Oh. Could you check with Kelleye? Please?"

A moment later, Grace returned to the phone.

"Cora, darling, it looks like you and I have fallen into the perfect teenage plot. Colleen tells you she's going to be here. You call here. Kelleye tells you she's in the shower or something. Kelleye knows where Colleen is and calls her there. Colleen calls you back and says she was in the bathroom doing number two or something."

"Except this time they got caught."

"What are you going to do?"

"What do I do? Does Kelleye know where they are?"

"She wouldn't tell me. I am her mother, I can make her tell me. I can withhold her medication until she cracks."

"No Grace, I can't go charging after her. Oh, and I definitely can't tell Cameron."

"Tell me what?"

"We're having a last minute sleep over."

"Oh."

Cameron walked back into the bedroom.

"Cora, do you still think this sleep over is a good idea?"

"Yea Grace, bring him over. I need all the witnesses I can get so I don't kill that girl."

Cora hung up the phone and dialed Genie.

"Hello."

"Genie, it's Cora. Is Jeremy asleep?"

"No."

"How would you like the night off? We're having a last minute sleep over. Send him over."

"He's on his way."

Within five minutes, Jeremy was packed and down the street at Cora's. Genie seized the opportunity and picked up the phone.

Miranda walked over to Jo Ann.

"You're home late."

"Don't change the subject. I didn't know you had a date with the Commissioner."

"Another date, actually. His name is Peter."

"Well, excuse me."

"Listen, I was going to have a drink with him, but Chad scared him off. Care to join me?"

"Sure."

"By the way, how did you like the champagne I sent over?"

"That crap? We dumped it down the toilet."

They both giggled as they walked inside together.

"Hello."

"Charlie, it's Genie. What are you doing tonight?"

"I'm ashamed to say nothing. After all, it's Saturday night."

"Why don't you come over and we can do nothing together."

"Where's your son?"

"At a sleepover."

"Give me an hour."

Charlie smiled to himself. Suddenly, he felt funny.

"Hey, does this make me a whore?"

"Absolutely not. We're just two people with nothing better to do on a Saturday night than have wild, uncommitted sex."

"Well, since you put it that way."

Charles hung up the phone feeling awkward. On the one hand, he was a young guy. What was wrong with getting lucky with a hot older woman? On the other hand, was he that available? She calls him for sex and he's over there within the hour? His good sense was overpowered by the growing feeling in his jeans. He quickly showered and drove to Sherwood Circle.

Ten minutes after she hung up the phone, Grace Moore was dropping Eric off at Cora's. She motioned for Cora to follow her into the kitchen.

"I broke her down. I know where Scott and Colleen are."

"Do I want to know?"

"Well, you were right about not telling Cameron. They're at the Hotel Bentley, the same hotel where the prom was. Kelleye and Colleen didn't know where they were going to end up, but called her when she found out."

"Does she know which room?"

"Cora, do you really want to know?"

"Yes."

"Room 501."

"Thanks Grace."

"Cora, you're not going to do something crazy are you? You're not going over there to confront them?"

"I can't now, I've got the boys."

"Please. I can tell you now that Chris, Chris, Eric and Jeremy have done just fine by themselves before."

"What would you do?"

"I don't know. If you confront her, you lose her trust. She has to be reprimanded though. She has to know she can't lie to you."

"Thanks again Grace."

Cora walked Grace to the door, fuming. She hid her feelings well in front of the fellow soccer mom, but wanted to kill her daughter. She calmly went to the bedroom where Cameron was watching television.

"Cam, I'm going out for a while. I have an errand."

"Why don't you just bring your boyfriend here and we can have a threesome?"

Cora rolled her eyes, she had no time for jokes.

"The boys are watching a movie. Keep an eye on them and be sure they don't get into any of *your* movies."

"Do they know where they are?"

Cameron suddenly felt very uncomfortable about his sons finding his porn collection.

"They're thirteen year old boys, I'm sure they do."

"I'll keep an eye out."

Cora got into her car and, against her better judgment, sped into the city to the Hotel Bentley.

Miranda was leaving Jo Ann's when she saw her brother-in-law pull into the circle and drive up to number eight.

"Charlie!"

She had had two strong drinks with Jo Ann and was feeling a little tipsy. Despite the fact that alcohol made her tired, she had to know what Oren's brother was doing at Genie's at eleven o'clock at night. He pretended not to hear her. She ran across the street, yelling his name.

"Charlie! What are you doing here?"

Charlie hadn't knocked on the door yet.

"Nothing."

"Yeah, what are you doing at Genie's house in the middle of the night?"

Slowly, but surely, Miranda caught on.

"Is this a booty call?"

"Keep your voice down!"

"Charles, she is old enough to be your mother."

At that moment, Genie opened the door.

"Miranda, would you mind keeping your voice down?"

She pulled Charles inside and slammed the door in Miranda's face. Once the door was closed, Genie busted out laughing.

"Did you see her face?"

"Genie, you don't think this is weird?"

Genie kissed him hard on the mouth, unbuckling his pants and sliding them down around his knees. She looked him right in the eye.

"Not at all."

The speedometer inched toward seventy five as Cora sped toward the city. She didn't see the small dog, contemplating crossing the street. As she caught sight of him, she swerved to miss him, flipping her car and sending it into a series of rolls. Cora screamed and, before she blacked out, she realized she was upside down.

Chapter 11

Phone calls in the middle of the night are enough to scare any parent, but Cameron Mayhelm wasn't surprised when his phone rang after eleven thirty. He expected a call from either his daughter or wife. The way Cora ran off, there was no telling what kind of trouble she had gotten herself into. He picked up the phone, laughing.

"Is this the Mayhelm residence?"

"Yes it is."

"Whom am I speaking to?"

"Cameron Mayhelm."

"Mr. Mayhelm, your wife was involved in an accident."

Cameron's heart stopped.

"Is she dead?"

"No, but her condition is critical. She's been taken to Gulf States Memorial."

"I'm on my way."

Cameron hung up the phone and called Colleen's friend Kelleye. The prom ended an hour ago and Cameron needed Colleen to come home immediately. Grace Moore picked up the phone, sleepily.

"Grace, it's Cameron Mayhelm, I need to speak to Colleen."

Grace had no idea what to say. She knew Cora hadn't told Cameron about Colleen.

"Cameron, she's ah…"

"Grace, it's an emergency. Please."

"Is something wrong?"

"Cora was just in an accident. She's been taken to the hospital in critical condition."

"Cameron, I hate to be the one to tell you this, but Colleen isn't here."

"She's supposed to be."

"I know. Did Cora tell you where she was going?"

"No."

Cameron began to lose his patience. He was obviously out of the loop and Grace Moore was keeping something from him.

"Cameron, Colleen and Kelleye lied to us. Colleen is with Scott at the Hotel Bentley. Cora and I figured it out tonight but she didn't want to tell you. She was probably going to the hotel to confront them."

"I need Colleen, do you know the room number."

"501."

"Thanks Grace."

"Do you need me to watch the boys?"

"Yea, thanks. I'll wake up Candice."

"No, don't do that. I'll stay over there."

"Thanks again Grace."

Cameron hung up the phone and immediately phoned the Hotel Bentley.

"Hotel Bentley."

"Room 501, please."

After a moment, the phone began to ring. Colleen, expecting it to be Kelleye, picked up the phone.

"Hello."

"Colleen, it's your father."

Colleen, shocked, couldn't speak. Cameron was furious, but kept his temper in check.

"I don't know what's going on, or why you lied, or what in the hell you're doing in a hotel room with a boy I hardly even know, but you'd better get your ass home immediately."

"I can explain…"

"Shut up. Your mother has been in an accident and was rushed to the hospital. I need you here with the kids."

"How bad was she…?"

"Now!"

Cameron slammed the phone down. Within minutes, Grace was there. Cameron thanked her again and drove the short distance to the hospital.

Colleen put the phone down and shook Scott awake. She couldn't believe what she had just heard.

"Scott, that was my dad."

"What's up?"

"My mom was in an accident. We need to get to the hospital."

Scott jumped out of bed and got dressed. Within ten minutes, they were on their way. Colleen called home and was shocked to hear Grace on the other line.

"Miss Moore, I'm on my way home, but I'm going to the hospital first. I just want to see what's wrong."

"I think that's best."

Grace's coldness came straight through the phone.

"Miss Grace, I'm so sorry…"

"This is a conversation you should be having with your parents. I've already dealt with Kelleye."

"I just wanted to…"

"I'm fine with the kids Colleen. You get to the hospital."

Before Colleen could say anything, Grace hung up.

Twenty minutes later, Colleen and Scott walked into the emergency room at Gulf States Memorial. Scott wisely stayed back when Colleen walked over to her father.

"Dad…"

Cameron turned around and, in a moment of hatred for his oldest daughter, slapped Colleen across the face. Colleen had never seen this side of her father and it scared her. She gathered herself together and straightened herself up. Cameron showed no sign of apologizing. Instead he spoke, his words dripping with contempt.

"I hope it was worth it."

Cameron shot a hateful glance over to Scott.

"Go home."

"What do I tell the kids?"

"Tell them nothing! Until I get news, don't tell them anything."

"Alright."

Colleen turned away from her father and went home to be with her brothers and sister. Once they got home, everyone was asleep. Grace, who was in the kitchen making coffee, came out when she heard the front door open. She immediately gave Scott an evil look.

"I told your father I'd stay with the kids."

"No, Miss Moore, I can stay."

Grace looked past Colleen to Scott.

"I really don't mind."

Colleen got the hint and turned to him.

"You'd better go. Call me tomorrow."

Scott nodded and left. Grace started to collect her purse.

"Tell your father to call me when he finds word about your mother."

"What about Mom?"

Grace closed her eyes, hoping she didn't hear what she had just heard from the small voice behind her.

"Candice, what are you doing up?"

"I had to use the bathroom. What happened to Mom?"

"Nothing honey, go back to bed."

Colleen was pushing her sister back into her bedroom.

"Colleen, can I sleep with you tonight?"

"Sure. Climb in and I'll be there in a minute."

Thankfully, Candice went off to Colleen's room with little protest. Grace started to leave and Colleen stopped her.

"Miss Grace, I know you said you dealt with Kelleye. Just know this was all my idea. She only wanted to help me."

"That doesn't excuse what she did, what either of you did."

Grace left and drove home, praying silently for Cora Mayhelm.

Two hours later, Dr. Lionel Washington came out to consult with Cameron.

"Mr. Mayhelm, the good news is that your wife's condition is stable. She's still in the ICU under observation."

"Is she awake? Can I see her?"

"You can see her but she is still unconscious. There is other news…"

"Bad news."

"I'm afraid so. The crash fractured some of your wife's vertebrae, severing her spinal cord. I'm afraid she may never walk again."

The words knocked the wind out of Cameron. He felt like he had been hit with a ton of bricks.

"She's paralyzed?"

"From the waist down. Of course, we'll know for sure once she wakes up and how much she can use her legs."

Tears formed and ran down his cheeks.

"Can I see her now?"

"Of course."

Cameron followed Dr. Washington into the ICU where Cora was lying, bruised and unconscious. He sat down next to her bed and held her hand.

Chapter 12

"The house is situated on the cul de sac, it has one of the biggest backyards on the street."

Hope and Allen followed the realtor into the backyard. Allen had sweet talked her into showing them some houses on a Sunday morning. This was the third house they had seen that morning and she was right, the backyard was huge.

"Do you two have any children?"

"Actually, we just found out we were pregnant."

"How exciting. You can see the yard has plenty of room for a pool or a swing set…or both."

Hope squeezed Allen's hand. This house had everything they wanted. The garage had been turned into a den with a fireplace. All the appliances were new. Both the roof and the air conditioning systems were less than five years old. Allen turned and smiled at his wife. There was no doubt this was the house she would push for. She loved the fact that it was next to her brother. He loved the fact that it was three blocks from church and school. Mentally calculating, he figured it was well within their price range.

"Can I speak to my wife privately?"

"Certainly."

Allen took Hope aside. She was positively giddy.

"What do you think?"

"Well, even at the price it is now, our payments will be about five fifty. That's not too bad."

"Should we make an offer or go and take it now?"

"I would prefer to take make an offer…but I know how much you want this house and I'd hate to miss it if we got outbid. Let's take it now."

Hope jumped up and threw her arms around her husband.

"Is that good news?"

"We'll take it."

"Fantastic. I'll get the paperwork started."

An hour later, Hope caught up with her mother before noon mass.

"Mother, listen, I have two great pieces of news. I would have told you about the first one last week but we were so busy with Father Tom's party."

"What a fiasco. I told Bea I would help her, but she wanted to do everything herself. And it showed."

"I thought it went well."

Muriel giggled to herself.

"What was your news Hope?"

"First of all, Allen and I got the house next to Gretchen and Ben's."

"That is a fantastic neighborhood. Do you really need something that big?"

"Well, the second thing is…we're having a baby!"

"Darling, that's wonderful! My baby having a baby. We'll have to start shopping next week. Oh wait. I hope you're going to be due before February because your father and I are cruising the Mediterranean."

"Mother, do you think this is more important?"

"Well, darling, we're going with a tour group."

Hope rolled her eyes. Her mother and father were totally content sailing around with a bunch of rich old snobs. She couldn't imagine how she and Ben had turned out so well grounded.

"Well mother, I'm going to the doctor next week and I'll let you know about the due date."

"Listen; let's have lunch after the doctor. We need to start decorating the new house."

"We have everything we need in our apartment."

Again, Muriel giggled to herself.

"Of course you do darling, see you inside."

Muriel went inside. Allen went up to her, noticing she was upset.

"What was that all about?"

"Just my mother being herself. I told her about the baby."

"Was she excited?"

"Yes, as long as it doesn't interfere with her cruise."

Allen laughed.

"That's your mother alright. Come on, let's go inside."

Father David West paced frantically. He knew what he was doing, he had said Mass hundreds of times before, but never in front of his own parish. Never in front of a group of people so accustomed to their old pastor that he felt them wishing him to fail, all eyes sizing him up in judgment. Once he heard the opening song, he took his place and proceeded down the aisle.

Halfway through the homily, he started to relax. He had formally introduced himself and gave information on his background. He found a few people smiling at him and focused on them.

Gretchen looked around the church and whispered to Ben.

"I don't see Cora and Cameron here. I wonder if they went to Mass earlier."

Ben shrugged. He had never known Cora, no matter how good she was, to be able to get all the kids up early enough for the eight o'clock service.

"Maybe, I don't know."

"Daddy, shhh."

Ben looked at Tim and put a finger to his lips. He almost burst out laughing, being reprimanded by his three year old. Tim laughed out loud and Ben saw his mother looking over her shoulder from her place of honor in the first row. Gretchen saw this too and elbowed her husband in the ribs. As Mass was coming to a close, Father David approached the microphone for an announcement.

"Ladies and gentlemen, I'm asking you to join me in praying for one of our families. Last night, Cora Mayhelm was involved in a car accident and taken to Gulf States Memorial in critical condition. Her husband called me this morning to tell me her condition is stabilized but they still don't know the extent of her injuries. Please keep the Mayhelm family in your prayers."

Gretchen took Ben's hand. She couldn't believe what she was hearing.

After Mass, Malcolm York went up to his daughter and held her tight.

"Darling, your mother just told me the news. When are you due?"

"I'm guessing sometimes in February."

"Well, we'll have to change that."

Before she could protest, Malcolm continued.

"And I hear you bought a house? Right next to Benjamin?"

Gretchen's eyes lit up.

"You never told us you were taking it!"

"Well, we signed this morning. We move in at the beginning of next month."

"You're not moving anything."

"I know."

Hope smirked at Allen.

"Your mother and I insist on taking everyone to lunch to celebrate."

Everyone agreed with Malcolm and the group walked to the parking lot. Ben smiled for his sister, but nobody on Sherwood Circle would ever forget what happened at number six nine years ago.

Cameron was walking back from the coffee machine when his cell phone rang.

"Hello."

"Dad, I know you don't want to talk to me right now but…"

"Actually Colleen, I apologize. I know it won't be easy to forgive me, but I acted out of anger, something I've tried to teach you not to do."

"You just scared me that's all."

"I was angry. We still need to talk about what happened last night."

"Speaking of that, I know you told me not to tell the kids anything, but you need to tell them something. I bought them off for a while telling them you and Mom went off for a few days."

Cameron smiled in spite of himself, God his daughter was a good liar.

"But Candice woke up and heard me talking to Miss Grace last night. She knows something is up."

"I'll check with the doctor and be home in about an hour."

"Dad…"

Colleen was almost afraid to ask.

"How is she?"

"Not good. Stable, but not good."

"Isn't it horrible about Cora Mayhelm?"

Gretchen nodded, trying to keep her boys in line. Muriel looked at her two grandsons with a disapproving eye.

"Gretchen, really, you'd think they had never been in a restaurant before."

"Muriel, that's why I suggested The Breakers, Mariners is great, Benjamin and I love it here, love the linen tablecloths, love the ten piece place settings, but it's not a place for children. I told you that."

Hope couldn't believe her sister-in-law had stood up to her mother like that. She couldn't believe her brother would sit there and let his mother talk about his kids like that. She tried to intervene but chose the wrong topic.

"Dad, what did you think of the new priest? You weren't there for his welcoming party."

Muriel interjected immediately.

"That party was for Father Tom, not this new kid."

"I thought he was okay."

Muriel rolled her eyes.

"Well, Bea told me he's a total slob around the rectory."

"So you and Bea are talking again? After the mess she made of the going away party?"

Muriel appeared to ignore her daughter.

"Anyway mother, he's a young bachelor. Give him a break. I think he'll do wonders for the youth program, maybe even bring some young people back to the church."

"I'd love a youth choir."

Gretchen knew the choir was made up entirely of Muriel's friends, headed by Bea de la Roche. Muriel looked at her over her wineglass, not saying a word, but secretly despising her daughter-in-law.

Cameron pulled into his driveway, not knowing what to say to his children. He got out of the car and was met at the door.

"Where's Mom?"

Cameron sat down and put Candice on his lap. He took a deep breath.

"Guys, your mom was in a car accident last night. She got hurt real bad and they brought her to the hospital."

"Is she alright?"

"I don't know Chris. The doctor told me before I came home that they were moving her to her own room. That's good…"

"But…"

"She injured her spinal cord and may not be able to walk again."

"Ever?"

"Ever."

"Is Mommy going to die?"

Cameron squeezed his youngest child.

"No honey, she's not going to die."

"When can we see her?"

"We can go over there now. Get ready."

The three oldest children began to get ready. Candice, with all the innocence of a six year old, looked up at her father.

"Dad, are we still going to camp?"

"Of course."

Cameron smiled at his daughter, not wanting to upset her, not wanting to shatter her whole world. She had no idea how all their lives would be changing soon enough.

Chapter 13

Jeremy walked into his mother's room when he heard the shower running. It was way past noon and she was running late for work. He had come home early from his sleepover and was wondering what to do with his day alone. He knocked on the door and walked in, calling to Genie. What he didn't know was that Genie had left for work earlier and it wasn't his mother in the shower.

"Mom, are you off of work today?"

Charlie stood motionless. He had overslept and knew Genie didn't want him home with her son. He wasn't expected back till later on the day. He stood there silent, not knowing what to do.

"Mom?"

When he got no answer, Jeremy smiled to himself. He went and filled a pitcher up with ice water and crept back into the bathroom. He climbed on top of the toilet and dumped the ice water over the person in the shower, assuming it was his mother. Startled, Charlie yelled out and threw open the shower curtain, careful to keep his lower half hidden.

"You're not my mom!"

"No I'm not. Can I finish in here, please?"

Not knowing what to say, Jeremy nodded and left the bathroom.

Cameron led the children to their mother's room. As they were about to go in, Father David stepped out.

"Father."

"Mr. Mayhelm."

"Please, call me Cameron."

David leaned in.

"I would say call me David, but it probably isn't appropriate."

"Probably not."

"I was just in with Cora, praying with her."

"She's awake?"

"She woke up during the Joyful Mysteries."

Cameron opened the door and let the kids in, staying behind to talk to Father West.

"Does she know anything about her injuries?"

"No. How bad is it?"

"They say she may never walk again. She's damaged her spinal cord."

"Well, everyone at church is praying for her. Cameron, call me if you need anything."

"Thanks David."

Cameron hugged his priest and went in to see his wife.

A few minutes later, Charlie came out of the bathroom, fully dressed. Jeremy was on the sofa watching television.

"This is awkward."

"No it's not. You're the guy sleeping with my Mom. I'm not an idiot. Is that why she's not getting back with my dad?"

"Beats me."

Jeremy got up and went to the kitchen.

"Do you want something to eat?"

"What?"

Charlie couldn't believe his ears.

"Yea, do you want something to eat? I man, you can hang out if you want. You appear to be not much older than I am and I'm sure you've worked up an appetite."

"Uh."

"Don't worry, it's cool. I hope when I'm as old as my mom, I'm still having sex."

"Are you having sex now?"

"This minute?"

Jeremy laughed at his own joke.

"No way dude, I'm only thirteen."

Jeremy got the pans out.

"How about hamburgers?"

"Uhm, alright."

Jeremy smiled to himself. If he kept this jackass eating, Genie would walk in on them and have a fit.

"That was a pretty good trick with the ice."

"I learned that at summer camp."

"Pretty sneaky."

"You haven't seen anything yet."

"Guys, why don't you go downstairs and get us something to drink."

Cora's kids raced out of the room, leaving their parents alone.

"Has the doctor been in to see you?"

"He did some test when he thought I was asleep. It can't be good."

"How's that?"

"I can't feel my legs. I didn't want to freak out Father David or the kids so I kept quiet. There is something wrong with my legs, isn't there?"

"The doctors say you may never be able to walk again."

"I figured that."

Cameron couldn't get over his wife's attitude.

"What do you want, Cameron? Do you want me to start crying, screaming, getting hysterical, beating my breast, cry why me? Why me?"

"I expected some kind of emotion."

"My emotion is that I'm going to have to learn to live with it. I have no other choice. If there's a no chance I can walk again, then I'll do what's necessary."

Cameron held back his own tears as he kissed his wife's hand.

"You don't have to put on a brave front for me, you know."

"I know."

After a moment of silence, Cora kicked back into Super Mom mode.

"What are we going to do about Colleen?"

"I'm afraid I didn't handle that too well."

"Neither did I, driving off into the middle of the night like that like some sort of crazy person. Look where it got me. You know, what was I going to do once I got there? Bust through the door in the middle of them having sex?"

"So you think…"

"Of course they did. An eighteen year old boy doesn't rent a hotel room on prom night with his girlfriend for any other reason. Well, she has to stop seeing him of course."

"Well, in the least, she isn't staying at home when we bring the kids to camp. She's coming with us."

"And she's going to stop seeing him."

"Are you sure that's the wisest thing to do?"

Before Cora could answer, the four kids came back into the room. They jumped on the bed and chatted for a few minutes before the doctor came in.

"Cora, this is Dr. Washington."

"Hello."

"Guys, your mom and I need to talk to the doctor, wait outside for a while."

Once they were alone, Lionel pulled a chair up to the bed, When giving bad news to people, he was careful never to look down on them.

"Mrs. Mayhelm…"

"Cora, please."

"Cora, most of your injuries are already taken care of. You got a mild concussion, that's what made you black out. You separated your shoulder, but we popped it back with no problem. Your cuts have been treated and your bruises will heal. The injury to your spinal cord is permanent. It's too extensive and risky to operate and the chance that it will heal itself is highly unlikely."

Cora squeezed Cameron's hand.

"I've arranged for a wheelchair, one of the smaller ones that will make it easier to get around your house. I've also set up appointments with a physical therapist in your home. You're going to have to build up your upper body strength."

Cora nodded.

"When do I get to leave here?"

"Soon."

"Good."

Cameron looked at Cora.

"Well, Cameron, I have to be home. The boys' last day of school is this week and I promised I'd make muffins. Candice's graduation is ten o'clock Thursday morning…"

"I think you're going to have to slow down."

"I can't. I can't play the poor crippled woman. I'm not going to let this change my life."

"It has changed your life, you have to accept that."

Lionel interjected.

"Cora, I think your attitude is great. Until you become adjusted to life in a wheelchair, you need to slow down a little. I'll come by to see you before you're released."

Lionel Washington's smile faded as he left the room. The entire family's life was about to change and he hated to see what would happen when Cora's family realized she would never walk, or drive, or dance again.

Jeremy smiled as the door to his house opened. Genie called out to him as he answered her, bracing himself for the upcoming scene.

"Do you have any idea what you want for…?"

Genie stopped dead in her tracks. She couldn't believe her eyes. There, at her table, was her thirteen year old son casually having lunch with her twenty five year old lover.

"Charlie, what are you doing here?"

"Oh, should I assume you two know one another?"

"Jeremy, don't be a smartass."

"It's cool, Mom, really."

"Charlie, can I see you in the bedroom, please?"

"Haven't you seen enough of him in the bedroom?"

"Jeremy, shut up!"

Genie walked down the hall with Charles right behind her. Was she going to scold him? If that was it, he was gone. He was not her child. Genie closed the door behind them and, before Charlie could say anything, she had her tongue down his throat. His hands fondled her breast and she could feel him growing harder beneath his jeans.

"I want you so badly."

She finally got the strength to push him away.

"Charlie, we have to be more discreet."

"I'm sorry, Genie. I overslept."

"That's alright. I should have seen this coming. Jeremy is no idiot. Oh god, if he tells his father…"

"Genie, relax. We can meet at my place after work. We can handle this."

"Is this all we are? Secret meetings for casual sex?"

He had asked himself that same question.

"Is that so bad? Come on, do you really see us having a serious, long term relationship? I'm young enough to be your…"

"Don't finish that sentence."

She kissed him once more and walked him to the door. She went into the kitchen and tried to decide how to deal with her son.

Tears ran down Colleen's face as she went to the farthest payphone from her family and called Scott. He picked up on the first ring.

"Colleen?"

"It's me. We're at the hospital."

"How is she?"

"She's awake. Oh god, Scott, she's paralyzed. She may never walk again."

Scott couldn't believe what he was hearing.

"Ever?"

"That's what my dad told us."

Scott remembered the scene in the hospital the night before. Colleen cried all the way home after her father slapped her.

"Have the two of you talked?"

"He apologized. Scott, it's my entire fault."

"Our fault. You weren't alone last night. And you're wrong, it wasn't our fault, it just happened."

Colleen dried her eyes when she saw Gretchen and Ben walking down the hall.

"Listen, I have to go. I'll try and call you later once we get home."

"Colleen, I love you. No matter what happened, last night was the most romantic night of my life."

Colleen smiled.

"Are you sure that was your first? You sure seemed to know what you were doing."

"I could say the same thing for you in the swimming pool."

Colleen smiled through her tears.

"I love you too, I have to go."

Colleen hung up the phone and turned to her neighbors.

"Colleen, Father West told us in church what happened. How's your mother?"

"She's pretty bad. She's in five seventeen."

Colleen watched as they walked down the hall and went into her mother's room.

"What did you think you were doing?"

Jeremy sat eating lunch, unfazed, as his mother approached him.

"What was I supposed to do? I walk in on the guy buck naked in the shower. I figured the least I could do is offer him lunch. Would you have rather we had just come to the restaurant?"

"Young man, I don't like your attitude!"

"Whatever."

Jeremy rolled his eyes at his mother and walked past her to his bedroom.

"Jeremy Michael, you get back here this minute!"

Jeremy slammed his bedroom door and called his father.

"Breakers Inn."

"Oren, you're the assistant manager. What are you doing answering the phone?"

"Waiting for Gage to come out of the bathroom."

Oren hated when Miranda called him at work. It either meant the car was broke or the house was on fire. Thankfully, they didn't have any kids to get sick.

"What's wrong?"

Miranda rolled her eyes.

"Now why does something have to be wrong for me to call you at work?"

"Because the only time you ever call me is when something is wrong."

"Well, nothing is wrong worrywart. Quite the opposite actually. How would you feel about spending a few days in Miami?"

"That sounds great. How did you pull it off?"

"My boss has a condo on the beach. He said we could use it if we wanted. All we would have to pay for is the air fare."

"I'll have to clear it with Caryn first."

"Clear what with Caryn?"

Like mental telepathy, Oren's boss came through the front doors. Oren covered the mouthpiece with his hand.

"Miranda's boss has a condo in Miami. He's letting us use it for a few days."

"Ooh, I love Miami. Let me know where it is and I'll let you know where to eat."

Oren turned his attention back to his wife.

"Sounds like it's okay to me. Call Atlantic International."

"I'm on it."

Oren hung up the phone and turned to Caryn.

"Thanks Caryn."

"Well, you do get two weeks of vacation. Just give me a few days' notice."

Gage came out of the bathroom.

"What did I miss?"

"Nothing. Pre-authorize these arrivals."

"Hello."

"Dad, it's me. Listen, I know why Mom doesn't want to get back together. She has a new boyfriend."

Geoffrey smiled to himself. He had secretly wondered if Genie was seeing someone but didn't want to ask his sons.

"Is that so?"

"He's younger than Patrick."

"Really?"

"Can I move in with you?"

The question took Geoffrey totally by surprise. Was this the son that wanted to beat him up a few weeks ago?

"Is it that bad at home?"

"Well, I figured Mom getting laid would loosen her up a bit, but lately she's been a total bitch."

"Hey! Watch your attitude toward your mother young man."

"Sorry."

"Listen, let me talk to your mother and I'll get back to you."

"Don't wait too long. Hey, are you still living at the hotel? That would be so cool."

"Actually, I'm moving out next week. Sorry."

"Anyway, talk to Mom."

Jeremy hung up. Geoffrey smiled to himself. Genie had herself a boy toy. It was about time. He wondered if Patrick knew anything about this. He picked up the phone.

Melissa picked up the phone immediately.

"Hello."

"Melissa, it's Geoffrey."

"Oh."

"Is something wrong?"

"No, I was waiting for the hotel to call. That's all."

Melissa wondered if her father-in-law knew it was her idea not to have Geoffrey stay with them. Patrick had let his father down easily, not even mentioning his wife. Geoffrey was no fool. He knew the daughter-in-law he had never met had to have had some ill feelings toward him, despite the turn around in his son's attitude.

"It won't take long. Is Patrick in?"

"Hold on."

After a moment, Patrick picked up the line.

"Hello."

"You're not in the office today?"

"Lucky for you, no."

"Listen Pat, has your mother mentioned anything about a new man in her life, one that's considerable younger?"

"Not that I of. She's never mentioned anything to me."

"Apparently, she's seeing someone and it's upset your brother so much that he asked to move in with me."

"Well Jeremy hasn't told me anything. Are you going to let him?"

"I need to talk to Genie first."

Geoffrey heard Melissa say something in the background and he assumed she was pushing him to get off the phone. A second later, she was on the line.

"Melissa, I'm sorry…"

"No, it's not that. Geoffrey, we'd like to have you over for dinner. How's tomorrow night?"

"Sounds good to me. Can I bring anything?"

"Wine would be nice."

"Sure thing."

"Do you need to finish up with Pat?"

"No. Tell him I'll see him tomorrow."

"Seven o'clock?"

"Sure thing."

Melissa hung up the phone, smiling. Extending the olive branch was the right thing to do.

Geoffrey immediately called Genie.

"Hello."

"Genie, it's Geoffrey. What's up with Jeremy?"

"Why don't you tell me? His attitude is totally out of line lately."

"He tells me you have a new boyfriend, boy being the operative word."

Genie rolled her eyes. How dare her thirteen year old run to her ex-husband and tell him about her relationship. Jeremy needed to be put in line. Pronto.

"Yes, I am seeing someone and yes, he is slightly younger than me. Why does this concern you Geoffrey?"

"Because our son asked if he could move in with me?"

Genie was shocked into silence.

"Genie, are you still there?"

"I thought you were living at the hotel."

"I'm moving out next week. I found a place to rent near the museum where I'm working."

"Are you still restoring art?"

"Yeah."

"Well, what should we do?"

"Well, I know you're going to hate the idea. Let him move in here. He'll be finished school in two weeks."

"What is he going to do all day?"

"That's the point. When he figures out how boring it is here, he'll be dying to come home. He'll never see his friends and he'll be miserable."

Genie was about to agree.

"But isn't this giving into him, giving him exactly what he wants?"

"Tell him I asked you about it. He doesn't know that you know he wants to move out."

"Yea. You and I thought it would be a good way for him to get to know you."

"Exactly."

"Good idea Geoffrey. I'll talk to him about it tonight."

"I'll get everything ready over here."

Colleen pulled into the driveway at number one to find her father hard at work. She walked to the door, taking in all the lumber and supplies.

"Be careful not to step on any of these nails. I've spent enough time in the hospital these last few days."

Cora had been kept in the hospital longer than anticipated. The doctors were running a few more tests before they released her.

"Dad, what are you doing?"

"Building a ramp for your mother's wheelchair."

The words hit Colleen like a ton of bricks. She had been walking on eggshells the past few days, dreading when she would be alone with her father. She hadn't said two words to her mother. She couldn't bear the thought that she was responsible for her mother's accident. Scott had called twice since the accident to see how Cora was doing and both times, Colleen had refused to talk to him. Overwrought with guilt, she worked at the store as much as possible. The problem was, it was just as hard to avoid Scott there.

"Oh."

She walked past him toward the door when Cameron asked the question he had been dreading.

"Why did you lie?"

"What, Dad?"

Cameron stood up and dusted the sawdust off of his pants.

"Why did you lie?"

"Why does anyone lie? I was doing something I wasn't supposed to be doing and I didn't want to get caught."

"It's just rotten luck your mother has to pay the price."

"Don't do this to me. I have to live with this guilt for along time, okay, probably the rest of my life. I don't need you to make it worse."

She stormed past him and into the house. Holding back his own tears, Cameron finished up and went to get ready to pick Cora up from the hospital.

"Good news, Ben's sister and her husband are moving next door to us."

Gretchen was arranging the flowers she had brought for Cora.

"Is she the one that's pregnant?"

"Yes. My mother-in-law was ecstatic. She wants a granddaughter. That's all she talked about at lunch, when she wasn't criticizing my children."

"Gretchen, that's what mother-in-laws do. Does she, your sister-in-law, does she know about what happened there?"

"No. I doubt she does. It isn't exactly something the realtor fills you in on."

"Yea. The last two people who lived here died here."

"The fact is, they didn't just die."

"I know."

"Let's talk about something cheerier. When are you getting out of here?"

"Getting out so I can spend the rest of my life in a wheelchair?"

Gretchen had no idea what to say to her friend. Cora realized she had made her uncomfortable.

"I'm sorry, Gret. Cameron should be here any minute to pick me up."

Gretchen took her hand.

"Well, if you need anything, call me. I'll be right over."

"Please, I'll need help getting on and off the toilet. You know, I don't think Cameron has any idea what's in store for us."

"Cora, you have a strong marriage and a great family. You'll get through this."

"Thank you."

"Anybody home?"

Ben stuck his head in the room. Cora smiled.

"Your wife was just telling me about your new neighbors."

"Yea, I haven't decided if my sister living next door to us is a good thing or a bad thing."

"At least you'll always have a baby sitter. Between her and Colleen, you'll have all your bases covered."

"Speaking of that, Gretchen, we've got to go. The kids are tearing this place up."

Gretchen kissed Cora goodbye. She turned to leave, but stopped at the door.

"By the way, you're going to love the new priest."

"Good homily this week?"

"I wasn't paying attention. My mother-in-law hates him so that's good enough for me."

"She hates him already?"

"Already."

Gretchen passed Cameron on the way out of the room. Cameron went over to his wife and kissed her.

"Are you ready?"

"I'm just waiting for Dr. Washington to bring in the chair.

Chapter 14

The next day, Genie finally got Jeremy to stay in the same room without scowling at her. She took that as a good sign and decided to break the good news.

"Jeremy, your father called me yesterday.

"Oh."

"He asked if you could spend the summer with him and I said yes."

""'Just the summer?"

"Yes."

"Why not longer?"

"Because this is where you live and once school starts, I need to know where to find you."

"Whatever. When can I leave?"

"When school ends in two weeks."

"Cool."

Jeremy got up to call Christopher.

Cameron pulled the van into the driveway. Cora stared at the entranceway to their home.

"What did you do?"

"I built you a ramp, and I took the screen door off. The only door you have to get past opens inward."

"Thanks, I guess."

"I wanted to make it easier for you. I'm sorry."

"Well, help me down from here so I can try it out."

Cameron went around and lifted Cora out of the van. He tried to push her but she turned and swatted his hands away.

Doris stopped eating her sandwich and went to answer the door. She peeked through the peephole and got nervous when she didn't recognize the young man on the other side. She cracked open the door.

"Can I help you?"

"Yes ma'am, is Herb Shepherd home?"

"I'm Doris Shepherd, his wife."

"May I speak to your husband please?"

"Herb is dead, he died years ago."

The young man looked broken hearted.

"This was the last address on the list."

"What are you talking about?"

"My name is Kevin Ryan. Herb Shepherd is my father."

Doris started to close the door.

"Ma'am, was your husband a pilot for US West?"

Doris stopped closing the door. Herb had been a pilot when the two of them met in nineteen sixty one. She had just turned twenty. They dated for a year before they got engaged and married on her family's farm in Iowa. She despised the lonely nights, but the money and affluent lifestyle of a pilot's wife was something she had gotten used to. Herb had retired in eighty nine and died six years later. They had lived in San Diego until Herb had the seniority to fly when he wanted. After that, they moved to New Orleans to be with his family. They bought their house on Sherwood Circle in nineteen seventy three, right when the subdivision was being developed.

"Yes he was."

"Did he ever fly to Boston?"

The San Diego-Boston flight was one of Herb's favorites. Doris couldn't believe what she was hearing.

"Mrs. Shepherd, before my mother died last month, she told me who my real father was. She said he was a pilot for US West by the name of Herb Shepherd. She told me lived in New Orleans. I went through the phone book and this was the last Shepherd on the list."

"Your mother lied to you."

Doris began to shut the door again. The young man stopped her, frightening her. Why had he come here and what did he want?

"Mrs. Shepherd, please, here's my card. If you want to talk, I'm staying at a place called The Breakers Inn. I'd like to talk to you once this settles in."

Doris shut the door in the young man's face. It couldn't be true, it couldn't. How could Herb have done that to her, to their marriage? She wanted to look through the peephole to see if he was still there, but was afraid to look into those blue eyes, the exact eyes of her husband. Oh god, how could Herb have done this?

That night, Melissa opened the door to Geoffrey with a smile on her face.

"Geoffrey, come in. I'm so glad to finally meet you."

"Really? I'm sure you have some not so pleasant pre conceived notions about me."

Embarrassed, Melissa kept smiling.

"Well, we'll have to use tonight to clear up some of those."

"I brought wine."

Melissa took the bottle from him.

"Let's open this baby up. I think Patrick is in the kitchen, follow me."

He followed her through the foyer of their house and was immediately impressed. The house was very nicely decorated, everything matched. The draped matched the carpet, went with the sofa, coordinated with the placemats that complimented the dishtowels. It looked like something out of a magazine shoot, yet was comfortable and inviting at the same time.

"Did you study decorating or do you just have a flair?"

"Oh, I just pick things up here and there."

Geoffrey didn't believe her. Every detail in the house had been seen to. Melissa was readying herself for a life as a successful lawyer's wife. Patrick was in the kitchen finishing dinner when his wife and father came in.

"Dad, I'm glad you came."

"I'm just telling your wife what a beautiful home you have."

"That's all her. I just nod and smile."

Melissa smiled at her husband's compliment.

"Pat, your father brought wine. Why don't you open it and I'll give him a tour of the house."

Melissa took Geoffrey by the arm and led him through the kitchen and up the stairs. Patrick was glad to see that their first meeting, so far, had gotten off to a good start.

"Cameron, honey, you have to let me get used to getting around like this."

Cora chided Cameron's attempts to help her make dinner. She wheeled herself around surprisingly well. Cameron knew this would be the easy part. Cora hadn't used the bathroom, taken a shower, or gotten into bed yet. Colleen had stayed in her room during Cora's homecoming, too guilty to watch her mother struggle. Scott had called earlier, wanting to come visit, but Colleen thought it better if he stayed away for a while. Once a welcome visitor in the Mayhelm home, Scott would be seen differently as the man who deflowered their daughter and cost Cora the use of her legs.

"I've been traveling. I'm an art restorer."

Melissa nodded. She was enjoying meeting her father-in-law. She wanted so much to like him, but despite Patrick's change of attitude, couldn't forget all the bad stuff she had heard about him over the years.

"How did you get into that?"

"I've always loved art. I studied it in college and formed a career out of it."

"I thought you got married right out of high school."

"I did. I went to college when Patrick was still in grade school. I finished before Jeremy came along."

"That must have been hard, going to school and supporting a family."

"It was. Thank god I had a good wife to support me."

"And still you left."

Patrick couldn't believe Melissa had said that. He shot his wife a hateful glance before trying to change the subject.

"Melissa, that's not why we're here."

"That's alright Pat. She has a right to know, she is family now."

Geoffrey sipped his wine.

"Melissa, I never wanted to go through life thinking 'what if'. I got married way too early and hated feeling tied down. Hell, I had never even been on an airplane. I had never been out of state. When Genie got pregnant, we did 'the right thing' and got married. I wasn't miserable at first but started seeing all the things I was missing out on. I thought going to college would help and for a while, it did. But I was going to school full time and working two jobs. When I wasn't studying, I was working or sleeping. I never saw my son or my wife. I finished school and began traveling in my field. Right after Jeremy was born, I was chosen as part of a team to restore the *David.* It was the biggest honor of my life and when I got back from Rome, I hardly knew my wife and children anymore. I finally told Genie I couldn't do it anymore and we separated. Our trial separation lasted seven years, in that time, Genie filed for divorce. I put my work ahead of my family and I lost them. Seeing the world doesn't compare to seeing your children grow up."

Oren walked into his house and dropped his bag on the dining room table. Miranda peeked out of the kitchen.

"Get that off there, I just dusted!"

Dutifully, he obeyed his wife. He walked into the kitchen and put his arms around his wife.

"Miami, huh?"

"Yes. Doesn't that sound great? Greg's condo is on the beach. He says you can hear the waves from the bedroom. How soon can you get off?"

"The sooner the better."

"Is next week too soon?"

"I'll let Caryn know tomorrow."

"I'll call Atlantic International and book for Monday. How does that sound?"

"Sounds great to me."

"Have we even taken a vacation since our honeymoon?"

"No."

"Four years is too long."

Miranda smiled at her husband.

"Speaking of too long, I had better turn this chicken before it burns."

She kissed him and went back to finishing dinner. Oren started setting the table. He hated eating so late, but figured it was worth the price to eat together.

Over dessert, Geoffrey got to know his daughter-in-law.

"I have three sisters and one brother. My parents have been married for thirty six years. I went to college for business administration and have been working at the Hotel Bentley for four years now..."

"How did you and Patrick meet?"

"We were both on a cancelled flight in Houston. We got bumped from one flight to another and finally had to spend the night at the airport. Everything was full. We had dinner and talked. We slept a little on the floor, remember that?"

Patrick nodded, smiling.

"The next morning, we waited for the first two flights. We finally gave up and rented a car to New Orleans where we talked another seven hours en route. When we got here, we exchanged numbers. A few days later, we had our first date."

"Hey, I always considered Hot Dog Hacienda on Concourse D our first date."

Melissa smiled.

"And there was no way to get you home?"

"There was a hurricane in New Orleans and every flight that did get out was oversold. The airline confirmed us three days after our original flight. We couldn't wait so we gave up and drove home."

"How romantic."

"Actually, it was."

"What was your wedding like?"

Patrick rolled his eyes while Geoffrey laughed. Melissa smacked Pat's hand.

"It was a theme wedding. It was at a plantation outside the city and we wore period dress. All my girlfriends hated me because of the dresses I made them wear. They were big with hoop shirts, hats and parasols. You'll have to watch the video sometimes."

"Yea, we make everyone sit through it at least once."

Geoffrey smiled and checked his watch.

"I'd love to see it tonight, but I have to be on my way."

He got up and Melissa kissed him goodbye.

"It really was good to meet you Geoffrey."

"I hope we can get together more now that you're back in town."

"We'll do that."

She hugged him and started clearing the table. Patrick walked his father to the front door.

"Patrick, your wife is fantastic."

"I think I'll keep her."

"You have no idea how much this means to me."

Patrick nodded and hugged his father. Geoffrey opened the door, but before he left, he turned back to his son with a puzzled look on his face.

"Parasols?"

Patrick laughed and waved goodbye. After Geoffrey was in his car and on his way, Patrick went back inside to help Melissa clean up.

Miranda and Oren were finally sitting down to dinner.

"Hey, do you know that lady that lives at number eight?"

"Genie? She's a waitress at The Breakers."

"How does she know your brother?"

"Charlie? I introduced them at our housewarming party. Why?"

"Because I think they're sleeping together."

Oren nearly chocked on his fried chicken.

"What makes you say that?"

"I saw him sneaking over there one night. When I asked him about it, he got real stupid."

"That's no proof."

"Well, when Genie saw that I had caught them, she slammed the door in my face."

"Again, no proof. What's it matter anyway?"

"It doesn't. I just thought you might want to know, that's all."

"I don't want to know about my brother's sex life, especially if it involves someone old enough to be our mother."

Chapter 15

The next morning, Doris sat at her kitchen table, staring at Kevin Ryan's business card. She replayed their conversation over in her head. Could Herb actually cheated on her? Could he have a child he never knew about, or even worse, knew about but never told her about. She shook her head, fixed a second cup of coffee and picked up the phone.

"Cameron, I need you to help me get out of bed."

Cameron picked up Cora out of bed and set her in her wheelchair.

"I guess we have to make some sort of adjustments."

"Adjustments? Like a roll in shower or a toilet with bars?"

"Unless you want to go through what we went through last night."

"No way. The physical therapist comes in today. Let's see what he suggests."

"How do you know it'll be a guy?"

"It had better be a young, hot guy."

Cameron rolled his eyes and went behind his wife.

"Do you need help?"

"No. I've got it."

Cora wheeled herself down the hall and into the kitchen. Cameron watched as she reached for something in the cabinets.

"I guess we have to make some adjustments in here too."

Cora smiled.

"Could you please get me the pancake mix?"

Cameron thought it better that Cora not try to cook but knew better than to try to stop her. She needed to try to do as many things on her own as possible. Chris and Chris came in, hot and sweaty.

"Now honey, these are two hot guys. What are the two of you doing up so early?"

"Cutting the grass across the street before it gets too hot."

"Go clean up and tell your sisters we're having a late breakfast."

"Is Colleen back?"

"Back from where?"

Cora couldn't believe Colleen would have sneaked out to see Scott.

"I don't know. I was sweeping and I saw her walk out the house and down the street."

"Did she say when she'd be back or where she was going? She may have been going to work."

Chris shook his head.

"No uniform."

Cameron and Cora exchanged glances.

"Let's give her some time before we jump to conclusions. In an hour, I'll call Grace Moore and Scott."

Cameron nodded and went to wake Candice.

Colleen walked into the office at Mary, Mother of God and walked to Bea's desk.

"Mrs. De la Roche, is Father West busy?"

"Why?"

Colleen hated the old bitty. It was none of her damn business why Colleen was there.

"I'd like to talk to him if he has a minute."

"I'll see if he's awake."

With great effort, she pulled herself up from her desk. Just then, David came in from the kitchen.

"Of course I'm awake. I've been jogging."

Bea sat down and forced a smile.

"Father West, I was wondering if you had a minute to talk."

"Call me Father David. I have a few minutes…"

"Colleen. Colleen Mayhelm."

The name immediately registered in David's mind. He hardly recognized her from the afternoon in the hospital but knew her mother was the one paralyzed in the car crash. Colleen followed the young priest into his office. Guilt overcame her as she caught herself checking out his legs and butt. She couldn't help herself. She was so used to ancient Father Tom that she forgot this young man was her priest, the head of her church parish, the one who said her graduation Mass. David sat down and motioned for Colleen to take a seat across from him.

"You'll have to excuse the fact that I'm not in priest garb. I usually go running every day and today I'm a bit behind schedule. Would you like something to drink?"

He motioned to a small refrigerator behind her.

"No, thanks."

He nodded to her and sat back in his chair.

"So, Colleen, how's your mom?"

"Alright, I guess. I haven't really talked to her since the accident."

"She's probably going to need your support now more than ever, your help too. You have three other brothers and sisters, right?"

"Yes. The twins, Christopher and Christian are thirteen, almost fourteen and Candice is six."

"Two Chrises. Doesn't that get confusing?"

"It used to. Do you anything about my mom's accident?"

"Not the details, no."

"I caused it."

"How?"

"It was prom night and I was with my boyfriend…"

"With him, with him?"

Colleen lowered her head.

"I know what you're going to say."

"I'm going to say that pre-marital is a sin and the fact that everyone is doing it isn't an excuse that isn't going to go over well with God. It doesn't make you the worst person in the world, though."

"I also lied to my parents about where I was going to be. When my mother found out, she came after me, she had the accident on the way to the hotel."

David nodded. He had heard the rumors spread through the parish but didn't want to entertain them. Colleen started to tear up.

"How can I ever look at my mother and father again? I feel guilty over what I've done, but at the same time, I'm angry that I can't see Scott anymore. I really do love him."

"I think you need to rebuild your relationship with your parents first and then move on to the relationship with your boyfriend."

Colleen nodded.

"I feel like I should do something good. Does that sound silly?"

"Not at all. First, you need to talk to your mother."

He dried her tears. He put his arm around her and walked her to the door. Bea eyed them curiously.

"Everything is going to work out fine. Let me know."

Before she left, Colleen turned to him.

"Father David, do you go jogging every morning?"

"Seven sharp, usually."

"Ever want company?"

"I'm usually passing your street around seven ten. I'll keep an eye out."

Colleen hugged him, causing Bea to raise an eyebrow.

"Thanks, Father."

David smiled and went inside to shower.

"Mrs. Shepherd, I'm glad you called me."

"Come in, Mr. Ryan."

Kevin walked past Doris into her living room.

"I made some tea. Won't you sit down?"

Kevin sat down across from Doris and tried to look relaxed. Ever since she had called him, his heart had been racing. Was he finally going to find out something about his father? He already knew he was an adulterer.

"Mrs. Mayhelm, I'm Andrew Tyler, your physical therapist."

Cora wheeled herself out of the way.

"I see you're getting along fine with the chair so far."

Cora smiled. Her expression changed when she saw Colleen walking up the walk.

"Colleen, where have you been?"

"I went for a walk."

"I was worried."

"Don't worry mother, I wasn't with Scott."

Cora looked at her daughter angrily, then remembered her manners.

"Mr. Tyler, this is my daughter Colleen."

Colleen nodded and went off to her room.

"Would you like something to drink?"

"Sure."

Andrew followed Cora into the kitchen, assessing her every move, trying to decide where to go with her treatment. They spent the next hour talking. Andrew needed to know what kind of lifestyle Cora had led thus far. From what he heard, she led very busy life.

"You have the four children?"

"Well, my house is usually full of kids. My daughter's boyfriend is usually here. The boy down the street is here a lot…"

"You have a full house."

"Tell me about it."

"What did your mother tell you about Herb?"

"That he was an airline pilot. She never told me he was married, she probably never knew."

"Didn't you wonder why he never married her?"

Doris sipped her tea.

"I think she knew…that he was married."

"But you just said…"

"In her heart. I thing she knew the truth. I guess it embarrassed her to be the other woman."

"It should have."

"You're right."

"Mr. Ryan, you still have no proof."

Kevin took two photos from his wallet.

"This is the only picture my mother had of the two of them. The second is of my mother and me."

Doris took the photos and covered her mouth to hide a gasp. It was her husband.

"That's Herb. That's my husband."

"I'm sorry."

"Me too."

Kevin spooned more sugar into his cup, waiting for Doris to offer more info. He wasn't sure she was going to. He waited.

"Of course you look just like him."

"I know. Did you and your husband ever have any children?"

"No. We never did."

"What was he like?"

"He was so handsome. I always thought we had the perfect marriage, but I'm guessing we didn't. Was your mother a flight attendant? I always figured if he ever cheated on me, it would be with a flight attendant. Of course, they were called stewardesses back then."

"No. She was a waitress in the airport coffee shop."

"How convenient."

Kevin smiled.

"I guess so."

"What about you Kevin? Does your mother have any other children? With pilots from Pacific Pride or Colonial maybe?"

"That is my mother you're talking about."

"Well, that's my husband your talking about!"

Kevin stood up angrily.

"I'm sorry to have bothered you."

He walked toward the door and Doris stopped him.

"Look, do you have any idea how hard this is for me? I find out yesterday that my husband cheated on me and had a child with someone else. What does that say about the thirty three years we were married? Does it void them? Does he have children all across the country?"

"I think you need to focus on the good times in those thirty three years. Think of your husband as the good man you remember him to be."

After a moment of silence, Kevin continued.

"Mrs. Shepherd, I'm leaving for Boston today. I'd like to take you to lunch first."

"No, I don't think that would be a good idea."

"Please."

"The thing is Kevin; I don't go out much any more. Thank you for the offer.

"Would you mind if I called you sometimes?"

"Sure."

Kevin walked back to his car. Doris went to her bedroom closet and took her wedding album down. Tears ran down her face as she remembered the good times with her husband, unable to believe the nights she had spent alone, assuming him to be faithful.

Chapter 16

"This is so cool, you moving in with your dad."

Two weeks later, Christian was helping Jeremy pack his things.

"I know. I still can't believe my mom is letting me do it."

"How long are you going to be gone?"

"All summer."

Chris couldn't hide his disappointed look. Jeremy noticed this and tried to cheer him up.

"Do you still think I could come swimming some time?"

"Sure."

Geoffrey honked his horn and Jeremy raced outside, followed by Chris and Genie. Genie handed Jeremy some money.

"Call me if you need anything."

"Mom, I'll be just across town."

"I know, but I'll still miss you."

She kissed him, embarrassing him greatly. Chris made fun of him.

"Aw, isn't that cute."

Genie put him in his place.

"Christopher Mayhelm, I know for a fact that your mother kisses you every day before school."

"I'm Christian, Miss Genie."

"Whatever."

Jeremy laughed at his mother and jumped into the car. Genie waved goodbye and went to get ready for the late shift.

Oren stowed his bag and settled into seat 2F next to wife. The flight was pre-boarding and Miranda had already ordered drinks for the two of them, one of the perks of flying first class. Oren took her hand and kissed it.

"What do you think of making a baby on this trip?"

Miranda smiled broadly.

"If you think we're ready."

"We'll never be ready, but let's go for it."

"Okay."

Cameron loaded the last of the kids' bags into the van. He and Cora were taking the kids to camp and he wasn't looking forward to the three hour drive ahead of them. He watched as Christian walked home from Genie's house.

"Why the long face, Chris?"

"Jeremy's going to be gone all summer."

"You'll be at camp for a month. You won't even notice."

"I guess."

"Now, go get your sister and brother and tell them we're ready to go."

Cameron followed his son into the house and went to find Cora. She was in Colleen's room. Cora had found out that Scott was in Europe with his parents and would be gone two weeks. They had decided to let Colleen stay home alone.

"Now Kelleye can come over and that's it. I left the number where we'll be staying if you need anything. I'll call you when we get there. Are you working this weekend?"

"No, I got lucky. Somehow."

"Well, we'll be leaving in a minute so tell your sister and brothers goodbye."

After Colleen left the room, Cameron began to massage Cora's shoulders.

"You know what tonight is?"

"No."

"Our first night alone together with no kids in years."

"I can't believe years."

"Years."

Cameron left the room, leaving Cora wondering what he had on his mind. She hoped it wasn't sex. She hardly felt sexy anymore. Being carried to bed like in a romance novel was one thing. Being carried to bed because you were crippled was quite another. She wheeled herself to the car and waited for Cameron to put her in. Andrew had been working on her upper body strength, but it tired her out. This morning, she had lifted herself onto the toilet and it nearly killed her.

"I can't believe you're not tired of me yet."

Jo Ann was walking Peter to his car. They had just had lunch together. Their relationship had progressed nicely over the last few weeks. They still hadn't slept together, something Jo Ann was really careful about. She didn't want to rush the relationship and that was a major hurdle they hadn't crossed. Besides, there was another hurdle waiting for them.

"So when should we introduce the kids?"

"Do we have to?"

"I think if we want to move on to the next level, we have to look at blending our families."

"I don't know. You know Chad can be…difficult."

"So can Paul. They'll get along great."

"I don't…"

Peter took her face into his hands.

"Jo Ann, you're not saying no because you're unsure about us, are you?"

"No. No."

She kissed him lightly on the lips.

"No."

She was spared from any more talk on the subject by a giant van pulling into Sherwood Circle. Hope and Allen were moving in and it looked like the whole neighborhood had come out to meet them. Cameron was ushering the kids into the car. Jo Ann was walking Peter out. Genie was walking out to her car, heading for work. Even Doris was peeking out the window.

"Those must be the new neighbors."

"I wanted to have your grass cut by the time they got here."

"You can come by and do it tomorrow, but only if you take your shirt off before you start."

"You don't want me to get all dirty and gritty?"

"No, I want to see your bare chest glisten with sweat. It makes me hot."

Peter laughed and got into his car. Jo Ann leaned through the window.

"I wonder if June Cleaver is going to make them lasagna."

Peter wagged a finger at her and drove away.

"I can't believe someone would be stupid enough to but that house."

Doris was talking to herself as she watched the new people moving in across the street. She shook her head and went back to her sewing.

Gretchen and Ben went over to help with the moving. Gretchen wanted to be sure Hope didn't lift anything heavy.

"You guys, I wish you would have let us hire movers for you."

"My mother said the same thing. Don't worry, I'm not going to overdo."

Hope picked up a box marked bathroom and Gretchen tried to stop her.

"But I'm not going to sit here and let you all do the work."

Gretchen decided not to protest and followed Hope into the house with anther box.

Colleen raced inside when she heard the phone ringing. Assuming it was Kelleye, she immediately started talking.

"Get over here, now."

"Colleen?"

Her cheeks turned beet red.

"Father David?"

"Yea, listen there's something I wanted to discuss with you while we were jogging this morning."

"What is it?"

"If you're still looking to do something good, I'm putting together a youth choir at church. How would you like to help me start it up?"

"That sounds great."

"Great. Can you come by the rectory tomorrow around one?"

"I'll be there."

"Colleen?"

"Yes Father?"

"Do you still want me to come over?"

"No. That's no fair, I thought you were Kelleye."

"I'm not."

"See you tomorrow Father."

Colleen laughed as she hung up the phone. She went to the kitchen to find something to eat. She opened all the cabinets to find them empty. Overcome with guilt again, she realized her father had moved everything lower so Cora could reach everything. She bent over and pulled out some cookies, but wasn't hungry anymore.

After everything was unloaded, Hope looked around her new house. Overwhelmed with all the work left to do, she needed a break. She turned to Ben and Gretchen.

"You guys want food?"

She yelled to the back of the house.

"Allen, come on! We're going to eat!"

Allen came in from the back bedroom.

"We have all this work to do."

"We need a break. Let's go eat. We'll unpack when we get home."

It didn't take much persuasion for Allen to agree. The four of them packed up the kids and went to get lunch.

Three hours later, Cameron was bust getting the kids settled at camp. Christopher and Christian, being old veterans, didn't need their father's help and went off on their own. Candice, being a first year camper, needed her parents' help to get settled. Cora was worried how she would take it, being gone from home for so long. After meeting Candice's counselors and kissing her goodbye, they drove to the inn where they would be spending the night.

Camcron raised an eyebrow when he saw Cora wipe a tear from her cheek.

"Something wrong?"

"I just hope Candice does okay. She's never been to camp and a month is a long time."

"Well, before the boys ran off, I asked them to keep an eye out on her."

"They'll love that."

"I told them they didn't have to associate with her or anything, just check up on her from time to time. I also got her counselor's cell phone number."

"Really?"

"For emergencies only."

Cora smiled and took Cameron's hand.

Jeremy was already bored. There was nothing to do at his father's house. There were no kids around and most of his father's neighbors were old ladies. His father had already left him alone, having to run to thee museum to supervise a new shipment of antiques. Restless, he flopped down on the sofa and began to flip through the television channels. Yea, this was going to be some summer. He was jealous of the fun Chris and Chris would be having at summer camp.

"Your room is two fourteen."

The clerk handed Cameron the keys and looked over at Cora, suddenly feeling terrible. The Bedford Inn didn't have any rooms on the first floor available. Months ago, when Cameron made the reservations, he didn't need to consider that. Now things had changed.

"Where's the elevator?"

"We don't have an elevator, sir."

"Are you sure there's nothing on the first floor?"

"No sir, Mr. Mayhelm. I'm sorry."

Cora's heart sank. She knew what was coming next and it was killing Cameron. She wished the regular front desk clerk was working. They had been coming here for years and were on a first name basis with the owner and half the staff.

"Sir, is there anything around here that has rooms on the first floor?"

"The Budget Inn, about four miles from here."

Cora looked at Cameron and tried to cheer him up. The Budget Inn was a national chain

Of motels that catered to truckers and weary travelers.

"Thank you."

Brokenhearted, Cameron grabbed the bags and followed Cora out to the car. He helped her in and they drove in silence to the Budget Inn. Turning her head toward the window, Cora hid the tears that were starting to form. Once they were checked in, Cameron tried to make the best of the situation.

"You know honey, we could go to dinner at the restaurant in the inn."

"If you don't mind, I'd rather rest for awhile. I'm tired."

"Take a nap. We'll decide what to do when you wake up."

"Whatever."

Awhile later, when Cora was asleep, the phone rang. Cameron picked it up quickly as not to wake her.

"Hello."

"Mr. Mayhelm, this is Clark, the owner of The Bedford Inn."

"Yes, I remember you."

"I saw you cancelled your reservation once you arrived. Was there anything wrong?"

Cameron hated giving the details but needed to talk to someone. He and Cora had been going to the inn for years and were on a first name basis with Clark Young, the owner.

"Actually, Clark, Cora had an accident a few weeks ago and is in a wheelchair."

"For how long?"

"Forever. The doctors say the damage to her spinal cord is so extensive that it will never heal."

"There has to be some hope."

"They don't give us much. She's been working with a physical therapist."

"Cameron, I feel horrible."

"Anyway, we dropped the kids off at camp, as usual, and went to check in. We didn't realize there were no elevators or rooms on the first floor."

"No, the rooms on the first floor have been out of service for weeks. We had a major plumbing problem and had to change all the carpet and upholstery. We've never had an elevator though."

"I guess we never needed one, so we never noticed."

"And now you're at the Budget Inn."

"Yes."

"Cameron, don't let this ruin your evening. If Cora is up to it, please come and have dinner at the inn as my guests."

"That sounds very nice. I'll see if she's up to it."

"Up to what?"

Cora stifled a yawn as she woke up.

"Dinner at the inn."

"Is that Clark? Tell him I said hello."

Cameron relayed the message and hung up the phone after promising they would try to get there for dinner. He turned to his wife.

"What do you think?"

"I guess I'll start getting ready. Can you help me to the tub?"

"Sure thing."

Cameron, glad to see her nap had changed her depressed state, went to help Cora in the bathroom.

Geoffrey's phone rang and Jeremy picked it up after checking the caller id.

"Hey, Dad."

"Jeremy, I've got some bad news. I have to work late tonight so you're on your own for dinner."

"But I thought we could hang out."

"I have to work. This new exhibit is very important. There's frozen pizza in the fridge. Fix that for tonight and we'll do something special tomorrow night."

"Alright."

"Jeremy, I've got to go. Be in bed by the time I get home."

Jeremy hung up the phone without saying a word. Some great summer this was going to be. Day one was already a disaster.

Clark's face lit up when the Mayhelm's entered the dining room. He ran over to them, pumping Cameron's hand enthusiastically and kissing Cora on the cheeks.

"It's good to see the two of you. I'm so sorry about today's mix up. Please enjoy dinner, again, courtesy of the inn."

Clark ran off to get a bottle of champagne, leaving them alone. Cameron reached across the table and took Cora's hand.

Jo Ann picked up the phone and dialed Peter's number. After a few rings, he picked up.

"Hey, it's me."

"Hello, me."

"Listen, Peter, I was thinking of what we talked about this afternoon. I think it's time the boys met. What do you say about going on a picnic tomorrow?"

"That sounds great."

"Meet us in Torres Park tomorrow at eleven. I'll bring all the food."

"What should we bring?"

"We're bringing two boys to the park. Bring a football, a ball and bat, that kind of stuff."

"Sounds good to me. See you at eleven."

"Bye now."

Mary walked in to see the glow on her daughter's face.

"Who was that, as if I even have to ask?"

"Peter. We're taking the boys on a picnic tomorrow."

"Oh."

"What's that mean?"

"That's a big step, introducing the kids. How serious are the two of you?"

"Do you mean, could I marry him? Yes I could."

"You'd better be sure the kids get along first."

"Chad is always my first priority, you know that."

Chapter 17

The next morning, Colleen let herself into the rectory, calling out for Fr. David. She went into the kitchen, looking for a soda. David, not having heard her, came into the kitchen wrapped in a towel, dripping wet.

"Colleen?"

"Father! Oh my god! I'm so sorry."

She turned around, embarrassed.

"Is this improper?"

"No, just a little embarrassing. Wait in my office. I'll get dressed and be out in a minute."

Colleen walked toward the office as Bea came in.

"Miss Mayhelm, what are you doing here?"

"I'm helping Father David with the new youth choir."

"Where is he?"

"In the shower. He'll be dressed in a minute."

Colleen walked past her and into the office, shutting the door behind her. She realized what she had said and found it hilarious. She smiled to herself, not realizing the extent of the damage Bea de la Roche was about to cause.

That afternoon, Jo Ann noticed Chad's uncharacteristic silence as they drove to the park. He had been quiet ever since they had come back from Phoenix. Jo Ann hoped that having another little boy to play with might open him back up, but not too much though. She could live without the hard to handle, rambunctious eight year old he had been before the abduction.

"I hear Paul is a pretty good baseball player. Maybe you guys could get a game going."

"With two people?"

"Peter and I could play."

"Whatever."

Chad kept his eyes on the window, not even looking at his mother. They pulled up to the park and Peter and Paul were already there. Jo Ann got out and waved. They walked over and Peter introduced the boys.

"Paul, this is Jo Ann's son, Chad. Chad, this is my son, Paul."

The boys politely said hello.

"Chad, why don't you go over and see the stuff we brought to play with. Peter and I will set up the food."

Without a word, Chad followed Paul to the sports equipment leaning up against the tree. Peter looked at Jo Ann and sighed.

"Muriel, you will never guess what I just walked in on."

Bea kept her voice down. Colleen and Father David weren't in his office two minutes before she picked up the phone and started the calls.

"Colleen Mayhelm was coming out of Father West's bedroom. She told me he was in the shower."

"Did it seem like anything inappropriate was going on?"

"I couldn't tell, but what was she doing there and why was she here so early on a Saturday morning?"

"I'm not sure Bea, but I'm going to get to the bottom of it."

Later on that evening, Cora wheeled herself through the front door, calling out for Colleen. Colleen came out from her bedroom.

"What are you yelling for?"

"I just wanted to be sure you were home. I called earlier this morning and didn't get an answer."

"I was with Father David picking out songs for the new youth choir."

"That sounds nice."

Cora wheeled herself into the kitchen, not wanting to be in the room when Cameron came in with the bags. As she expected, Cameron had tried to make love on the trip. She wasn't into it, but went along with it. When the time came, Cameron couldn't perform. It had happened before in their marriage, he may be too tired or have too much on his mind. Cora understood, but wondered if she was the reason. She wondered, as a cripple, if she would ever arouse her husband sexually again. The ride home had been shrouded in uncomfortable silence.

"That was fun wasn't it?"

Jo Ann and Chad were on their way home.

"I guess. Mom, are you going to marry Peter?"

Jo Ann was taken aback by her young son's question. Apparently, he and Paul talked about more than sports.

"Who told you that?"

"Well, are you?"

"I'm not sure, Chad, we've only been going out a few weeks. How would you feel about that?"

"You were married to Daddy."

"Chad, Daddy and I had a lot of problems. He was your daddy and he loved you, but he wasn't always the nicest person to live with."

"Is that why he killed himself?"

"I don't know why he killed himself."

"If you marry Peter, is he going to be my new dad?"

"He'll be your step-dad. Paul will be your stepbrother."

"I guess that would be alright. He taught me how to throw a spiral today."

Jo Ann smiled and Chad's attention returned to the window. When they got home, Chad ran to his room. Mary pulled Jo Ann aside.

"How did it go? Did the kids hit it off?"

"I think so. I think the two of them discussed Peter and me getting married."

"Well?"

"We haven't gone that far yet."

"You mean you haven't slept together."

"Mother! No we haven't."

"Don't wait too long."

Gretchen picked up the phone on the first ring.

"Gretchen, darling, I've told you never to answer the phone on the first ring."

"Sorry, Muriel."

"I have some questions about your neighbors, Cora and Cameron."

"Well, I would say ask them yourselves, but…"

Gretchen looked out her window and noticed the van in the driveway across the street.

"…oh yea, they are home. They must have just gotten back."

"Where were they?"

"Cora and Cameron brought the kids to camp. I think Colleen stayed at home."

"By herself?"

"Muriel, this really isn't any of my business, but I think she was alone. She is eighteen years old."

"Uh huh."

"What's wrong?"

"Nothing dear, just something I'm working on for church. Do you know if Hope and Allen got moved in okay?"

"Yes. Have you talked to them since they moved in? It might be nice to call them."

"Uh huh. Listen, Gretchen, I've got to go. Give the boys my love."

"Bye, Muriel."

By the next morning, Bea and Muriel had spread the torrid tale to all the choir members from the noon Mass. Colleen followed her parents into church and immediately felt uncomfortable. Were the choir women watching her? She couldn't be sure. She sat next to her father and smiled when Muriel turned to smile at her. After Mass, Colleen continued to feel uncomfortable.

"Do you want to have lunch at Mariners?"

"Dad, I'd rather just go home, if you don't mind."

"We'll meet you at the car."

Cameron wheeled Cora to the van. Colleen followed them but stopped when she ran into Scott. The two of them had barely talked since the accident.

"Scott, I don't see you at work too much anymore."

"I never get out of the deli."

"Tell me about it. Listen, Scott, why don't you let me ask my mom if you can come over for dinner. The kids are at camp and it'll just be the four of us."

"I'd better not. I still feel uneasy around your parents."

"Well how about..."

"Colleen, I have to go. I'll call you."

Scott ran off to catch up with his mother, who had heard the story form her cousin who was in the noon choir. Scott's mother quickly spread the story to Scott, as well as everyone at the hair salon. Colleen stood alone, mystified. Father David came up to her from across the yard. Bea walked up to Muriel and whispered in her ear.

"Colleen, do you think you would be free Wednesday evening? We're having a meeting for anyone who's interested in the youth choir."

"Sure, Father."

"Around six."

"Why not earlier?"

"Parents aren't off of work. The kids would have no way of getting to the meeting."

"Good idea, I'll see you then."

Colleen walked toward the van, noticing Muriel York watching her again.

"Jeremy, put on something nice. We're going to brunch at Mariners."

Geoffrey stuck his head in his son's room.

"Did you hear me? Get dressed."

Jeremy got up and went through his bags, looking for something suitable for Mariners. His dad was probably trying to make up for missing dinner the night before. Fifteen minutes later, they were on their way.

That afternoon, Muriel and Malcolm were having lunch at Allen and Hope's with Gretchen and Ben.

"I don't know, Muriel, we've know the Mayhelms for a long time and I don't think Colleen would do anything like that."

"Either way dear, it doesn't look good for the young priest to be consorting with the young women of the parish. Anyway, Benjamin, didn't you tell me they go jogging every morning?"

Gretchen turned to her husband, waiting for him to stand up to his mother's overreacting antics and almost died at what came out of his mouth.

"Yes. Every morning."

"Ben, that is totally innocent!"

Muriel continued.

"I told Bea we would have problems with a young priest."

Hope shook her head. She couldn't believe her mother and was shocked by the way her brother went along with her. She looked at her sister-in-law and saw the same reaction on Gretchen's face.

Geoffrey led Jeremy into the dining room at Mariners. He spotted a table of people in the far corner and waved at them. Jeremy knew exactly what was going on the minute they waved back.

"Dad, I thought we were having lunch?"

"We are. We're just meeting some friends of mine from the museum. Is that okay with you?"

"I thought it was going to be just us?"

"Next time, bud."

Geoffrey put his arm around Jeremy and led him to the table. Jeremy put on his best smile and acted nice for his dad's friends, despite being secretly hurt. He mentally calculated the days until Chris and Chris came back from camp.

"Genie, there is a hottie at D10 asking for you."

Genie looked through the window at the table and saw Charlie sitting down and looking over the menu. She smiled and turned to Park.

"Park, that's him."

Parker looked at D10 and raised an eyebrow.

"He is cute. Are you sure he's not…"

"I'm sure."

Genie grabbed her pad and tray and went to the table.

"Can I get you something sir?"

Charlie looked up and smiled.

"What are you offering?"

Genie smiled, remembering Geoffrey had once made the same joke.

"You look nice."

"I just came from church. I'll have an iced tea."

"What are you doing for dinner tonight?"

"I don't know."

"Why don't you come over? Jeremy is saying at his father's. I can cook."

"Jeremy isn't at home? Did it have anything to do with me?"

"You mean, him finding you naked in the shower? That didn't help."

"I'm sorry."

"No, it isn't you. You know, single mother, teenage son. There's bound to be issues."

"What time tonight?"

"Seven?"

"Should I bring something?"

"Just those sexy boxers you sleep in."

"Sleep in? If memory serves, they usually end up on the floor next to the bed."

Genie blushed.

"You are terrible. I'll be right back with your tea."

"Cameron, do you think if I sat with my feet in the pool, I'd be able to feel the cool water?"

"What?"

"Nothing, it was just a thought."

Cameron walked over to his wife and kissed her.

"If you want to get in the pool, I'll help you."

"And what? Roll me onto the deck like a carp?

Cora laughed, relieving Cameron. Things had been tense for them since the trip.

"I would have to get you out somehow."

Cora smiled.

"Well, since your daughter didn't want to go out, what should I fix for lunch?"

"She didn't want to go out. I say we leave her to sulk in her bedroom and you and I go get an early dinner."

"Sounds like a plan."

The phone rand and Cora wheeled herself over to it.

"Hello."

"Cora, it's Grace Moore."

"Grace, we've been friends for twenty years. You can say Grace and I'll know who it is."

"I hate to call like this, but I was wondering if you know what's been going around church?"

"The flu?"

"Worse."

"Grace, I hate to be a gossip."

"So do I, Cora, but it's about Colleen and it's not good."

"What about Colleen?"

"Was she home alone this weekend?"

"Yes."

"Did she see Father West?"

"They're working together on the new youth choir. Grace, get to the point."

"People are saying they spent Saturday morning alone behind closed doors and they are drawing their own conclusions."

"Who would say something like that?"

"You know who. Bea de la Roche, that's who. She probably couldn't wait to pass the story of the hot new priest and the young teenage girl."

"This happened yesterday?"

"Cora, you know this town."

"Well, talk is cheap."

"Yea, but the price can be high if it's true. Talk to Colleen."

"I will. Thanks."

Cora hung up the phone. Cameron came out of the bedroom, changed for dinner.

"Hold that thought, Cameron. I need to talk to Colleen."

Cora wheeled herself into her daughter's bedroom.

"And you just sat there."

"I happen to agree. I think it's inappropriate."

Gretchen and Ben were home after lunch, fighting. The church gossip, barely two days old, was already dividing families.

"You don't agree. You're just afraid to go against your mother."

Ben turned and started to walk away.

"Benjamin, don't you walk away from me! Why are you walking away?"

Ben turned to his wife, fuming.

"You want to know why I turned away? Because in nine years of being married, I've never felt like hitting you…until now."

He turned away from her again and stormed into the bedroom, slamming the door behind him.

Next door, Hope and Allen were having the same conversation, with different results.

"I feel the same way Gretchen does. We've know the Mayhelms from church for years. How could my mother think Colleen would be capable of doing something like that? And my own brother? Colleen watches his kids. How could he believe such trash?"

"Hope, there's no reason to convince me. I agree with you."

He slipped her arm around his waist.

"Besides, I don't want you to get too excited. Don't let your mother or your brother stress you out. Besides, we have better things to worry about."

He patted her stomach. She turned around and kissed him.

Jeremy was silent the entire ride home. During lunch, he had been the perfect gentleman, even though his father and his friends had excluded him from the entire conversation.

"I guess I should have told you we were meeting friends."

"I guess so."

"I'm sorry Jeremy. I'm just not used to having kids around, being a father. I guess you realize that."

More silence.

"If you want to go back to your mom's, I'll understand."

"No, not yet."

Chapter 18

That Monday morning, once Colleen and Cameron had left for work, Cora relaxed and sipped hot tea, waiting for Andrew to arrive. He came at nine o'clock, as usual, and joined her for some tea before starting their session.

"How are things going?"

"Fine. I can finally get myself on the toilet and in bed without help. Not that you would want to know the details."

"No, I need to know how things are going. How is the family adjusting?"

She paused before answering, telling Andrew all he needed to know.

"Things are tense…between Cameron and me."

"As expected."

"We had a night alone together this weekend when we brought the kids to camp and that didn't go well."

"Cora, I am not the one to give advice on relationships. I was seeing a very nice girl and put my career first."

"Who was she?"

"Her name was Eva. She was a flight attendant for Transcoastal. Airlines."

"And what was the job?"

"Head of physical therapy at a hotel in Chicago."

"Impressive."

"Yes, but I hated the seventy hour work weeks. I was headed for a mental breakdown, so I moved back here."

"I'm glad you did."

Andrew smiled.

"Are you ready to start?"

Peter and Paul were walking through Barristers Department Store when Peter casually steered Paul toward the china department.

"What are we doing here?"

"Hey guys."

Jo Ann called out from behind the desk and walked over to them. She kissed Peter hello and smiled at Paul.

"I thought you worked in an office building?"

"That's my other job. I clean offices at night."

"Like a maid?"

Jo Ann could tell by his tone that he didn't approve but was glad to be making conversation.

"Kind of."

Peter interjected before his son could offend his girlfriend.

"We were just wondering if you and your family wanted to come over for dinner tonight, Mary, too."

"Are you sure about that?"

"Yes."

"Well then I accept, for all three of us."

"Six?"

"Works for us. Bye, Paul."

Jo Ann went back to her desk. A moment later, Peter came up behind her.

"Jo Ann, I need to talk to you about something."

"So talk."

"Did Chad have a good time at the picnic?"

"Yes, he did. Did Paul?"

"Yes. The two of them did a lot of talking."

"I kind of got that idea from Chad. How was Paul's reaction?"

"He was cool with it."

"Cool?"

Peter smiled.

"You know what I mean."

Jo Ann nodded.

"What I really wanted to talk to you about was this, do you think you could get some time off of work?"

"From work? I'm not really sure. They were really lenient when I flew off to Phoenix with an hour's notice."

"A few days?"

"I'll see. What do you have in mind?"

"A weekend away, just the two of us."

Peter wondered if he was moving too fast. Jo Ann had already had one bad relationship and, until now, they had moved at her pace. He wanted to move things forward and hoped she felt the same way. Her smile was all the confirmation he needed.

"That sounds nice; I'll talk to my bosses."

He kissed her again and went to find Paul.

Later that evening, Colleen came home and plopped down on the sofa. Cora wheeled over to her.

"Mom, how was therapy?"

"I'm very tired. Colleen, have you talked to Scott lately?"

"Why?"

"No need to get defensive. I was just wondering if you'd like to have him over for dinner."

Colleen sat up.

"Actually, I'm not sure Scott is speaking to me right now. I mentioned the same thing after church and he started acting all weird."

"I'm sorry honey. Guys can be jerks sometimes, especially young guys."

"I don't want to think he's one of those guys who got what he wanted and dumped me right after."

"Well, it's a difficult and awkward situation, for all of us."

Cora kept thinking about what Grace had told her. She wondered if Scott had heard the rumors and had drawn his own conclusions.

"Did you and Kelleye have a good time this weekend?"

"Actually, I spent a lot of time with Father David."

"I heard the announcement about the youth choir. That sounds like a lot of fun."

"Yea. There's a meeting on Wednesday night for any interested kids. It's a shame Candice is at camp. I think she would enjoy it."

"So, you'll probably be spending a lot of time at church."

"Yea, why?"

Cora didn't know how to proceed without asking straight out if there was anything funny going on. She wouldn't let herself believe the rumors and didn't want to offend her daughter.

"I just wanted to be sure it doesn't interfere with your job. That's all."

Colleen smiled at her mother. It was the first nice, relaxed conversation they had had in a long time.

"It won't."

"Mary, it's so good to see you again. This is my son, Paul."

Mary smiled at Paul. Chad followed his grandmother into the house.

"Paul, take Chad into your room and show him the new video game we bought today."

The two kids went to the back of the house. Jo Ann went into the kitchen. Peter followed her in.

"Can I help you?"

"Everything smells so good. I'm just looking for the take out containers."

"You will find no such things. I'm offended."

He kissed her and she pushed him away."

"Not in front of my mother."

Mary laughed and Peter remembered his manners.

"Mary, would you like a glass of wine?"

"Do you have any beer?"

"Mother!"

"What?"

"Here we are dressed up, about to have a nice dinner and you're acting like we're at a truck and tractor pull."

"You know what, Mary; I think I'll have a beer, too."

Peter stuck his tongue out at Jo Ann.

"Children! That's what the two of you are, children!"

Cora wheeled herself into the living room, took the remote and turned off the television. Cameron protested.

"What are you doing? I was watching that!"

"We need to talk."

"I hate these conversations."

"Not about us. It's about Colleen."

"I'm listening."

"People are talking."

"About?"

"Apparently, she spent time with Father West this weekend getting stuff together for the youth choir and it was misinterpreted."

"By whom?"

"The whole damn parish. Grace Moore told me everyone is talking."

"You sound like you're in the third grade."

"I'm just telling you."

"We need to talk to her. We need to tell her what people are saying."

"She's going to hate us."

"I'll take that chance. Colleen!"

Cameron called out to his daughter.

"Yea."

"Come in here, please."

Colleen came in from the back of the house.

"What's up?"

Cora got right to the issue.

"Colleen, people at church are talking about you and Father West."

"What about us?"

"They think it's inappropriate that the two of you are spending so much time together. They are speculating that the two of you must be having some sort of relationship."

"Because we jog together every now and then?"

"That and the closed door meetings..."

"About the youth choir."

"Honey, we know. We need to know if there's anything going on between the two of you."

"No, he's a priest."

"We know. We just want to know the facts before we confront people."

"Why confront them? Let their evil little minds thing whatever they want."

"It doesn't bother you?"

"No, because it's not true."

Colleen got up and turned to face her parents.

"Let them say what they want."

She walked out of the room, leaving Cora and Cameron staring at each other.

Later that evening, after everyone was gone, Peter got a phone call.

"It's all settled."

Jo Ann was on the phone. She had juggled her schedule and had gotten the weekend off.

"You actually got off of work?"

"Yes and it was surprisingly easy. What are the plans?"

"I pick you up Friday afternoon and we hit the road."

"Where is this exotic locale you have in mind?"

"It's a surprise."

"Well, I'll arrange everything with mother and I'll be waiting Friday afternoon."

"See you then."

Peter hung up the phone and saw Paul staring at him.

"Are you going somewhere?"

"I'm going off with Jo Ann this weekend."

"Oh."

"How do you feel about that?"

"I said, *oh*."

"That's not a feeling."

"Do you even know what Saturday is?"

"What?"

"I didn't think so."

Paul turned and walked without a word to his room. Peter thought frantically and then ran over to the calendar. June twenty third. Not his birthday, not Paul's. Why would that date be important? Of course. The coming Saturday was the day his wife Dana was killed, the day her flight to Hong Kong was destroyed. God, how could he have forgotten? He immediately picked up the phone and called Jo Ann back.

Gretchen slid in bed next to her husband, who appeared to be sleeping.

"Ben? Ben? Ben, are you still mad at me?"

Getting no response, she covered herself up and tried to get some sleep. Ben, wide awake, pondered his wife's earlier words. Had he let his mother cloud his own judgment?

"Honey, I have to cancel this weekend."

"I haven't even had a chance to talk to my mother."

"I know, but this Saturday is the day Dana was killed. Paul and I usually go to the cemetery and spend the day together."

"Peter, don't hate me for asking this, but, if Dana was killed when the plane blew up, what did you bury?"

"An empty casket."

"Oh."

"Jo Ann, I'm so sorry."

"Peter, I understand. It's very important you and Paul spend the day together."

"What did I do to deserve such an understanding woman?"

"I don't know. I'll get back to you. Besides, I feel I owe it to you for crying on our first date."

"It was our second actually."

"Well, if you want there to be anymore, you'd better hang up."

"Alright. I get the message."

"Peter, I want our relationship to move on to the next level. I'll understand if Paul isn't cool with it."

"Give him timc. This is a hard time of year for him. I've been so happy, I hadn't noticed."

"Call me tomorrow."

"Bye."

Peter hung up the phone and went to see his son.

That Friday afternoon, Oren and Miranda came back from Miami, tanned and relaxed. They had made love every night, hoping to make a baby.

"I'm glad we both have tomorrow off, I need a day to relax."

"I'm going to bring Mrs. Shepherd the wind chimes we bought her."

"What about the ones for Jo Ann?"

"I'm saving those for a wedding present."

"Don't get ahead of yourself."

Miranda laughed and ran across the street to number five. She knocked and waited for Doris to answer. She opened the door a crack and smiled when she saw her new friend standing there.

"Miranda, come on in."

"I brought you a souvenir from Miami."

Miranda sat the bag on the coffee table and pulled out the dolphin shaped wind chimes. They tinkled lightly under the breeze from the ceiling fan.

"Miranda, they're beautiful. You really didn't have to do that."

"I wanted to."

"Won't you stay for some iced tea?"

"I really can't. You know how it is when you come back from vacation, tons of laundry."

"Actually, I wouldn't know."

"I didn't want to say anything, but you don't seem to get out much."

"I haven't left this house in almost fifteen years."

This is the story. This is the story Cora Mayhelm had hinted to at their housewarming party. Miranda sat down.

"Alright, Doris, I'm intrigued."

"Then maybe, you'll want some tea after all."

"Peter, it's Mary, Jo Ann's mother."

"Mary, how are you?"

"I just wanted to thank you for dinner the other night. I enjoyed meeting your son. He seems like a nice young man."

"Thank you, Mary. We were glad to have you."

"Peter, I want to know what's going on with you and Jo Ann. What are your plans? Do you see a future with her or are you just stringing her along?"

"Mary…"

"I know it's none of my business, but my daughter has already been through one bad relationship and I hate to see her getting into another one."

"Mary, I assure you, I'm nothing like Louis Mott. Jo Ann and I had plans for this weekend but I had to cancel because of a prior commitment. I want to take this to the next level and, be assured; I would never do anything to hurt Jo Ann."

"Be sure that you don't. I like you, Peter, but I don't want to have to have you taken care of."

Peter wasn't sure if she was kidding or not. He smiled and laughed anyway to cover his doubt.

"I'm agoraphobic, Miranda. I haven't left the house in over ten years."

Miranda sipped her tea, her eyebrows raised.

"Never?"

"I'll go into my backyard, but never out in front. I tried walking to the end of the driveway one day but couldn't do it."

"That's so psychological. Do you know anything about it?"

"I learned a lot on my computer. It can usually be traced back to one event. One traumatic event that scares you into staying inside."

Miranda nodded. She was dying to know what the event was, but wasn't sure if Doris was going to tell her.

"I know you're dying to know, so I'll tell you."

"Doris, you don't have to tell me if it's too personal."

"It is personal. I was carjacked and raped one night after work."

Miranda nearly dropped her tea. She had no idea Doris would reveal something so personal.

"The one thing I could never understand is how a man, a boy in this case, he couldn't have been more than twenty. How can a boy be sexually stimulated when the person they're on top of is crying, screaming and hitting them? How can you keep a hard on?"

Miranda shook her head. Suddenly she was very uncomfortable. She wanted to leave.

"Did they ever catch him?"

"No. He dumped me and left me for dead. They found my car three days later, stripped clean. Knowing that he's still out there was the main reason I was afraid to go out. It got progressively worse. Now my mind is so screwed up that I make myself physically sick if I even think about going out."

"Doris, that's horrible."

"Everyone around here just thinks I'm the nosy old lady that never leaves the house…"

"If they only knew"

"It isn't something I advertise."

"Have you ever talked to anyone about it?"

"I joined a counseling group online, two actually. One for agoraphobics, one for rape victims"

"Wow."

Doris sensed the tension.

"I'm sorry Miranda; I've turned a pleasant situation into an embarrassing and awkward situation. Why don't you go home, I'm giving you an escape clause. Come back tomorrow and see the wind chimes once I put them up."

Miranda, glad to get out, thanked Doris for the tea and headed home. She had no idea how a man could find a struggling, unwilling, old lady sexually stimulating. She shook her head wondering what kind of world she and Oren were trying to bring children into.

Chapter 19

Saturday morning, Cameron went outside to get the mail. Something out the corner of his eye caught his attention. Spray painted in neon orange, across his entire lawn, was the word WHORE. Cameron stood there for a moment, unsure of what to do. Cora opened the door.

"Did the gas bill come yet?"

She noticed her husband staring at the grass. When she saw the orange paint, she wheeled herself out to see what the deal was. When she read the entire message, she nearly screamed in fury. Holding herself back, she looked at Cameron, who still hadn't said anything.

"Has Colleen seen this?"

Cameron shook his head. As if on cue, Colleen came walking out the door.

"I'm leaving for work. What are you guys staring at?"

"Colleen get back inside."

"Why?"

Despite Cora's efforts, Colleen looked at the message.

"Who did…"

She stopped mid-sentence.

"I guess that's supposed to be me."

Finally, Cameron spoke up.

"Colleen, you'd better get to work."

"Dad, I'm sorry."

"Just get to work. Your mother and I will take care of it."

Colleen got into her car and drove to the store. Cora turned to her husband.

"What should we do?"

"Well, the grass is kind of high with the boys at camp. Maybe if I cut it close, you won't be able to read it."

"Is there anything I can do?"

"Find out who did this."

Without a word, Cora wheeled herself into the house.

At the cemetery later that afternoon, Jo Ann pulled up and watched as Peter and Paul stood by Dana's grave. She got out of the car and lit a cigarette, staying back a respectable distance. After a few minutes, she saw Paul wipe his eyes and start back to the car, followed by Peter. She had thought twice about coming out but drove out despite her better judgment. If Paul was thinking about his father marrying her, he had to know she respected his former life. She walked up to him and smiled.

"Hey, Paul."

"What are you doing here?"

His question lacked the attitude she was expecting.

"Paying my respects to your mother. Your father told me what today was. I hope you don't mind me coming out. The thing is, my cousin was a flight attendant and it could just as easily been her on that flight."

Peter looked strangely over his son's shoulder. He had never heard that story before.

"Oh."

"Have you eaten yet?"

"No. We were on our way to get something."

"I'd like to take you to lunch if you'd let me. I'd understand otherwise."

"No. I think that would be nice."

Paul walked ahead to the car. Peter slipped his arm around Jo Ann's waist and kissed her cheek.

"That was very nice, coming out."

"I wasn't sure. I know it's a special day for the two of you."

Peter shook his head.

"I didn't know your cousin was a flight attendant."

"She wasn't. I didn't want him to think I was some desperate woman who couldn't let her man spend the day alone with his son."

"Aren't you?"

"No. I care about the two of you and I didn't want you spending the day alone."

"You're something else, you know that?"

"That's why you love me."

"I do. Love you, you know that."

Jo Ann smiled at him.

"I haven't felt this way about a woman in a long time."

Jo Ann squeezed him tight.

"Come on already, I'm starving!"

Paul yelled at them from the car, anxious to get to lunch.

"How long do you think it'll take us to get pregnant?"

"Who do you think I am, Superman?"

“No. I was just wondering.”

Oren and Miranda were lying in bed, enjoying the last day of their vacation. They had just made love for the third time that day and Oren was exhausted. When he suggested having a baby, he had no idea Miranda would take it so seriously. Now she expected him to be some sort of machine.

“Give it some time. Enjoy trying. When you get pregnant, your sex drive may be so messed up and we may not have sex for months.”

“Or it could turn me into a nymphomaniac.”

“I couldn’t handle that.”

Oren went into the kitchen and came back with drinks for both of them.

“By the way, how did Mrs. Shepherd like her wind chimes?”

“Oh my god, I found out why she never leaves the house. She’s agoraphobic.”

“What does that mean?”

“She is actually afraid to leave her house. She makes herself physically ill just thinking about it. She’s a prisoner in her own home.”

“That’s horrible.”

Colleen was half way through her shift at Sav-U-More. The last few hours dragged by as she racked her brain to figure out who would do such a thing to her house. She was glad the kids were at camp. She couldn’t imagine explaining to Candice what that word meant. She cringed when she saw Bea de la Roche walk up and start unloading her groceries. She nearly laughed aloud when she saw the douche next to the Geritol. She nearly gnashed her teeth when Bea started, what seemed to be, casual conversation.

“I didn’t realize you worked here.”

“For the past few months, until I leave for college.”

“I figured with all the work you and Father West have been doing for the youth choir, you wouldn’t have time for anything else.”

“I have time for both.”

“Well, we’ll certainly miss you when you go off to school.”

“Thank you.”

Colleen finished checking her out and handed her change.

“Have a good day.”

“See you in church, dear.”

“Get dressed, we’re having a guys’ night out.”

Jeremy couldn’t believe his ears.

“Just us?”

"Yes. Bowling and then pizza."

"Alright."

Geoffrey finished getting ready and ten minutes later, was still waiting for Jeremy. He went into the bathroom and found his son gelling his hair.

"What are you getting all spiffed up for? You're going to make me look bad."

"Leave me alone."

Geoffrey smiled at his son, but wondered, at fourteen, how much Jeremy knew about sex. Did he have questions? Was he prepared to answer them?

"Are you looking for love in a bowling alley? That sounds like an old country song in the making."

"You never know who you might run into. You have to be prepared."

"Words of wisdom."

Later that night, Cora lay next to Cameron. She turned on her side and began to rub his back. Only a few days ago, she had been turned off by the thought of sex, but something about tonight was different. She felt the need to be near him. She secretly wondered if she would be able to feel him once he was inside her and wondered what would happen if she couldn't. Cameron stirred.

"What's up over there?"

"What's up over *there?*"

She reached around and stroked him gently.

"Not tonight honey, I'm exhausted. Fixing the lawn was harder than I thought it would be."

"Alright then. I love you."

"I love you, too."

Cora kissed Cameron on the back of his shoulder and rolled over. Cameron felt horrible. He was afraid to try to make love to her after the incident at the motel. He wondered how long he could put Cora off.

Across the street was a different story. Hot and sweaty, Miranda screamed out as Oren filled her then collapsed on top of her. He rolled over and got up.

"Where are you going?"

"To get a drink. You want one?"

"Sure."

So much for cuddling, Miranda thought. Oh well, the job was done. She picked her legs up over her head, letting gravity do its job. She hoped she was pregnant soon. Unbeknownst to her, Oren was in the kitchen thinking the exact same thing, but for different reasons.

"I saw you talking to that girl."

Jeremy turned red. He and Geoffrey were on their way home, guy's night a complete success.

"She was looking for the right sized ball."

Geoffrey bit his tongue. That wasn't the kind of joke you make with your fourteen year old son.

"Well, she was too old for you anyway. How old was she, seventeen?"

"I didn't get to ask her."

Geoffrey shook his head and laughed.

"My son, the lady killer."

"Dad. Stop, you're embarrassing me."

"In front of who? It's just us. How would you like to have dinner with Patrick and Melissa tomorrow night?"

"Two nights in a row? Watch out. I might move in permanently."

"I don't think your mother would appreciate that."

"She's been too busy with her new friend to even notice."

"You should really be happy for her. She's been alone for too long, no thanks to me."

"This isn't your fault."

"I know but…"

"But she's having sex right in front of me. If she's not married, then it isn't right. At least that's what she keeps telling me."

"Are you listening?"

"News flash, I am a freshman in high school! You've got me flirting with older girls and sleeping around. You don't know me very well."

"Well, that's what tonight all was about, right?"

Geoffrey feared insulting his son. He tried to change the subject.

"Where did you learn to bowl so well, by the way?"

The next morning, Colleen was dressing for church. Cameron and Cora were having coffee when she finally came out. With everything out in the open about what people were saying, she decided to talk frankly with her parents.

"Do you think people will be staring at me again this week?"

"I'm sure people have forgotten all about that."

Cora felt like a fool as soon as the words left her lips.

"Mother, look at the lawn! Apparently, it's just beginning. You know, I didn't realize people were staring at me last week, but once I thought about it, it all made sense. Can't we go to St. Louise?"

"And let Bea de la Roche and Muriel York win?"

"I wonder how long it took Scott to hear the news. No wonder he wouldn't have diner with us."

"Well then, he's a jerk."

"Do I have to go?"

"Yes, finish getting ready."

As expected, all eyes were on the Mayhelms as they entered church. Furious, Colleen fought the urge to turn and leave. Her mother was right though. That would be admitting she had done something wrong. She took a seat next to her father and tried to ignore all the stares. After Mass, Cora called out to Hope Boudreaux.

"Hope! Hope!"

Although new to Sherwood Circle, Hope was still a York and been involved with the church for years. She and Cora had worked together on a fundraiser year's back when the church was renovating. Hope smiled when she saw Cora wheel herself over. She liked the Mayhelms and refused to believe the rumors.

"Hope, was that you I saw moving into number six a few days back?"

"Yes, it was."

"How do you like living next door to your brother?"

"We haven't decided yet. Has Gretchen or Ben told you the good news?"

"What's the good news?"

"I'm pregnant."

"Congratulations. When are you due?"

"February."

"So you have a while then. If there's anything I can do, just let me know. Gretchen has my number, or just come over."

"Thanks, Cora."

Muriel walked over to her daughter.

"What was that all about?"

"I was telling Cora that if Colleen and Father West need someplace to be alone, they could use my third bedroom."

"Hope!"

"Give me a break mother. What do you want to do, not talk to her because you and my dim witted brother think she's the Whore of Babylon?"

"Your father agrees with me."

"Of course he does."

Muriel stood dumfounded. She couldn't believe her daughter would talk to her like that. Allen came up and rescued his wife.

"What's going on?"

"Nothing. I want to go home so you can massage my feet."

"Will do. Muriel, have a good afternoon."

They walked to the car. Muriel looked for Ben and Gretchen and saw them across the parking lot, ushering the kids into the car. From across the parking lot, she could sense the tension between her son and his wife.

Genie waved at the Mayhelms as they entered The Breakers for Sunday brunch. Once they were seated, Genie, who knew their drink orders by heart, went over with the tray.

"I'm not used to seeing such a small group at this table. How are the campers? Any letters home?"

"Candice wrote to us about something she made in arts and crafts, the boys won't write until they're made to."

"I know what you mean; Jeremy hasn't even called since he moved in with Geoffrey."

"What?"

"Just for the summer. He had issues with my new friend."

Genie looked nervously over at Colleen. She wondered if she should be discussing her sleeping arrangements in front of an eighteen year old.

"It gives him a chance to get to know his dad."

Colleen got up without saying a word and went to the buffet.

"Was it something I said?"

Cora looked around before confiding in Genie.

"Muriel York has been spreading rumors about Colleen and the new priest at Mary's."

"Well, if you ask me, she had better stay in good terms with any priest she comes in contact with. Didn't her daughter just move into number six? Next to me?"

"Yes."

"Well, I can guarantee you full disclosure was not part of that real estate deal."

"Speaking of deals, what *is* up with you and your new friend?"

"My God, Cora, he's young enough to be my son."

Genie caught Oren coming through the door.

"Speak of the devil, here's his brother."

"Oren is his brother?"

Cameron waved him over.

"What arc you doing?"

"Being a good neighbor."

Oren came over to the table. Cameron stood up.

"Oren, why don't you join us for lunch?"

"I wish I could, Cameron, but I have a lot of work to catch up on.

"On a Sunday?"

"Don't you notice my tropical tan? Miranda and I have been in Miami all week."

"Business or pleasure?"

"Pleasure that turned to business. Miranda wants to get pregnant."

"Yea, when it turns into a job, it's no longer fun."

Oren caught the hateful glance Cora shot to her husband.

"Genie, could you go check my order? I have to be getting back."

Genie and Oren left the table. Cora turned to her husband.

"So, is that how you view sex with me now? As a job?"

"Cora, that has nothing to do with us."

"That would explain why you haven't been able to make love to me since the accident."

"Can we talk about this later?"

Colleen came back to the table.

"Mom, do you want me to fix your plate?"

"Yea, you know what I like."

Cameron grabbed his plate and followed Colleen to the buffet.

Later on, Genie rolled over and answered the phone.

"Mom, it's Patrick. What are you doing?"

"Resting. I just got off of work and I'm lying down for a few minutes."

"Do you want to come over for dinner tonight? Dad and Jeremy are coming over. I thought you could bring your friend."

"Are you trying to start drama?"

"Mother, we all know about your new boyfriend. Why can't we just have a nice family dinner?"

"I'll be there, but I can't promise Charlie."

"See you for seven."

"Bye, Patrick."

Genie hung up the phone and set her alarm. She was going to try to get a nap in before dinner with her ex-husband and her new boyfriend.

Chapter 20

"Look, we won't stay long."

Genie and Charlie were standing on her son's doorstep, waiting to be let in.

"Do you really think this is a good idea?"

"Listen, my youngest son practically saw you naked and my ex-husband is the last one to be making judgments."

Before Charlie could interject, the door opened and Melissa let them in. She had never met her mother-in-law's new boyfriend and was shocked by how hot he was. She never figured Genie could land someone that hot.

"Charlie, this is my daughter-in-law Melissa Van Matthews. Melissa, this is a friend of mine, Charles Grant."

"Nice to meet you."

"Likewise. Come right through here and let's get some wine."

Charles went ahead. Melissa whispered in Genie's ear.

"I assume he's old enough to drink."

"Stop that."

Melissa led Genie into the kitchen where Patrick was pouring wine.

Jo Ann was getting ready for bed when she was startled by a knock at the door. It was Peter, with a dozen roses.

"What are you doing here?"

"I figured we could salvage the last part of the weekend. You look like you're turning in early."

"I was going to."

"Change of plans. Get dressed."

She took the roses from him and let him inside.

"What are you up to?"

She kissed him hello.

"You're off until tomorrow night, right?"

"Yes."

"Then get dressed."

Jo Ann smiled, put the flowers down and went to get dressed.

Melissa was setting out the cheese and crackers when the doorbell rang again. She went to the door and let Jeremy and Geoffrey in.

"Melissa, whose car is out front?"

"Genie's friend, Charles."

"Well, I guess it's glad you offered to have dinner here instead of my house. I would never have room for an entire dinner party."

"It was Patrick's idea."

Melissa led them to the kitchen. Genie, trying to avoid initial awkwardness, jumped into the introductions.

"Geoffrey, this is a friend of mine, Charles Grant. Charlie, this is my ex-husband Geoffrey. You've already met Jeremy."

Charlie shook Geoffrey's hand and then Jeremy's, adding,

"Did you cook dinner tonight? I remember those hamburgers were pretty good."

"Not tonight?"

"Geoffrey, wine?"

Geoffrey smiled at his daughter-in-law.

"Do you have anything stronger?"

Jo Ann and Peter drove in silence for a few moments before Jo Ann spoke up.

"So where is your son?"

"At home. He's thirteen, he can stay by himself. He has the number of where we'll be."

"Where will we be?"

"You'll find out in a few minutes."

They drove for a little longer before pulling into the parking lot of the Breakers Inn. Peter opened the door and walked around to room 112. He opened the door and inside was a table set for two. Jo Ann smiled.

"When did you do all this?"

"This afternoon. I hope you haven't eaten yet."

"I had a bagel for dinner."

"Well, I cooked. I hope you'll be able to get your appetite back."

Jo Ann looked jokingly over to the bed.

"I don't think that'll be a problem."

In the middle of dinner, Patrick stood up and clinked his glass, calling for everyone's attention.

"Melissa and I had a reason to make this dinner with my dad a family occasion."

Genie grabbed Charlie's hand under the table. She knew what was coming next. Charlie knew too. He knew he was about to be sleeping with a grandmother.

"We're going to have a baby. In April."

Everyone applauded. Geoffrey got up to congratulate his son and grabbed his chest. He dropped to his knees and collapsed at Jeremy's feet.

"Geoffrey."

Genie jumped up and ran to Geoffrey's body. Patrick turned to Melissa who was already on the phone.

"Call 911."

"I'm on it."

"I can't feel a pulse."

She started CPR on him, willing him to wake up. After a few minutes, beads of sweat formed on her forehead and she began to tire. Charlie took over and, after a few minutes, the paramedics arrived. They attached an oxygen mask to Geoffrey's face and put him on a gurney. The one in charge turned to Genie.

"Ma'am, is this your husband?"

"Ex-husband. Geoffrey Van Matthews."

"May we ask you a few questions?"

The paramedic's eyes darted over to Jeremy, who had been silent thus far. Genie walked over to him.

"Jeremy, get your things. We're going to the hospital."

Jeremy sat staring at his father, unable to move.

"Jeremy!"

Melissa came out of the kitchen, having turned everything off in there. Patrick grabbed the keys.

"They're taking him to Gulf States Memorial."

Within minutes, Geoffrey was loaded into the ambulance. Genie went with him. Melissa ushered Jeremy into the car with her and Pat.

"Where's Genie's friend?"

"He's behind us. He's taking his own car."

"God, I hope your dad is alright."

Melissa grabbed Pat's hand and squeezed it tight.

"You want to tell me what that was all about in the restaurant today?"

Cora and Cameron were getting ready for bed. Neither one of them had spoken to the other since lunch. Cameron had no idea Cora had taken their lack of sex so personally.

"I was just lashing out."

"But that's how you feel. You don't think I'm sexually attracted to you anymore. You think that I think sex with you is a job now."

"Don't you? You haven't been able to touch me since I've been in this chair."

"What if you can't feel anything? What if I can't satisfy you anymore? What does that say about me as a man?"

"What does the fact that you don't even try say about us as a couple, about our marriage? We need to get past this, Cameron. Dr. Washington said this would test us. I think we're strong enough to pass, but I need to know you feel the same way."

"Of course I do."

Cameron walked over to his wife with tears in his eyes and hugged his wife. He couldn't believe they had let it go this far. Cora stroked her husband's back lovingly, then spoke up.

"I think we may have bigger problems on our hands. From what I heard whispered at church today, Colleen is now the town whore."

"I'm just glad the others weren't here to see the lawn yesterday."

"What should we do?"

Cameron shook his head.

"I can't believe it's gotten this bad in a week. I mean, they were so quick to judge and condemn the new priest. If you don't like him, fine, but don't ruin his career."

"Do you think that could happen?"

"That's exactly what could happen."

"We need to talk to him then. We need to let Father West know what's going on."

"I agree. Invite him over for dinner tomorrow."

Cameron lifted Cora into bed and kissed her softly on the mouth.

"I love you so much. I'm sorry I made you feel the way you did."

"It's my fault as much as yours. We can get through it though."

Cameron climbed into bed with his wife, putting his arms around her. Cora had never felt as loved as she did at that moment.

"So where did you order all this from?"

Peter stared at Jo Ann, offended.

"I cooked all this from scratch. Paul helped me."

"So those Imperial Gardens take out containers in the trash are left here from the previous guests?"

Peter rolled his eyes.

"Damn."

"Caught you."

"I really can cook though. It's just once I decided to do this, there wasn't much time. The dishes are from my house though."

"The good china? I'm impressed."

"I'm glad."

Jo Ann stared into Peter's eyes. She was in love with him, there was no doubt. She had never wanted someone so much but had waited so long. She had jumped into bed with Louis and it turned out to be a nightmare. She was glad she had waited with Peter and was sure she was doing the right thing.

"So impress me more."

"Are you sure?"

"Yes, I've never been surer."

Peter took Jo Ann's hand and led her to the bed. He stripped her slowly, taking in every inch of her body, treating her as gently as a porcelain doll. He pulled his shirt off. She sat on the bed and unbuckled his belt. He slid his pants off and climbed on top of her. He kissed her passionately, starting with her neck and making his way down to her breasts. Although Jo Ann could tell he wasn't well endowed, he more than made up for it as he dove between her legs, setting her thighs on fire. She quivered as he entered her, their bodies locked together. She screamed out his name as they finished together, lying spent in each other's arms.

"Let's get married."

"You don't have to marry me to sleep with me silly."

"I'm serious."

Jo Ann kept silent. She had thought about it but was still unsure.

"I have to talk it over with Chad."

"Of course."

"And I'd have to consider mother."

"I saw her eyeing up my guest room."

"She would never leave Sherwood Circle. I would have to be sure she was taken care of."

"You would be able to quit that two job shit."

"I would still work two jobs. I would use the money from cleaning to take care of her."

"What about Barrister's?"

"Are you going to pay all the bills?"

"Sure. Jo Ann, let me take care of you and Chad. Let someone take care of you for a change."

"I couldn't let you do that."

"I want to. I love you."

Peter smiled down at her.

"Peter, you know my answer is yes. Let me break the news to Chad before we make any plans."

"Plans?"

"Of course. I want a huge wedding."

Peter looked at her, not sure if she was kidding or not.

"I'm kidding, Peter. I do want something nice, though."

"We'll plan whatever you want."

He kissed her forehead. She snuggled up close to him, not being able to get close enough.

Genie was stopped at the door as they wheeled Geoffrey into the exam room. Once they had his shirt open, they hooked him up to the monitors. She watched the flat line creep across the monitors. The paddles came out and Geoffrey's body convulsed from the electric shock. A flat line. Paddles. Compressions. Nothing. Genie held her breath as she watched them cover him up and turn off the monitors. She was unaware of Patrick, Melissa and Jeremy standing behind her.

"Mom, why are they covering him up?"

Genie couldn't say anything.

"Mom? Mom, why did they stop? Why are they covering him up?"

Genie turned to her youngest son with tears in her eyes.

"We need to talk to the doctors."

Before they could walk away, a nurse came over and closed the blinds to the room. A tall doctor came out and addressed Genie.

"Mrs. Van Matthews?"

"Yes."

"I'm sorry, but we couldn't save him."

Genie nodded, tears running down her face. Melissa took Patrick's hand, giving him the strength to stay strong for his mother and his little brother. He's the one who did the talking.

"Was it a heart attack?"

"Yes. And from the test we did on the way here, I can tell it wasn't his first. Had he been in good health prior to this?"

"We've been separated. I haven't seen him in seven years. He only came back to town a few months ago."

"Well, I can tell you the heart muscle was severely damaged. He's definitely had a previous heart attack, or two."

Jeremy was crying now. Genie put her arms around him, not knowing what to do next.

"What do we do now?"

"His body will be taken to the morgue. Call the funeral parlor and they'll pick him up from there."

"Thank you, doctor."

The doctor left them.

"Patrick, take Jeremy home please."

Pat led Jeremy toward the door. Genie took Melissa aside.

"Melissa, make sure Jeremy takes this."

She pushed a small blue pill into her daughter-in-law's hand.

"Cut it in half. It's a sleeping pill."

"Are you sure it's safe?"

"Cut it in half. I'll be home in a few minutes."

"Do you need a ride?"

Genie looked past Melissa and saw that Charlie was still waiting for her, giving her time with her family.

"No, I'll have Charlie bring me home."

"We'll be waiting up for you."

"Thank you."

Genie kissed her goodbye and went over to Charlie. She collapsed into his arms.

"He's dead. We were becoming a family again. It was never going to happen for us, of course, but we were starting to be civil, even friendly. He was reconnecting with the boys."

"I know."

"You really didn't have to stay here you know."

"I wanted to."

"Thank you."

"Are you ready to go home?"

"Yea, let's go."

Charlie put his arm around Genie and led her out to the car.

Chapter 21

The next morning, Patrick had taken over the funeral arrangements. The service was in three days and the death announcement was going in the next day's paper. Genie called in sick to the restaurant and Oren was standing there paying for his breakfast when Park took the message. Parker hung up the phone and turned to Oren.

"You live by Genie, don't you?"

"Why? What's wrong?"

"Her husband died yesterday, well, her ex-husband."

"Geoffrey?"

"Apparently, he had a heart attack and died in the emergency room."

Park shook his head in disbelief.

"If you see her, tell her to take off as long as she needs. Tell her to call me when the arrangements are made."

"Will do."

Oren grabbed his breakfast and went back to the hotel.

"Mary, Mother of God."

"Bea, this is Cora Mayhelm."

The uncomfortable silence on the other end almost made Cora laugh out loud.

"May I speak to Father West?"

"One moment, Cora."

Cora smiled as she was transferred. Within a minute, David picked up.

"Father West."

"Father, it's Cora Mayhelm. How are you?"

"Busy, actually. Genevieve Van Matthews's ex-husband died last night."

"Really?"

"I don't like to spread gossip, but I know she lives in your circle."

"Well, then it really isn't gossip is it? Speaking of gossip, do you think you would have time for diner tonight?"

"I think I could squeeze it in."

"Around seven?"

"I'll be there."

David hung up the phone as Bea was walking past his office. David shook his head. He had heard the rumors going around and wondered what his secretary had to do with any of it.

Jo Ann walked into her house cautiously. Mary surprised her.

"Where have you been all night?"

"Quiet. Where's Chad?"

"I sent him to Kathleen's so he wouldn't see you sneaking in."

"You told me to sleep with him."

"And now you listen to me?"

"Mom, he proposed."

"Let me see the ring."

"There is no ring. He proposed in bed last night."

"How sleazy."

"It was perfect."

Jo Ann kissed her mother.

"I'm going to take a shower."

Jo Ann danced down the hall. Mary couldn't help but smile.

Gretchen picked up the phone, afraid of waking the boys who were, thankfully sleeping in.

"Hello."

"Gretchen, it's Cora. What's the latest news going around the parish? I know your mother-in-law knows everything that goes on at that church."

"I don't want to be the one to tell you…"

"But?"

"Muriel is organizing a letter writing campaign to the archbishop alerting him of the inappropriate goings on around here."

"Are you serious?"

"I'm afraid so."

"Have you written your letter?"

"Cora, you know me better than that. I don't believe a word of that crap."

"Well, we're having Father West over for dinner tonight and we're going to set the record straight. Now for the real reason I called. Genie's ex-husband died last night."

"Genie from number eight?"

"Yes. I'll get the details of the service and let you know."

"Thanks, Cora. I'll tell Ben."

Cora hung up the phone, remembering Gretchen's words. She said she didn't believe that crap. Did Ben?

That evening, Cora opened the door for David.

"Father, I'm so glad you could join us."

"I'm glad to be here. Thanks for inviting me."

"Well, I'm glad you had the time. We need to talk, all four of us."

David walked in and kissed his host hello. Walking into the kitchen, he shook hands with Cameron and kissed Colleen hello.

"Would you like something to drink?"

"Iced tea would be nice."

"Coming right up."

Mary ran to the door and was delighted to see Peter on the other side. She threw her arms around him and kissed him on the cheek.

"Congratulations! Come in."

"I guess she told you."

"Of course."

Peter turned to Mary, embarrassed.

"I guess I should have spoken to you first."

"What is this, nineteen sixty three? You're both adults. I'm happy for you either way."

Peter smiled, not forgetting his previous conversation with Mary about him and Jo Ann's relationship. Jo Ann came out from the back of the house and was relieved when she saw her mother and fiancé smiling together.

"You know, I really screwed up this whole issue."

"Why is that?"

"What I should have done was..."

Peter pulled a velvet box out of his pocket and got down on one knee. When he opened it, Jo Ann gasped. As tears filled her eyes, she bent down and kissed Peter. Before he had a chance to get up, Chad came out of his room and walked in on the whole scene.

"What's going on?"

Peter looked at Jo Ann awkwardly.

"I haven't exactly talked to him yet."

Peter got up.

"Mother, could you show Peter that leaky faucet in the kitchen. Remember, you wanted to see if he knew anything about plumbing."

"Yea. Peter, follow me."

The two of them left the room. Jo Ann sat on the sofa.

"Chad, come sit here with me."

"What's going on?"

"Chad, Peter asked me to marry him last night. I said yes. Do you understand what that means?"

"Are we moving out?"

"Yes. We're going to live with Peter and Paul. You're going to have a bigger room…"

"Where is grandma going to be?"

"Grandma is going to stay here."

Chad was quiet for a moment. The silence worried Jo Ann.

"Is Peter my new daddy?"

"Well, he's going to be your step-dad. You can still call him Peter."

Chad shrugged his shoulders.

"I guess that would be okay."

"Are you sure?"

Peter had poked his head in the room, standing back as to not intrude in the moment. He wanted to be sure to give Chad as much room as he needed.

"Yea."

"Well, I think you need to help your mom put on this new ring."

Jo Ann held out her hand as Chad slipped the ring on her finger. She pulled him close and kissed his forehead.

"Father, I'm not sure if you know what's been being spread around the parish recently."

Dinner was going nicely but Cameron decided that it was time to discuss the current rumors.

"I have. I've ignored them because they're ridiculous. Is that why I'm here? Do you think I've behaved inappropriately with your daughter?"

"No. Not at all. Actually, we're so proud of the new choir you two are starting. I think it'll be good for the parish."

Colleen beamed with pride at her mother's words.

"Colleen has worked very hard. We have another meeting Wednesday."

"Well, Colleen thought we should ignore them too, the rumors. Then someone spray painted a word I won't repeat at the dinner table across our lawn. The situation isn't going to go away."

"Well, I certainly apologize for anything your family has had to go through, Cameron. I'll confront the parties involved."

"Are you sure that's wise?"

"I don't see anything else we can do."

Gripping the seat, Hope lurched forward. She got up, wiped off her mouth and walked into the bedroom.

"Morning sickness, my ass."

"Come lay down and I'll rub your feet."

"Thanks, sweetie."

"I was talking to the baby."

"You jerk."

Hope laid down next to Allen and put her arms around him. She was almost finished her first trimester.

"You know, we haven't talked about names yet."

"Well, if it's a boy, I want Allen Jr."

"Works for me. Can we call him A.J.?"

"Works for me."

"And if it's a girl?"

"Faith."

"Faith?"

"Hope and Faith. I think it's pretty."

"We'll see."

"Have you felt it move yet?"

"No, not yet. I'm waiting patiently, though."

Allen placed his hands on Hope's stomach.

"What are you doing?"

"Willing it to move."

"Give it up darling. You're not telekinetic."

Hope kissed him and rolled over to go to sleep.

Two days later, at Geoffrey's funeral, Genie sat next to the casket, surrounded by her family. Jeremy sat next to her. Melissa sat on her other side with Patrick standing behind them. Miranda and Oren stood away from the crowd. As Father West was finishing up and the casket was lowered, Cora wiped a tear from her eye. She remembered how Geoffrey had hurt Genie and the kids when he left seven years ago, but she wouldn't have wished him dead. She knew how excited Jeremy was to have his father back in his life and felt sorry for him most of all. Genie got up and accepted condolences from her family and walked over to where her neighbors had gathered.

"You know, we're having lunch at the house. I hope you all can make it."

"Genie, is there anything we can do?"

"No. Patrick and I are going through his papers tomorrow. Just come over for lunch."

Genie and her children walked back to the car and rode to the house. Cameron pushed Cora to the car. Miranda walked up to Jo Ann and Peter.

"I didn't want to say anything because of the circumstances, but I couldn't help but notice…"

She picked up Jo Ann's hand and flashed the diamond.

"When did this happen?"

"He asked Sunday and delivered the ring Monday."

"How is Chad with all of this?"

"He says he's alright."

Miranda smiled.

"We'll see you at the house."

Ben knocked on Genie's door and waited a moment. Jeremy opened the door and let him inside. Ben found Genie and Charlie in the kitchen and put the macaroni and cheese Gretchen had fixed on the buffet table. He went over to Genie and kissed her on the cheek.

"Genie, we're sorry we couldn't be there today. We couldn't find a babysitter. Hope and Allen had a doctor's appointment."

Cameron, who was nearby, spoke up.

"Ben, Colleen could have watched the kids."

Genie noticed Ben ignoring Cameron's comment and changed the subject.

"Have you met my friend? Benjamin York, this is Charles Grant. He's Oren's brother."

The men shook hands and Genie noticed Jo Ann leaving.

"Excuse me."

She walked away from the kitchen, wondering what was up between Benjamin and Cameron. They had always been friends. Ben had his own reasons for keeping his distance. Despite what Gretchen accused him of, he had his own opinions and believed that Cora and Cameron's daughter wouldn't be in the mess she was in if she had been properly supervised.

Later that evening, Jo Ann heard something going on in her front yard and went out to investigate. She found Chad and Peter covered in whitewash.

"What are the of you doing out here?"

"Well, I figured I took the whole day off for the funeral and I didn't want to waste the rest of the day. Your trim and shutters needed to be stripped and repainted. The paint was flaking off."

"You didn't have to do this."

"Well, I don't want my mother-in-law's house to be the trash of the neighborhood."

He winked at her and kissed her lightly.

"You jerk."

"I'm going to fix the backyard fence next weekend."

"God, our house is falling apart. We really are the trash of the neighborhood."

"Well, when my assistant and I are done, it's going to look like something off of television. I did however find a million cigarette butts in the grass."

"My fault."

Peter smiled at her.

"I didn't think they were Chad's."

Chapter 22

"You'll want to sing. It's fresh like spring. You'll want to pass it on."

Colleen sang along with the piano. David checked his watch. The choir meeting was supposed to start ten minutes ago, and, with the exception of the two sitting in the front row, nobody had showed up. Colleen's heart sank when she realized they were the only two coming. Apparently, the other children's parents didn't approve of her being in charge.

"Why don't you guys go get some cookies in the rectory."

The two kids ran off, leaving David and Colleen alone.

"You know, you'd better watch out. You and I alone together, people are going to start talking."

David laughed. Colleen started to tear up.

"You know, I really wanted this to work. I really thought I was doing a good job."

"I'm sure people just forgot. We'll make another announcement next week…"

"Father, people didn't forget. What they forgot is that I grew up in this parish. They know I'm not a bad girl. Why would they say this stuff about me?"

David put his arms around her and comforted her. She collapsed in his arms, sobbing.

"Colleen, we'll straighten this all out. I promise."

As Colleen was breaking down, Holly Stewart came into the church and walked in on them. She couldn't believe what she was seeing. Muriel York had been right. If she wanted a letter to the archbishop, she was going to get one.

"Excuse me."

"Dr. Stewart."

"I came to pick up Heather."

"She and Robert Shaw are in the rectory having cookies."

"Unsupervised?"

Before they could respond, Holly turned and left the church.

That Sunday before Mass, Muriel and Malcolm were standing outside church, surrounded by their little following. Hope and Allen went up to greet her parents and overheard her father.

"I had Bea take me off the schedule. I won't read with that boy on the alter."

"I know what you're saying. I can't serve for someone I don't respect."

Hope grabbed Allen by the arm.

"We're leaving."

Allen nodded and followed his wife to the car. Muriel saw them start to leave and stopped them.

"Hope, where are you going?"

"St. Louise. I don't want to be in the same room as you hypocrites."

"You need to watch your mouth in front of church people."

"They're not church people. Are you listening to yourselves? Mother, you don't serve a priest, you serve God!"

"Keep your voice down darling."

"Go to hell!"

Allen almost laughed out loud when he saw his mother-in-law's stunned expression. He went to the car and opened the door for his wife, never being more proud of her than he was at that moment. Benjamin and Gretchen walked toward the doors, Ben Jr. and Tim following close.

"Mother, what was that all about?"

"Nothing, Benjamin, let's go inside."

Genie sat at the break table smoking a cigarette. Parker found her.

"Smoking? Something must be wrong?"

"I'm done. I'm just resting."

"How's Jeremy doing?"

"Fine. He moved back home a few days ago. Listen, thanks for coming the other day."

"Of course. It was nice to see your friend there."

"My neighbors."

"No, your other friend, the hot one."

"Charlie? He's great isn't he?"

"I thought he was just there for fun?"

"He was. Now, I'm not so sure."

"Well, I wouldn't be jumping into any new relationships with Geoffrey fresh in the ground."

"Speaking of which, Patrick and I were going through Geoffrey's things and he had just drafted a new will. Guess who his lawyer is?"

"Who?"

"Devon McKenzie. Patrick's partner"

"He changed it since he's been back?"

"I wonder if that's why he came back. Did he know he was dying? I told you his heart had been damaged from previous heart attacks."

"You told me the doctor said that."

Genie crushed out her cigarette.

"Anyway, Geoffrey left everything to the boys. He did leave me his car though, which is good because the Ford is on its last leg."

"How much are we talking?"

"A lot. Apparently, Geoffrey was very good at what he did and made a lot of money doing it."

"Is it legal? You have no idea what he's been up to for the past seven years."

"I'm not thinking that way. Whatever it was, it paid for Jeremy's college tuition, his wedding and half his first house."

"Wow."

"No kidding."

Genie got up to go.

"Well Parker, I'll see you tomorrow."

"See you later."

Tired, Genie got in her car and drove home.

Colleen looked around the church and felt sick when she realized it was half empty. She shook her head, not believing the people she had grown up with could behave such a way. She saw Kelleye two aisles over and waved. She was relieved when she waved back. At least her best friend hadn't abandoned her the way her boyfriend did. Behind Kelleye and her family stood a priest Colleen didn't recognize. Colleen could swear he kept glancing in her direction. After Mass, everyone was filing out. The priest went up to David.

"Father West."

"Bishop O'Hara, I didn't realize you were coming out for a visit."

"I'm afraid this is business. Can we go inside and talk?"

"Sure."

Muriel York watched the exchange with a smile on her face. For the first time, Ben couldn't believe his mother. Is this what she had wanted all along? How could she do this to a priest? He was still a kid.

Once they were inside the rectory, the two men sat in the living room.

"So David, how is everything going?"

"Bishop, with all due respect, you can stop with the small talk. I assume this is about the rumors that have been going around my parish. Must say, I'm impressed they got to you so fast."

"They're not just rumors Father. In this past week alone, we're gotten over one hundred letters demanding your resignation."

David's heart sank. He was sixteen when he decided to become a priest. He had graduated at the top of his seminary class and went on to earn his masters in psychology. At the age of twenty-seven, he had worked hard and had achieved everything he had dreamed of. Last spring, when he was assigned his own parish, his head filled with dreams to do God's will and touch people's lives. Now, nearly four months after being assigned, his dreams were collapsing. He wanted to hate. He wanted to cry. He kept his composure in front of his boss.

"So I'm fired?"

"Reassigned. You'll be going back to St. Matthew's."

David got up and walked across the room.

"Tell me I'm not a failure."

"You're not a failure. I know nothing happened with that girl. Anyone who knows you knows nothing happened, but the parishioners demanded action and we had to respond."

"Alright."

Bishop O'Hara got up.

"You'll be expected at St. Matthew's on the first of the month. I hate to drop this news on you and leave, but…"

"I understand."

David shook his hand and walked him to the door. After he was gone, he went to his bedroom and collapsed on the bed. He wondered how he was going to leave gracefully, hiding his feelings, his hatred for the gossiping, meddlesome old bitches that had cost him his job.

Ben Jr. and Tim ran inside, anxious to change into their swimsuits. Ben grabbed his wife's arm and led her to the bedroom.

"We need to talk."

Gretchen sat on her bed, tired of fighting, and looked at her husband.

"What about?"

"I was wrong, about my mother. You and Hope were right all along. I think she maliciously spread rumors because she didn't like the new priest. And now she's ruined his reputation."

"And Colleen's."

Benjamin nodded.

"This reminds me of something I need to do."

Ben took his wife's hands.

"I'm sorry we've been fighting."

"I'm sorry, too. We were both wrong."

Ben kissed Gretchen and went to the door.

"Where are you going?"

"To right a wrong."

Jo Ann took a pan of enchiladas out of the oven. She plated them up and called her mother and the kids to lunch. Peter sat at the table, pouring sangria for the adults. Jo Ann had worked all morning to prepare the perfect Mexican fiesta. Mary walked into the kitchen.

"I hope you don't intend to leave all this crap in the kitchen. I just cleaned up."

"You're welcome mother. Sit down and eat. Peter will do the dishes."

"I didn't volunteer for that."

He winked at her as she put the food on the table. Paul and Chad came running inside, smelly and sweaty.

"Go wash up you two."

Jo Ann sat down. Mary smiled. She was glad to see her daughter so happy.

"So, have the two of you set a wedding date yet?"

"Labor Day."

"That's six weeks away!"

"I know and we have a lot of planning to do. I need to find something to wear."

"What kind of wedding? Big? Small?"

"Well, Peter had a big wedding the first time. You know me and Louie got married at the courthouse. We have no idea."

"I told her, Mary, that whatever she wanted was fine with me."

"I've already asked Kathleen and Miranda to stand up with me. Chad will, of course, walk me down the aisle. And I'm assuming Paul will be your best man?"

"Of course."

"I have to call the church, the caterers, the florist, the photographer…"

"Watch out, Peter, you've created a monster."

"I don't mind."

He took Jo Ann's hand.

Cameron got up from eating lunch and went to answer the door. He was surprised to see Ben standing on the other side of it. After the chilly reception he got after Geoffrey's funeral, he figured Ben would never talk to him again. Frankly, if Ben and Gretchen bought into the lies going around the church, he had nothing to say to him anyway.

"Ben."

"Cameron, may I come inside?"

"Cora and I are eating lunch."

"What I have to say involves Cora, too. It's very important that I say it. It won't take long."

Cameron opened the door and let Ben inside. Cora wheeled herself into the dining room.

"Hi, Ben."

"Not today, Cora. I just came from church."

Cora laughed. Cameron was losing his patience.

"What's this about, Ben?"

"I came to apologize for the way I've been acting. I'm afraid I let myself believe the rumors about Father West and I've treated my friends badly."

"I thought you were acting funny the other day."

"I'm sorry. I was a jerk."

"Yes, you were?"

Cora spoke up.

"How does Gretchen feel?"

"She feels like I was a jerk, too. She never believed what they were saying. What my…"

"What your mother was saying."

"Yes."

"And now you realize what she was saying was ridiculous."

"Yes."

Ben felt like a schoolboy being reprimanded by the nuns.

"Well, Ben, I think you should be apologizing to Colleen. Unfortunately, she's at work."

"I will. You know, I hope things can get back to the way they were. You guys were always so good to us and the kids. I hope I haven't ruined it for good."

"No, you haven't."

Cora answered before Cameron could say anything. She was afraid he wouldn't be able to forgive so easily.

Chapter 23

The next Sunday, Father West stood at the podium with a heavy heart. He had worded his speech carefully, citing a transfer rather than a demotion.

"I have been asked to take over the psychology department at St. Matthew's Hospital, the same hospital I came from. Next Sunday will be my last Sunday at Mary, Mother of God."

Whispers came from the crowd. David continued.

"In my short time here, I got to know many of you and will remember you fondly. It's with a heavy heart that I leave here, but look forward to my future endeavors. I trust the next pastor will receive the same warm reception and welcome I got when I came here."

David's eyes bore down on Muriel York, seated in her place of honor in the first row. Everyone knew exactly what he was talking about and the church became so silent, you could have heard a pin drop.

"Please stand for the closing prayer."

Benjamin York eyes his mother with contempt. He couldn't believe it had come to this. At that moment, he squeezed Gretchen's hand. She smiled at him lovingly.

David stood outside the church accepting well wishes from the congregation. He wondered to himself how many were sincere and how many had come from the same people that had sent letters against him. Hope and Gretchen stood outside the church watching Malcolm and Muriel shaking hands with Father David.

"Can you believe them?"

"No."

Their husbands came up just then, towing the kids behind them.

"Honey, Allen has just invited us to a barbeque."

Hope raised her eyebrows.

"Really? Where?"

"Your house."

Hope rolled her eyes.

"I guess I have worked to do."

"Why don't wc go to Sav-U-More and pick up some stuff at the deli."

"Good idea."

Hope kissed Allen on the cheek.

"Darling, you go get the fire started. We're going to the store for provisions."

"What about the boys?"

"They're staying with you and Ben."

Hope and Gretchen went to the car, never giving Malcolm and Muriel another thought for the rest of the day.

"Flowers. Check. Caterer. Check. Photographer. Check. I'm sure glad I got my bonus check from the department store this week."

"You're tiring yourself out. I wish you would let me do some of that, or at least pay for some of it."

Jo Ann and Peter were reviewing the wedding list when Jo Ann glanced at her watch.

"Nonsense. I have to pick up Chad from the therapist."

"Let me do it."

"It's alright."

"Really. I want to take his shopping."

"For what?"

"I'm redoing the guest room to his bedroom and I have to know what he wants."

Jo Ann slipped her arms around Peter and kissed him.

"You're terrific, you know that."

"I just don't want him to feel like he's moving into my house. I want him to have his own space."

"How's Paul feel about that?"

"He's excited. He was a bit peeved when I took Dana's picture down."

"Don't do that. Peter, you can't get rid of his mother. I am not replacing her. He'll despise me."

"He's thirteen. He despises everything."

"Well, you pick Chad up then go home and put Dana's picture back up."

"You know, you're pretty terrific yourself."

"I'm not always this nice. Just wait."

Peter was getting ready to leave when Jo Ann stopped him.

"By the way, I was at Sav-U-More last week and Gretchen York herself told me how nice the house looked."

"See, you're moving up, babe."

The four adults sat around the table outside while Ben and Tim played in the sprinkler. Their Aunt Hope and Uncle Allen didn't have a pool like they did, but they didn't care. They were wet and happy.

"So, Father West is leaving."

"I can't believe it came to this."

"I can. Those people can be monsters. And we all know who was at the head of it."

"Gretchen, please. I don't want her mentioned for the rest of the afternoon. It's been too nice a day. Let's talk about something a lot nicer. Allen and I have decided to ask you and Ben to be the baby's godparents."

"Really?"

"Yes. We talked about it and decided last night."

"We'd love to do it. We're honored."

"Honored my ass! Hope, I'm your only brother. If you had asked anyone else, I would have kicked your ass."

"Well, thank god I spared myself that pain."

Hope winked at her brother and poured more iced tea for everyone.

"Well Hope, are you going to find out the sex of the baby?"

"No."

"How exciting. What abut names?"

"Allen Jr. if it's a boy and Faith if it's a girl."

"Faith and Hope. I like that."

"We thought it was nice."

"Give it back Tim!"

Gretchen rolled her eyes and went to see what her sons' issues were. Ben smiled and looked at his sister.

"Think twice before you have two."

Later that week, Genie found an invitation in the mail. It was for Jo Ann's wedding. She was tickled to be invited and marked her calendar. She wondered if anyone else in the neighborhood had been invited. She was sure Gretchen and Ben weren't. They had been nice to Genie and Jeremy but downright snotty to Jo Ann and her family. She was sure Oren and Miranda would be there, not so sure about the Mayhelms, and the people next door at number six. Nobody knew much about them except that they were related to Gretchen and Ben somehow. She smiled when she saw Jeremy's handwriting on the calendar. Chris and Chris were coming back from camp next week and it was nice to see Jeremy getting excited about something again. He hadn't talked much since Geoffrey's funeral. Genie sat down and slipped off her shoes.

Andrew was exercising Cora's legs, keeping them from turning into toothpicks from not being used.

"Andrew, do you think Colleen's going away to school in the fall will look like she's running away?"

Cora had confided in Andrew about the whole situation.

"I thought you told me the priest got sent away?"

"Next week will be his last week. People will still talk."

"For a while. It'll blow over. But no, I don't think people will think that at all."

"I used to think people would be crazy to believe that I would raise a child who would have an affair with a priest. That's what half the parish thinks."

"You know your daughter better than that. Fuck what they think."

"I've never heard you talk like that."

"I'm being a rebel today."

He alternately bent her feet and legs back and forth.

"Do you feel anything?"

"I've given up on that a long time ago."

"How are you and Cameron doing?"

"God, I do tell you everything, don't I?"

"I'm glad you feel comfortable enough with me to confide."

"Well, things are much better. We talked."

"Anything else?"

"Not yet, but we've been very busy."

"You have one child instead of four. How busy can you be?"

"He's been busy. He's been short a man at the garage lately and has to do everything himself."

"Avoidance?"

"I don't think so."

Damn Andrew for putting that into her head. Cora had to seduce Cameron, soon.

"Chad, how did you like going shopping with Peter the other day?"

"It was okay."

"Did he show you your new room?"

"Yea."

"Did you like it?"

"It was okay."

Jo Ann lit a cigarette and sat across from her son.

"You know, Peter and I are getting married in a few weeks and we'll be moving out of grandma's house. How do you feel about that and don't tell me it's okay."

"I'll miss grandma."

"You'll still see her."

"It won't be the same."

"I know."

Silence.

"Chad, you can talk to me you know. It's not good to keep things inside. Isn't that what Dr. Kirby says?"

"It'll be cool, having a new brother, a new room, and a new school."

Peter had arranged for Chad to attend St. Augustine's, the private school Paul attended. Jo Ann wasn't worried about Chad's friends. He didn't have many friends and the ones he had were bad influences. She hoped he would meet some nice boys from nice families there. Mary watched from the living room, tears filling her eyes. She had watched Chad grow from infancy and was going to miss him terribly.

"Well, I'm very excited."

She ruffled his hair, finished her cigarette and went to her room, passing her teary mother on the way.

"What's up with you?"

"Nothing."

"Well, stop it."

Cameron came home that night and called out to Cora.

"I'm in the bedroom."

Cameron walked into his room and smiled when he saw his wife. Cora was lying on the bed covered with rose petals. The straps of her nightie had slipped down her shoulders.

"I hope you're not too tired."

He smiled again and glanced at her leg, propped up, and letting the teal silk reveal the silk that was her upper thigh. She noticed this and laughed slightly.

"Don't get too excited. It took me five minutes to pull my leg into this position."

He walked over to her, placing her hand on his already hard crotch.

"You look like that and tell me not to get excited."

"I'm glad I've still got it in me."

"Not yet you don't."

Cameron stripped off his shirt.

"I should take a shower."

"No. Colleen will be home in an hour. I don't want to waste any of the time we have together."

She reached up and pulled him closer, covering his mouth, her tongue caressing his. He pulled away and unbuckled his pants, letting them fall to the floor. Poking out of his boxers, he climbed on top of her and separated her legs. She pulled him closer, afraid that she wouldn't be able to feel him. He kissed her breasts and entered her with full force. She cried out in pleasure and relief as she felt every inch of him fill her up. She longed to wrap her legs around him. Sweat dripped from his body as Cameron came closer to the anticipated moment. His whole body tensed as Cora dug her nails into his back and, with a moan, they finished together. Cameron rolled over and watched as Cora pulled herself up on the pillows.

"That was a nice surprise."

"Well, we made up, but we didn't make up."

"I'm glad we made up."

"Me, too."

"Now, I'm starving."

"Dinner is on the stove. Get it and come in here and eat with me. We can watch television and go to bed early."

"Food in bed?"

"I know, but Candice isn't here to see it, so we'll keep it our secret."

Cameron kissed her again and walked naked to the kitchen, stopping for a quick shower on the way.

The Mayhelms weren't the only ones with seduction on the mind. As Oren lay in bed, he felt Miranda's hand creep across his waist and into his underwear.

"Lay off honey, I'm tired."

"Isn't the woman supposed to say that?"

"What is that supposed to mean?"

"I didn't mean anything. What I meant…"

"What I meant is that I worked almost fifteen hours today. Caryn is out of town and I'm running the whole motel myself. I need some sleep!"

"But it's my fertile time."

"Well, then you have a few more days. Let me sleep."

Miranda's fingers kept playing below Oren's waistband. Pissed off, he threw the covers off of him and grabbed his pillow.

"Fine! If you can't understand, I'm going to sleep on the sofa!"

He stormed out of the room, leaving Miranda fuming mad.

The next morning, Miranda walked into the kitchen as Oren was fixing coffee. She went up to her husband, put her arms around him and kissed his neck.

"I'm sorry about last night."

"Me too."

"I guess I never realized how much I wanted a baby until we stated trying."

"Well, we both work really hard. We need time to just rest. It's only going to get worse after we have a baby."

"I know. Promise me you don't think I'm a freak."

Oren turned around, wrapping his arms around her.

"I always knew that."

"Do you think we can try again tonight?"

"Yes."

He kissed her lightly and left for work.

Chapter 24

The weeks passed quickly until Labor Day was finally upon Sherwood Circle. That Friday morning, Jo Ann and Chad were loading the rest of their things into a van to be taken to Peter's. Cora was outside getting the mail when she saw Jo Ann and wheeled herself over.

"So tomorrow's the big day? Jo Ann is there anything you need me to do? Can I help move boxes?"

"No, Cora, this is the last of it."

"Are you excited?"

"Excited, nervous, scared. I'm worried about mother being alone; I'm worried about putting Chad in a new school..."

"He'll do just fine."

"Speaking of school, How's Colleen doing up at North Lake?"

Colleen had left for the University of Louisiana at North Lake two weeks before.

"She must be having a good time. She didn't come home for the long weekend."

"She is so brave, going away where she doesn't know anyone. I don't think I could do that."

"Well, she needed to get out of St. Bernard for a while."

Jo Ann nodded. She didn't go to church but had heard the rumors secondhand.

"Is everything set for tomorrow?"

"Yes, finally. I never had a big wedding the first time and I'm glad to be doing it, but I'll be glad when it's all over."

"I know. Cameron and I had about three hundred people at our wedding and it was a nightmare. I was glad when it was over and we went on our honeymoon."

"Where did you go?"

"On the Caribbean Star. We cruised the Bahamas."

"Peter and I are going to be roughing it in a cabin outside of Birmingham."

"I wouldn't be caught dead roughing it."

Jo Ann shrugged.

"We like it."

"What about Chad."

"Kathleen is watching him and Peter's son for the whole week."

"His son, too?"

"Yes."

Cora caught Andrew pulling in the driveway.

"Well, Jo Ann, if you need anything, just call. We'll see you tomorrow and don't be a stranger."

"I won't."

"And don't worry about Mary, we'll take care of her."

"Thanks."

Jo Ann went back into the house, sorry she hadn't been closer to Cora and her family.

That night, Peter and Jo Ann's rehearsal party was in full swing. Miranda had arranged for the private dining room at Mariner's. It was a small, intimate gathering for about ten people.

Jo Ann had spent the entire day setting up everything in the house and she was exhausted. Cora was right, she would be glad when it was over. She walked to the balcony, overlooking the lake, and lit a cigarette. Her sister followed her.

"You guys having a good time, Kath?"

"Yea. We're leaving soon though. The kids are exhausted and they have a big day ahead of them tomorrow."

"Tell me about it."

"I just wanted to spend some sister time with you and tell you that I am very proud of you. You deserve to be happy Jo Ann, you deserve so much."

"Actually, I wasn't terribly unhappy before, but I never knew I could be this happy. I know, the awful first marriage, the abuse, the drugs, moving back home..."

"Working two jobs to support the three of you."

"I won't miss that. I'll still be working to help Mom out."

"I'm glad you mentioned that. Jerry and I were discussing finding a place for mother to live."

"She already has a home."

"I know, but with you moving out, we thought she'd do better in a senior facility."

"She isn't ninety, Kathleen."

"I know, but the place we're looking at is an apartment style complex. She would still be on her own, but security and health care provided when she needs it. It isn't like a rest home or anything."

Jo Ann ran her fingers through her hair. She tried to maintain her temper.

"What are you doing, Kathleen? What do you mean dropping this on me the day before my wedding?"

Kathleen tried to defend herself, but Jo Ann stopped her.

"No. You know what? We're going to shelve this and discuss it with mother after I come back from my honeymoon."

Jo Ann walked away from her sister, shaking her head.

Cora picked up the phone on the third ring.

"Hello."

"Cora, it's Gretchen. Can I ask a favor?"

"Sure. What?"

"Can you watch the boys tomorrow?"

"Honey, we can't. We're going to be at the wedding too."

"What wedding?"

Oops. Cora never realized that Jo Ann hadn't invited everyone in the circle to the wedding.

"Jo Ann from next door is getting married. I assumed you got an invitation. Genie got one and I know Miranda is in the wedding."

"Oh. No, we didn't get invited."

"Oh."

"Well, you know she never liked us."

"That's because you called her white trash to her face."

Gretchen shrugged off the comment, knowing it was the truth.

"Well, I'll try someone else. How's Colleen doing in school?"

"Great I think. She's trying out her independence. You remember."

"I do. Have fun tomorrow."

"Okay."

Cora hung up the phone feeling horrible. Gretchen was furious. She yelled to Ben.

"You'll never guess who is getting married tomorrow, whose wedding we weren't invited to."

"Whose?"

"Jo Ann Mott."

"Thank god. Maybe she'll move that little juvenile delinquent across town."

"It doesn't piss you off?"

"No. Good riddance."

"Well, I think it's rude."

Gretchen turned to find that her husband had already left the room.

"Now don't think about getting any ideas tomorrow, okay."

Genie and Charlie were lying in bed.

"I'm done being married."

"Me, too."

"Charlie, you've never been married."

"Well then, I don't intend to."

Genie sat up, letting the sheets slip down, revealing one still firm breast.

"Oh, I don't know. I think you might find a nice girl one day, someone you want to have children with. Hell, you may meet her tomorrow."

"I would never pick up another woman when I'm with you."

"Whatever makes you happy. I want you to be happy."

"You want to know what makes me happy? Being here with you. That's what makes me happy."

Genie smiled. In the back of her mind, she wondered how serious Charlie was getting. They had agreed on a casual relationship, but she was worried.

The next morning, Miranda was getting dressed.

"Oren, could you get my necklace out of my purse. Do you know the one? The ones she gave Kathleen and me to wear."

Oren went to his wife's purse and shifted through it. Shocked, he pulled out a brochure for the St. Bernard Fertility Institute. He flipped through it, unable to believe what he was reading. Miranda came out of the room and stopped when she saw what Oren was reading. He turned to her and held it up, unable to say anything.

"I was waiting for the right time to talk to you about that."

Oren shook his head, threw the brochure on the table and went to finish getting ready. Miranda chased him into the bedroom.

"Oren, talk to me."

He turned around and grabbed his wife by the shoulders.

"You need to stop with all this damn pressure!"

"It was your idea to try and get pregnant."

"And it hasn't happened yet. So what? Do you expect me to go jump through some hoops like some lab rat? Go jerk off in some cup to see if I'm the reason we haven't gotten pregnant?"

"Honey, we've only been trying for a few months."

"So lay off! Let's start living our lives for another purpose and if it happens, it happens. Remember having sex just for fun? Do you even remember what that's like?"

"Don't be so angry darling."

Oren looked at his watch.

"You'd better finish getting dressed. It's almost time for you to head to Jo Ann's."

Miranda knocked on Mary's door and let herself in. Jo Ann was standing in the kitchen in full bridal regalia, smoking.

"Do you think that's a good idea?"

"Are you kidding?"

Miranda smiled despite being furious with Oren. She looked over Jo Ann's dress. It was ivory and cut just to the knee. It was simple and elegant and looked great on her. The pale green bridesmaids' dresses were similar.

"What do you think about the hat? Do you think it's too *Gulf States International*?"

Mary came in from the back.

"It looks great. Phyllis wore one just like it when she remarried Jonathan. It looked good on her, but great on you."

"Jo Ann, what did you wear to your first wedding?"

"A fucking tank top!"

Miranda exploded with laughter.

"I was six months pregnant."

Jo Ann checked the clock.

"Chad Michael, get in here."

Chad came out of his room, dressed in a little tux.

"You look great, sweetheart."

Kathleen came through the door and stopped when she saw her sister.

"Jo Ann, you look beautiful."

"Thanks. The cars should be here soon."

Jo Ann nervously went to the window and looked out.

"Somebody must have died."

A few minutes later, Ben Jr. peeked out his kitchen window.

"Why do you say that, Ben?"

"There's a limo across the street."

Gretchen went and opened the blinds. The limousine pulled up in front of number three and, moments later, Jo Ann, Chad, Mary, Kathleen, and Miranda came out the house.

"No, Ben, it's just someone getting married."

Despite being ticked off at not being invited, Gretchen had to admit that Jo Ann looked great. Ben was right, though, good riddance. Now maybe the old lady would move out and they could get some more young people on the street. Lord knows the old lady at number five was never going to go anywhere.

Doris watched out the window as everyone got into the car. She had no idea Jo Ann was getting married but smiled for her anyway. Better get online and get some candlesticks or something from Barrister's.

Oren turned around and wasn't surprised to see his brother come in with Genie. He waved them over and the three of them sat together. Oren whispered in his brother's ear.

"Don't you two be getting any idea?"

"That's exactly what we talked about last night...in bed."

Oren rolled his eyes.

Peter stood in the side room and straightened Paul's tie. Peter and Jo Ann were getting married at The Ivory Palace, a reception facility where you could have your wedding and reception at the same place. They had looked for a church, but Jo Ann wasn't Catholic, so it posed a problem. At the front of the room was a grand staircase where the preacher was waiting. Paul went to the top and Peter waited on the bottom. One of his friends from the police department was standing up for him as well, but Paul was the best man. The music started and Miranda entered the room. Taking her place at the lower part of the stairs, she was followed by Kathleen who went up the stairs and took her place across from Paul. The bridal march began and Jo Ann and Chad entered the room. Gasp were heard as the two of them walked down the aisle. Jo Ann had never looked more beautiful in her entire life. She kissed Chad at the bottom of the stairs and took Peter's arm. They ascended the stairs like royalty. Once they were at the top, Chad went and sat next to Mary. The ceremony was beautiful and as Peter and Jo Ann joined their two families, the guests broke into applause as they walked down the aisle in the same grand fashion as they walked up.

Oren took a glass of champagne from a passing waiter and drank it down. This was his third glass and, despite having food in his stomach, he was already feeling a buzz. He walked over to Cameron and Cora.

"I thought Ben and Gretchen would be here."

Cora answered in a hushed whisper. "They weren't invited."

"Oh."

"They were never really close to Jo Ann. You know, suburban drama."

"Yea. Do I know drama."

He took another glass of champagne from a waiter and emptied it down.

"Perfect neighbors, perfect marriages, nothing is ever as it seems."

Cora began to get uncomfortable. Oren was well on his way to being full fledged drunk.

"Oren, have you tried the chocolate fountain?"

"Not yet, but I will. I think right now."

He turned and stumbled away. Cora took Cameron's hand.

"What was that all about?"

"Problems at home maybe?"

"I hope not. I like them."

Cameron shrugged.

"What do you say, we blow this party early and go home and fool around?"

"Why sir, how you do go on."

Cameron shrugged again.

"Get the kids together and I'll go say goodbye to Jo Ann and Peter."

About forty minutes later, Jo Ann was talking to some friends from work when Mary came up behind her, angry.

"So, that's the plan?"

"Mom, what are you talking about?"

"How dare you? You get married, start a new life, and ship me off to some rest home!"

"Where did you hear that?"

"I took you and Chad in when you had nothing and now you think you can kick me out of my own house!"

Mary was yelling now and people started to watch.

"Mom, I just found out about this yesterday."

"Jerry, told me it was your idea!"

"Would you keep your voice down?"

"The hell I will."

Jo Ann wanted to kill her brother-in-law. What has it his business to tell Mary when they hadn't discussed it as a family yet.

"Alright mother, fine. I'll yell too. I didn't know anything about this. Kathleen sprung this on me last night at Mariner's. All I agreed to is that we would talk about it after I get back from Alabama."

"If you think you can control me because you pay my bills, think again! I'm staying in my house and I don't need your damn money!"

Mary turned and ran out of the room. She flagged down one of her cousins that was leaving and got a ride home with them. Jo Ann turned to Peter, stunned.

"Where is my sister?"

Before he could answer, Jo Ann stormed off in Kathleen's direction.

"Oren, I think you've had enough."

"I don't think I have."

Oren slurred the words to his wife. She tried to pull the last glass of champagne out of his hands and he pulled away, spilling it on the floor. Charlie and Genie noticed this from about ten feet away and went over to investigate.

"Miranda, is something wrong?"

"Oren just had a little too much to drink."

"Oren, let's go. I'll take you home."

"No! Listen here little brother, you and your girlfriend or lady friend, whatever you call her, can just move on. This is between me and my wife."

Hardly insulted, but a little embarrassed, Genie looked away. She knew Oren was drunk and had no idea what he was saying.

"There's no reason to be insulting."

"It's not my problem you're sleeping with someone old enough to be our mother."

Oren leaned into his brother.

"Is it true though? Can you teach an old dog…"

Before he could finish the sentence, Charles cocked back and punched his brother square in the jaw, sending him falling backwards into Miranda. Peter came to see what the commotion was.

"What's going on?"

"Nothing. We're leaving."

The ladies exchanged glances of apology as Charles led Genie out of the building and into the car.

"We're leaving too. Tell Jo Ann to call me when y'all get back."

Miranda guided her husband to the car, furious at him. She threw him in the passenger seat and sped home. Once they were at the house, she threw him in the shower, suit on, and showered him with cold water.

"What are you doing?"

"You stay in there and sober up you son of a bitch! I have never been so embarrassed in my entire life. I just hope Genie can forgive you, although I sure as hell don't see why."

She left him in there and slammed the door shut.

Jo Ann missed the entire episode, having followed her sister into the ladies' room.

"Kathleen, what do you think you're doing?"

"I was reapplying my lipstick."

"That's not what I meant. Mom just left, angry at me for wanting to put her in a home."

"I never said anything."

"Jerry told her it was my idea!"

"Why would he do something like that?"

"I don't know. You tell me."

Jo Ann sat there while her sister tried to make excuses.

"You know what? I don't care. This is all on you. I'm leaving for my honeymoon tonight and I want all this fixed by the time I come back."

"Jo Ann, you know how mother can get. She was just overreacting."

"You will fix this, Kathleen! You will tell mother the truth."

Determined not to spoil her day, Jo Ann turned and stormed out of the room, rejoining her guests. When she saw Peter again, he filled her in on the whole Oren-Charles spectacle.

"Well, this certainly had been a wedding to remember.

Hours later, it was all over. Peter and Jo Ann were in Birmingham. Kathleen had picked up the boys and fell asleep with the help of a muscle relaxer. Oren passed out naked on the bed and it was Miranda's turn to sleep on the sofa. Only Cameron and Cora enjoyed the rest of the evening. Once the kids were asleep, the two of them had made love and fallen asleep in each other's arms.

Chapter 25

"You ruined my suit."

"No, I didn't. I've already taken it to the cleaners. You embarrassed me in front of our friends and insulted your brother."

Oren popped three aspirins in an attempts to kill his hangover.

"I'm sorry."

"Tell that to your brother. Tell that to Genie. I'm tired of hearing it."

"You're one to talk. You're hardly an angel of virtue and you know what I'm talking about."

She knew. A few years back, Miranda suspected Oren of having an affair with Serena Bentley and had sent Serena's mother Janet a letter airing her suspicions right before Serena's wedding to Gage. Serena found out the truth and the two women ad argued, resulting in the fall that caused Miranda to miscarry her and Oren's baby. Oren knew about the letter but nothing about the fight.

"You still need to talk to your brother."

"I'll see if he's at Genie's."

Oren left the house and walked over to number eight.

"Mother, you can't fault Jo Ann. With the wedding and all, she hasn't been thinking straight."

Kathleen was setting the record straight with Mary, putting all the blame on Jo Ann.

"Why would she think it's okay to do that to me, to make those decisions for me?"

"I talked to her yesterday and convinced her to wait before making any decisions. You should see how you like living alone before she goes off and puts you in a home."

"I'm not that old, Kathleen."

"I know mother, I know. Just let her adjust to her new life. Forget it never happened and we'll wait. If the situation presents itself and it's something your interested in, we'll discuss it as a family before anything is decided."

"I guess you're right. I'll give your sister the benefit of the doubt."

"That'll be best for everyone."

Kathleen kissed her mother and went home to fix lunch for her kids.

Charlie was getting out of his truck as Oren walked toward Genie's house.

"What are you doing here?"

"Apologizing."

"Oren, this isn't a good time."

"Why not?"

Charlie took a deep breath.

"I got a call from work yesterday. They're building a new office building and they want me to be one of the leads on the project."

"That's good for you."

"In Pittsburgh."

"Wow, does Dad know?"

"I haven't told him yet. I hate to leave but the money they're offering…"

"I understand."

Oren finally put two and two together.

"Genie doesn't know."

"And I'm telling her now. That's why it's not a good time to apologize. I know you're an asshole so it didn't bother me."

"But the things I said about the two of you, that isn't one of the reasons you're leaving?"

"No, I knew she was older. We've always known that. We've always known it was a casual thing, but I let myself care too much."

"How do you think she feels?"

"I hope she doesn't care for me as much. It'll make it easier."

Genie came out of the front door.

"I thought I heard you pull up. Hello, Oren. Did you enjoy the wedding?"

"Genie, I am so sorry for what I said. It was crude and out of line."

"That's alright. I figure you'll get what's coming to you from Miranda. Anyway, I've said a few things that were…uh…alcohol induced."

"You?"

"I called my mother-in-law a whore once."

"Wow."

"Geoffrey didn't appreciate that, so I know Miranda will take care of you for me."

"Well, I'll see you. Charlie, call me later."

"Will do."

Oren trudged to the house, happy for his brother but sad at the same time. Charlie put his arm around Genie, dreading her reaction to the news.

Miranda picked up the phone and was surprised who was on the other end.

"Miranda, I heard about Oren and his brother. What did I miss?"

"Jo Ann, you're on your honeymoon."

"I know, but Peter and I were just talking. Tell me everything."

"I'll tell you when you get home."

"Tell me now if you need to talk."

"Oren and I have been trying for a baby for the past few months with no success."

"It takes time sometimes."

"Well, I looked into a fertility doctor."

"Without consulting him..."

"He found the brochure right before we left for the wedding. He started drinking at the reception, got drunk, and had it out with his brother."

"Over what?"

"Oren's brother Charlie has been seeing Genie..."

"Seeing?"

"Sleeping with. Anyway, Oren made some comments about their age difference and Charlie decked him."

"I can't believe that. Good for Genie, though, Oren's brother is hot."

Miranda sighed, happy to get it off her chest, but sorry for ruining Jo Ann's honeymoon.

"Honey, trying to start a family can be one of the most stressful times in a marriage. Don't rush it. Just have fun and it'll happen."

"Advice from someone who knows?"

"Well, we certainly are having fun. Whether or not it happens is another thing."

Miranda smiled as Oren walked through the door.

"I have to go. Call me when you get home."

Miranda hung up the phone.

"Who was that? Your secret admirer?"

"Don't laugh. He just talked me out of killing you. Actually, it was Jo Ann. She wanted the details about your little dance with danger yesterday."

"Oh."

"Is something else wrong? Did Genie slam the door in your face? She's good at that."

"Charlie may be moving to Pittsburgh."

"For what?"

"Work."

"How's Genie taking it?"

"He's telling her now."

"First Geoffrey, now Charlie. Poor Genie."

Later that morning at work, Park noticed Genie was dragging at work. He called her into his office.

"Park, I'm busy."

"Nova can handle your tables."

"We both know that she can't."

"This won't take long."

She sat down across for him.

"What's wrong?"

"Charlie is leaving town. He told me this morning before I left for work."

"Where's he going? When?"

"Pittsburgh, in two weeks."

"Wow. There goes great sex."

Genie smiled.

"Trust me, after seven years without sex, these last few months with Charlie have me taken care of for the next decade."

Parker smiled.

"It's not just that. I started to let myself care for him. He was there for me when Geoffrey died, he got along with Jeremy."

Genie was shocked to feel a tear roll down her cheek. She wiped her eyes and smiled again.

"It's very good for his career. I'll miss him."

Genie got up and finished drying her eyes.

"You can go home if you want."

"No, I'll be fine. Thank you though.

Grabbing her tray, she left the office.

That night, Genie went home and sank in a hot bath. Jeremy was thankfully asleep already, earlier than usual. Miranda and Oren slept side by side, but could feel the communication of their marriage breaking down, fueled by the pressure to have a baby. Doris, sipping her tea, made a final run through her house, checking all the locks. Cora and Gretchen lay in their husbands' arms, safe in the security of solid marriages. Hope lay awake, unable to sleep as her second trimester progressed. As she felt the baby kick for the first time, she grabbed her stomach and placed Allen's hand on her belly. She soon fell asleep, content as the growing child inside her. As the sun set on St. Bernard, the residents of Sherwood Circle lay peacefully in the contentment of their lives. Summer was ending and the impending months would bring the winds of change to the entire community. Months, years would pass and families would grow; some would be destroyed. None of them were quite prepared for what lie ahead.

Four Years Later…

Chapter 26

"Colleen Elizabeth Mayhelm."

Colleen beamed as she crossed the stage to accept her degree from the Dean of the University and the head of her department. She was graduating with honors with a degree in psychology and a minor in social work. She gazed through the crowd, looking for her family. They were all clapping. She was sure Chris and Chris were bored but they didn't look it as they clapped enthusiastically along with her parents. She smiled and waved to them and went back to her seat, standing until the rest of her department had crossed the stage. At twenty-two, she was the first Mayhelm to graduate college. After the ceremony, she joined her family outside the auditorium.

"Congratulations, darling."

"Thanks. When do we eat?"

"We can go now."

"I want to put this in my car. I'll meet you at the restaurant."

Colleen walked to her car. She stopped when she heard a familiar voice calling out to her. She turned and hugged the man tightly.

"Father David. I'm so glad you came."

"I said I would. Congratulations."

"Thank you."

He handed her a small box. Inside was a beautiful crucifix on a gold chain.

"I figured you might need this later."

"Isn't it a part of the uniform?"

David laughed.

"Listen, I have to be getting back to St. Matthew's. I just wanted to say hello."

"Come have dinner with us."

"No. I have meetings all day."

"Alright then."

From across the parking lot, Christopher saw his sister with a man he thought he recognized. He was shocked to see Father David accept a kiss from her. This was the same man his sister had been accused of having an affair with. What the hell was he doing here?

Later that night, Chris confronted his sister.

"Colleen, what was Father West doing here?"

"Supporting me."

"After all the mess we went through?"

"We? Christopher you were at camp when all of that went down. It had nothing to do with you."

"You know what I mean."

"Not that it's any of my business, but I have been seeing Father David for a while now. He's helped me come to a major decision in my life."

"Aren't you the grown up."

"What about you little brother? I hear you have a girlfriend now. Is this how it works? You find someone to play with your little wee wee and suddenly you're the big man, telling me how to run my life?"

"That's none of your business."

"Neither is this."

Colleen walked away without giving her brother a chance to respond.

"Oren, can I see you for a moment please?"

Oren went into Caryn's office nervously. He searched his mind for something he had done wrong, but couldn't think of anything.

"Close the door."

This had to be bad. He closed the door and sat across from her.

"I'm leaving the hotel. Next week, you'll start training as general manager."

She said it like she was giving him her grocery list. He couldn't believe his ears.

"Where are you going?"

"My father is opening another hotel in Denver. I'm going to run it."

"Wow."

Wow was right. In the past seven years, Caryn had come in as a shipping heiress taking over the hotel as a favor for her father. She learned fast and made herself a good general manager.

"Here's your new salary."

Caryn slid a piece of paper over to Oren. He opened it and couldn't believe his eyes.

"That's very generous."

"Tell my father. I told him you weren't worth it."

Oren looked at her. Unsure of what to say.

"I'm kidding, moron."

"What about Gage?"

"He'll be promoted to assistant general manger. We want to keep people on who are already familiar with the property."

"And when do I start."

"I leave next month. You will train with me until then, but you already know how to do everything. You and I know you carry me around here. "

"Just that one time after the Christmas party."

"Our secret."

"Faith Muriel! Get back in here now!"

Hope yelled at her daughter. Four year old Faith had her father's features, jet black hair and blue eyes. She was born on Valentines Day and was the apple of her family's eye. Her birth had brought together the estranged York children and their parents. Malcolm and Muriel adored her. The fact that she was the first granddaughter in the family did not hurt either. A fact Muriel never let Gretchen forget. She came running in the back door.

"What are you doing without a coat on?"

"Playing."

"It is freezing outside. Go get your coat on right now, young lady."

Faith ran to her room. Hope followed her, making sure she buttoned it right. As she walked down the hall, a sudden chill swept over her. She checked the windows in each room to be sure there were no windows open. She walked in the other direction and noticed the chill yet again. She checked the thermostat and found everything to be working fine. Faith stopped in front of her for a quick inspection and then ran out to the back door again. God, She was still freezing all of a sudden. When Allen came home, She would have him recheck everything again just to make sure.

Chapter 27

Oren and Miranda Grant had begun to lead separate lives. In the past two years especially, their inability to conceive a child had torn their marriage apart. They had not made love in months and they were each waiting for the other one to end things. Oren, with his new raise, would never ask for a divorce now. With all the money he would be making now, she would surely get most of it. No way. She would have to ask him for a divorce and she was not making a dime. He was upset that they had not had a child but even more upset that it had caused so much damage to their marriage. They had tried counseling and it did not offer the help they so needed and wanted. Oren and Miranda were more like roommates these days. Roommates that didn't get along. He walked into the house, surprised to find Miranda home.

"You're home early."

"I wasn't feeling well."

"Oh?"

"I wasn't going to cook anything for dinner."

"That's fine."

Oren went to the pantry to see what he could throw together.

Allen came home to find Hope bundled up in a huge sweater.

"You know, we can afford to turn on the heater."

"The heater is on. I have been freezing all day. I just can't seen to get warm."

Allen felt her forehead.

"You are not sick."

"I know. I have felt a draft in this house all day."

"Did you check all the windows?"

"Yes. Gretchen came over earlier. She couldn't feel anything either. I must be going crazy."

Allen laughed and went to go get out of his work clothes.

"You know what this family needs, mother?"

"What's that?"

"A girl."

Mary looked up from what she was doing. The subject of her moving into a home was never brought up again after Jo Ann's wedding. Jo Ann had no idea what her sister had said and just assumed she had fixed the situation. Mary always resented Jo Ann after finding out, albeit falsely, that she was the one who wanted to put her away.

"Are you pregnant?"

Immediately after the wedding, Jo Ann got pregnant and had Peter Henry Graham Jr. almost nine months later, to the day, after their wedding.

"Peter and I wanted more children. I don't think I could take the chance with another boy. It's me, Peter, Paul, and Chad as it is. Hell, even the dog is male."

"I hate male dogs. every time they roll over or sit on you, you have to deal with their nuts and stuff right in front of you."

"That's gross."

"I'll tell you what's gross. Have you ever seen the dog with a hard on? It is the most disgusting thing I have ever seen."

"Mother!"

Mary shrugged and kept with what she was doing.

"I really would like another baby, though."

"You will have to take your chances then."

"I guess so."

A few days later, Cora and Cameron were having coffee, enjoying an empty house.

"Have you talked to Colleen, as to what her plans are now that she is done with school?"

"Are you in a hurry to get her out?"

"No, I was wondering what she intended to do with her life."

As if on cue, Colleen came through the door.

"Speak of the devil."

"And the devil appears."

"Sit down. Your father and I were just having a little talk about you, dear."

Colleen fixed herself a cup of coffee and sat across from her mother.

"Discuss."

"We were just wondering what your plans were now that your finished school."

"You want me out the house already?"

"That is not what we are saying."

Colleen's heart began to beat fast. Ever since she had made the decision, she had dreaded telling her parents the news. She got up and began to pace.

"Actually, I have been meaning to talk to you guys about this. I have decided to join the Sisters of the Holy Family."

Cora was sure she heard that wrong.

"What?"

"I am joining a convent. I want to become a nun."

"A nun? Are you sure?"

"Yes. I have prayed about this a long time, and before Christopher comes in and spills my big secret, I have been talking to Father West about this as well."

"You have seen him?"

"I went and visited him at St. Matthew's a few times."

Cameron had not said a work.

"Daddy, say something."

"Colleen, it is such a major commitment."

"So is getting married. If I had come in with a guy I had been seeing and told you I was getting married, you would have been excited. We'll, I am marrying God. I can't think of a more stable relationship."

Cora spoke up.

"I hate to be the one to bring this up, but you will have to take a vow of celibacy. Are you ready to not have sex ever again? Ever? For the rest of your life?"

"I have already though about that."

"And you will never have a family of your own?"

Colleen looked at her mother sadly.

"I though I already had one."

"That's not what I meant. I mean, your own children, someone who will call you Mommy."

"Mom, I have taken this all into consideration. I know that this is what I want to do. Please be happy for me. Or at least, support me."

Cameron walked over to his daughter and kissed her head.

"When do you leave?"

"Next month. I will study for two years and then I will take my vows."

"Whatever you need, just let us know."

"Thanks Daddy."

Colleen went off to her room. Cameron went to the cabinet and took out a bottle of bourbon. He started pouring it into a glass as Cora watched, laughing.

"To think I thought she was going to say she was a lesbian."

"I thought she was joining the army."

"I guess there are worse things."

He poured another glass and passed it down to Cora.

The next morning, Jeremy dropped Cora off at work so he could use the car. She walked into the Breakers and started getting her stuff together. She went to her first table and almost died when she saw who was sitting alone.

"Hey, Genie."

"Charlie."

Without thinking, she leaned over and kissed his cheek.

"What are you doing in town?"

"Visiting my Dad,"

Genie nodded.

"Are you still in Pittsburgh?"

"Yes. I just finished building a hotel over there."

"I am impressed."

"How is everyone?"

"Jeremy would love to see you, although you would not recognize him. He graduated last spring and is going to the community college here in town."

"Patrick?"

"He and Melissa had a boy. Geoffrey Patrick Van Matthews. He is a little terror. But he adores his Uncle Jeremy."

Genie was almost asking Charles if he wanted to get together when she moved out of the way for a lady and a small child. The lady stood facing Genie.

"You are blocking our seats."

"I am sorry."

This was the moment Charlie dreaded. Introducing the wife to the former lover. He had hoped Genie had not been working this morning for just this reason. The woman and small girl slipped into the booth across from Charlie.

"Did you order our drinks yet?"

"No, not yet. I wanted to introduce you to someone. Tina this is a good friend of mine, Genie Van Matthews. Genie, this is my wife, Tina, and daughter, Gabrielle."

Genie smiled despite herself and shook hands with Tina.

"Nice to meet you."

Before Charlie continued with the niceties, Genie went back to work.

"What did you want to drink?"

"Diet coke and small fruit punch."

Genie nodded and went to get their drinks. Tina looked at Charlie slyly.

"That's the one, isn't it?"Charlie nodded.

"I could tell."

Colleen came into the kitchen to find her mother making breakfast.

"Good morning. Do you want eggs?"

"Yes"

"Do you want coffee or juice?"

"Juice would be fine."

"Do you still want to be a nun?"

Colleen smiled at her mother.

"Yes."

"Who wants to be a nun?"

Christian ran into the kitchen having heard the last part of their conversation. Shit. Colleen was not ready for her brothers or sister to find out yet.

"I am becoming a nun."

"Is sex that bad."

Unlike his twin brother, Christian was still a virgin.

"No, you jerk."

"If you would ever pay attention in Church, The Catholic Church is short on women who want to answer the call. They need priest too."

She winked at her mother.

"Forget it. I am not ready to give up something I have never had yet."

"You do not have to decide now. I was not a virgin.

Cora groaned.

"Are two of my children talking about sex because I am definitely not ready for that."

"Who is talking about sex?"

As if on cue, Candice came in the room.

"Nobody."

"That's fine. I'll learn about it on television like everyone else."

"Learn what on television?"

Christopher came into the kitchen.

"Sex."

"Mom, is this appropriate breakfast talk?"

"Ask your brother and your sister, they started it."

Chris looked at Christian, eager to have the subject changed and fast, so he spilled the news out about Colleen.

"Colleen is going to be a nun."

"No way, a nun? Like with the black veil and the ruler and the sensible shoes?"

"It is called a habit. But, yes. One of those."

"So, you're my sister, and I get to call you sister, too?"

"You call me Colleen like you always have. I will be taking a new name though."

"What?"

"I don't know. Sister Mary something or another, I'm sure. I get it when I take my final vow."

Cameron came into the kitchen last, happy to see the whole family around for breakfast at the table.

"What's this about?"

"Colleen was just telling everyone her good news."

Cameron smiled at his daughter. Candice spoke up.

"Colleen, if my sister is a nun, does that mean I definitely get to go to heaven?"

Colleen smiled and ruffled her little sister's hair.

Genie was in the back refilling drinks when Charlie snuck up from behind.

"Genie, I didn't think you worked Friday mornings."

"That was four years ago."

"I guess things change."

"I'll say they do."

"This is awkward, isn't it."

"You know, why should it be? We have always been friends, among other things."

"Yes."

"And I really am happy for you, Charlie. You seem to have a nice family and your career seems to be going well."

"It is."

"Then enjoy it. You deserve everything that comes your way."

She kissed him on the cheek.

"Get back to your family."

That afternoon when Jeremy went to pick her up, Genie was uncharacteristically silent.

"What's wrong, Mom?"

"I feel old. My son's in college, my other son is making me a grandmother, and my boy toy is married with a child."

Jeremy knew exactly who she was talking about.

"You saw Charlie?"

"He came in for breakfast today, with his wife and daughter."

"Don't let it get to you. I know what would cheer you up, Imperial Gardens."

"Really honey. Just bring me home. I want to take a bath and go to bed early."

"Are you sure?"

"Yes."

Jeremy drove home is a very uncomfortable silence.

That evening, Gretchen walked across the street and knocked on Cora's door. Cora opened the door and smiled as her friend walked in.

"Cora, It has been too long since we have had coffee. I brought cake."

Gretchen went to the kitchen and put the cake saver on the table.

"Is it s a bad time?"

"No. Actually, I have some really big news to share with you."

Cora got plates out and started the coffee. Gretchen plated up two pieces of cake and, a few minutes later, after the coffee was done, the two ladies were sitting and gossiping.

"So, what's your big news?"

"Colleen is joining a convent. She wants to be a nun."

"You are kidding?"

"No. She is joining the Sisters of the Holy Family next month."

"How long does it take?"

"Two years and then she takes her final vows."

"Wow. And this just came out of the blue?"

"Shocked the hell out of Cameron and me. The kids think it is hilarious, but not in a mean way. They think it's cool, like now they have a guaranteed place in heaven or something."

Gretchen laughed. Cameron walked into the kitchen.

"What is so funny?"

"Cora was just telling me about Colleen."

Gretchen got up and got a plate and some coffee for Cameron. She and Cora had been friends for so long, she knew this kitchen like she knew her own. She set the cake in front of Cameron. He happily began eating.

"Gretchen, you make the best pineapple upside down cake I have ever had."

"Actually, Ben made it for his cooking merit badge."

"Well, tell him he can cook for us anytime."

"He will be glad to hear it."

After a few more minutes of talking Gretchen got up.

"Well, I just wanted to see how everyone was doing. We really don't get to talk outside of church anymore."

"We will have to fix that."

Gretchen kissed both of them and said her goodbye's. She walked back across the street. On her way home, Gretchen noticed Oren getting ready for bed, shirt off. She could not help but to stare. She was surprised he had such a nice body. She remembered him being a little pudgy when he and Miranda had moved in. Miranda walked into the bathroom and the two of them started fighting. Embarrassed to be watching something she shouldn't, Gretchen ran across the yard to her house.

Chapter 28

Three weeks later, everyone had heard Colleen's news and had gathered for a going away party for her at the Mayhelm's. About halfway through the party, Colleen was shocked out of her mind when Scott Winslow came through the door. She immediately went over to her mother.

"Did you invite him?"

"No. I figured you did."

"Why would I do something like that? He stopped talking to me altogether after the whole Father David mess. I'm getting rid of him."

Colleen left her mother and walked right up to her ex-boyfriend.

"Scott, what are you doing here?"

"Hello to you, too."

"Don't give me that. You have not spoken three words to me in four years. I loved you, but you chose to believe all that crap about Father David."

"Is that why you're doing this? To repent?"

"Go to hell"

"Is that any way for a nun to talk?"

Colleen stared at him, stunned.

"What happened to you? You were so nice. You had a body and looks to die for, but you were a nice guy. Is that what playing basketball in college taught you? How to be a prick?"

"No"

"Go home, Scott"

Without waiting for a response, Colleen spun around and rejoined her party. Defeated, Scott went out the front door with his tail between his legs. Grace Moore walked up to Colleen.

"Was that Scott I just saw?"

"Yes. I told him to beat it."

"Good for you."

"A nun? I would never have guessed it."

"Tell me about it."

Genie was standing in the corner talking to Mary and Jo Ann.

"I guess it makes sense. You know they have always been so church going."

"Whatever makes her happy. It has to beat waiting on tables."

Jo Ann clicked glasses with her friends.

"So, Jo Ann, any more children on the horizon?"

"We are in negotiations. I would like a girl."

"Forget it. Boys are much easier to raise. If I had had to raise a girl by myself, I would have killed her."

"Well, Paul graduates this year and Chad starts high school. Maybe it is too late for a little one."

"What about Pete? Don't tell me he's moved out and gotten a job?"

"No, but he does start kindergarten this year."

"Wow."

Jo Ann noticed Miranda come in, alone.

"Excuse me, ladies."

Jo Ann walked over to Miranda.

"Where's Oren?"

"He had to work late tonight."

Something in her friend's tone told Jo Ann she had been away from the cul-de-sac too long.

"Is everything alright?"

Miranda sighed.

"It has been better."

"I am sorry."

We have just seemed to grow apart, that's all."

"Oh Miranda, have ya"ll tried to talk to someone?"

"Yes. It worked for a while."

"What are you going to do?"

Miranda shook her head, tears forming in her eyes. Jo Ann hugged her close. Miranda could not believe that the people on Sherwood Circle could ever think of Jo Ann as white trash.

Hope and Allen were walking home from the party. Hope opened the door, and gasped. Her house stunk.

"My god, this house stinks."

"I don't smell anything."

"Allen, it smells like something died in here."

"I'm going next door to go get Faith."

He left her alone in the house and Hope went to investigate. She got on her hands and knees and searched the bottom of the pantry, thinking there maybe a dead mouse or something. She looked behind the refrigerator and stove with a flashlight and still found nothing. Allen came back with Faith and found Hope opening the windows.

"Hope, it's February! Why are you opening all the windows in the house?"

"I am trying to air the place out. I can not believe you can't smell it."

"No, I'm going to put her to bed."

"I'll be there in a minute. I just want to get some extra blankets."

The smell was almost gagging. Hope hoped that, with all the windows open, the smell would clear up in the morning. She wondered what was wrong with Allen. He had to be crazy not to smell it.

The next morning, the smell had subsided. Allen left for work and Hope was alone with the baby. She picked up the phone and dialed her sister-in-law next door.

"Gretchen, come over for some coffee."

"Be right there."

Within a minute, Gretchen was at the door.

"Hope, it's freezing in here."

"Do you smell anything funny?"

"No."

"Are you sure?"

"Yes. What's up? Did you burn the coffee or something?"

"Last night when we came home from Colleen's party, this house stunk so bad. I thought something had died in here."

"Maybe it was a mouse or something."

"We don't have mice."

"I didn't mean to offend you."

"Anyway, I already checked everything."

Gretchen sat down and stirred her coffee.

"Well I can't smell anything."

"Allen couldn't either. I opened the windows to air the house out."

Gretchen nodded.

"Gretchen, you're still in your robe."

"I know. I thought once Tim started school, I would be motivated to go back to work or something, but it has not happened."

"I get bored being a housewife. I can't wait for Faith to start school."

"No more children?"

"Maybe, we are still not sure yet."

"Well, Ben and I always joked that you can't call yourself a parent until you have at least two. Once you have enough that they start blaming one another for stuff, then the fun really begins."

Hope got up and poured a second cup.

"Can you believe Colleen?"

"I know. She has always been a good girl. I think she will make a great nun."

"When does she leave?"

"This afternoon."

That afternoon Colleen and her family were gathered at the train station. The two hour train trip would take Colleen to the convent of the Sisters of Holy Family. She would be there for two full years before taking her final vows and then coming home. She had leave for Christmas but would have to study straight through the summers. She hugged her family and said goodbyes to all before tearfully facing her parents.

"Well, this is it."

"Are you sure?"

"Dad, I have never been more sure."

"Send us your address and phone number when you get there."

"I will."

"Yeah, just because you are giving up pleasures of the flesh, does not mean you have to give them all up. I can still send cookies."

"Thanks, Mom."

"Can I talk to you for a minute, woman to woman."

"Sounds ominous."

"Just follow me."

Cora wheeled herself away from the family, Colleen right besides her.

"Colleen, I need to know that you are not doing this because you feel guilty."

They both know what she was talking about.

"You know, there was talk around the parish that you responsible for my accident. I want you to know, I have never felt that and I need to know you do not feel that way either."

"For a while, yes I did. But that is not what is drawing me to this life. I kept praying to God about my future and time and time again, this is how I saw myself. I want to do this Mom."

Cora reached up and hugged her daughter tight, tears running down both their faces now. The boarding announcement came on and Colleen pulled away slowly.

"I've got to go."

"Okay."

They rejoined their family with Colleen giving her last goodbyes before climbing aboard and taking her seat. As the train pulled away, she waved from her seat. Sad to leave her family and life she was used to, but excited about what lay ahead for her.

Hope was putting the finishing touches on her meatloaf when she heard the baby crying. She stopped what she was doing and tip toed to Faith's room. She cracked open the door and the crying stopped. Faith was napping peacefully. She closed the door and began walking away when she heard the crying again. She went and took another peek and, satisfied that her daughter was sleeping, went back toward the kitchen. She shook her head, sure she must have been imagining things, and went to finish dinner.

Chapter 29

The next few months passed quickly as summer came again to St. Bernard. Hope never did hear the baby cry again. Charlie and his family went back to Pittsburgh, never to see Genie again. Oren was busy adjusting to his new job. He was secretly stashing away money, money he would need to start over if Miranda ever asked for a divorce, which she still had yet to do. Doris was taking this opportunity to enjoy her garden when her phone rang.

"Hello."

"Mrs. Shepherd, it's Kevin Ryan. Do you remember me?"

"Of course Kevin."

Kevin Ryan was her husband's illegitimate son.

"I have some business in St. Bernard and was wondering if I could come see you."

"Sure. When?"

"Any particular reason for the visit? It's been four years."

"I have not had a reason to come down there. I was just hoping to get to know you better"

"Just call me when you are on your way."

"Thank you."

Doris hung up the phone, wondering why in the world would Kevin want to see her again. She shrugged her shoulders and went back to her gardening, protected by her back yard fence.

For four years, the Mayhelm boys had been cutting the grass for Miranda and Oren Grant. Miranda still remembered the small thirteen year old knocking on her door the day after she and her husband moved in. She could hardly believe time had passed so quickly, watching the two eighteen year old young men cutting her gross right now. Perfect bodies, sweat glistening in the sun. Miranda was in awe of the two hotties Christopher and Christian had become. Her pulse quickened as she watched them, Christopher taking off his shirt as his brother playfully wet him with the hose. She watched them from her bedroom window, partially hidden by the tree in the front yard. She moistened as she fantasized about the two of them. Christopher, sure of himself, strong, powerful able to satisfy her with his youthful agility. Christian, more innocent then his brother, just as hot, but inexperienced, open to everything she could teach him. Her nipples got hard and pressed up against her tee shirt. She heard Oren come down the hall and tore herself away from the fantasy and window. He walked into the room and he was hot. She went up to him and kissed him wildly. Surprised, he pulled away from her.

"What's this all about?"

"I've missed you."

She pulled off her shirt to reveal her firm breasts. Oren was hard himself within seconds. He was not sure what had gotten into her. He was sure she did not want him, but what the hell. He was not about to complain about getting laid. Even though it might confuse the situation. After all, they were still married.

"Make love to me Oren. Make love to me now!"

Oren undressed and climbed on top of his wife. Rolling around on the bed, Miranda fantasized about the two Chrises as she and her husband made love like two dogs in heat. It was not making love, it was full blown sweaty sex! When it was over Miranda lay in her husbands arms, wondering where it had all gone wrong.

Miranda was not the only one watching her hot young neighbors. From three houses down, Jeremy Van Matthews watched through parted drapes. After an embarrassing incident in the locker room his senior year which led him to quit the baseball team, he had admitted to himself who he really was. Nobody knew he was gay. Not his brother, not his mother, nobody. He was very careful about how he acted around people, making comments about girls when the right people were around. Strangely this summer, he found himself lusting after one of his best friends. Genie came in the kitchen.

"Jeremy, lunch is ready."

"I'll be right there."

Jeremy came away from the window and realized he had to adjust his shorts. He went into the kitchen and ate lunch.

Four days later, Doris had lunch set out for Kevin Ryan. He was on his way from the hotel. She still wondered why he felt the need to call her. Had he not destroyed her life enough four years ago when he dropped the bomb about her marriage? She heard his car pull up and went to meet him at the door.

"Mr. Ryan, please do come in."

"Thank you, Mrs. Shepherd."

"Call me Doris."

"Thank you, Doris."

He went past the living room and into the dining room. She indicated a chair and poured him some ice tea. She sat across from him and started to serve him.

"I have to admit Kevin, I'm a little confused about why you would come all the way out here to see me. I have nothing you could want. We're not related. If you are here looking for information about your father, I am afraid I'm not willing to give you information."

"That is kind of hateful, isn't it, Doris? You have every right to be angry at your husband or my mother, but why me?"

"Because seeing you reminds me of the fact that my husband, who I was faithful to for forty years, cheated on me with someone else, had a child with someone else."

"And seeing you reminds me of the fact that my father treated my mother like a cheap whore. He did not even bother to see if she was pregnant or not. He did not even bother to stay around to help her out."

Doris was stunned silent. She could not believe Kevin would talk to her like this. She knew he was right. He got real silent and hung his head. He sighed and looked up to her. She now knew he was hiding something.

"The thing is, Doris, my daughter is dying."

"You have a daughter?"

Kevin took out his wallet and flipped to a picture of his family. He had never mentioned them before.

"This is your wife?"

"Lisa. Chrissy is seven."

"She's sick?"

Kevin nodded.

"It's one of two diseases, each of which attack her immune system and travel through her body. It's genetic. We have yet to find a reason for it. The missing link is you husband, her grandfather. Can I ask how he died?"

Doris felt horrible. This young man was trying to save his daughter and she was going to give him a hard time. No way.

"Lung cancer. Herb was a two pack a day smoker."

"Oh."

"There was not any indication of any other illness or disease. He had tumors on his lungs, he smoked heavily, then he must have had lung cancer."

"Is there any way I could talk to his doctor?"

"Dr. Mixter? He has been dead for years."

Doris could see Kevin's heart breaking.

"You know, there was a nurse there that might still be around."

Doris got up and went to her phone book.

"Back then, she was the hot young nurse. Now she is probably the middle aged nurse that runs the whole office herself. Every doctor's office has one. I just hope the number's the same."

Doris dialed the number and waited.

"They may need to talk to you. They will need to know specifies about her condition and the doctor that takes care of her."

The nurse finally picked up.

"Yes ma'am, is Helen Sinclair still working in this office."

"Yes she does."

"May I please speak to her? This is an old friend of hers."

After a moment, Helen picked up the phone.

"Helen, this is Doris Shephard, Herbert Shephard was a patient of Dr. Mixter's about fifteen years ago."

"Believe it or not, I do remember you and your husband."

"How have you been?"

"Still here."

"I see that. Listen Helen, is there any way of getting access to Herb's files?"

"They should be on the computer."

"You have them computerized now?"

"Yes we are. Now, when did he die?"

"August of 1992."

Helen typed away.

"I have his records right here. What do you need?"

"Let me let you talk to my friend. His daughter is Herb's granddaughter…"

"Herb's granddaughter?"

"It is a long story. Anyway, she is having some serious medical issues and her doctor is looking for some sort of genetic link."

"Let me talk to him."

Doris handed the phone to Kevin and while they talked Doris went to the bathroom. She came out a few minutes later, Kevin had tears in his eyes.

"They are faxing his records to her doctor in Boston. Thank you, Doris."

She went over to him and hugged him tight, letting him cry in her arms.

"I hope they can find something Kevin. I hope it will help."

Kevin pulled away and dried his eyes.

"It helps more then you know."

"I want you to have something."

She handed him a framed picture of Herb in his US West uniform. He smiled when he saw it.

"The pride of US West, huh?"

"He looked so good in his uniform. I guess that may have been part of his problem."

Doris laughed and Kevin smiled again.

"I think every little girl needs something from her grandpa."

Doris and Kevin spent the next two hours sharing stories and laughing. It was the best she felt in years.

Chapter 30

"Jeremy, Jeremy!"

Jeremy sat in the food court of the mall, oblivious to the world around him. He finally snapped to it when he realized someone was calling him.

"I thought that was you. What are you doing here?"

"I took Geoffrey out for the day. Patrick is in court all day and Melissa is out of town."

Jeremy nodded to his nephew who was busy playing in the ball pit. He looked at Chris's bags.

"What about you."

"Shopping at Barrister's."

"Have you had lunch yet?"

"No."

"I was going to take him to Carlysle's. Do you want to come with us?"

"Sure."

"Geoff, Let's go."

The little boy, the spitting image of Melissa, came running over.

"Geoff, this is my friend, Mr. Chris."

The little boy smiled then hid behind his uncle. Chris looked at Jeremy.

"Mister?"

"Doris, I have to get going. My flight to Boston leaves in two hours."

Doris got up and walked Kevin to the door.

"Kevin, please call me with any news. Any time. I want to know she is alright."

"I will."

Kevin hugged her one last time and headed for the rental car. As he drove off, Genie was walking to her front door. She noticed Doris standing in front of her front door, not daring to step out of the safety of her home.

"Doris, are you hiding men in your house? No wonder you never leave."

Doris smiled and waved before closing her front door.

"Have you heard from Colleen?"

"No, not yet."

The guys were waiting for their food to arrive. Jeremy could not help but to stare at Chris.

"Have you declared a major yet?"

"In school?"

"No, you moron, in life. Yes in school."

"I don't know."

"You could major in sex. Most freshman do."

"Yeah, since I do so well in it now."

"Don't you?"

Chris rolled his eyes.

"I am not my brother. Jeremy, I have never had, well umm…well…you know."

Chris looked away embarrassed.

"You're still a virgin?"

"You're not?"

"I've gotten close."

"Close?"

"Once or twice."

"But you were dating…"

Jeremy shook his head.

"The rumors about her were just that, rumors."

The truth was, Jeremy's senior year girlfriend was more willing to go all the way. He was the one that resisted and he was the one to call thinks off, with just cause. Chris looked over at Geoff.

"Should we be having this conversation in present company?"

"He is not paying attention. Just tell him we are talking about Barney and he is cool."

Chris laughed. Jeremy had to turn away or chance being caught staring at Chris.

Two weeks later, Hope was soaking in the tub. Enjoying the day off. Gretchen had taken the kids to the park and Allen was still at work. She closed her eyes and smiled. She and Allen had been secretly trying for another baby and she was sure she was pregnant again. She was started by the sound of the baby crying again. She had not heard the crying in months and now it was back. She sat up and listened. It stopped and she tried to relax but could not. The crying started again and she got up out of the tub. Wrapped herself in the towel and went to investigate. The sound was coming from Faith's room, just as it had the previous time. She opened the door and found the room empty. She looked around, waiting for the crying to start again, but heard nothing. She did not realize Allen had come home early and was sneaking up behind her. He grabbed her from behind and she screamed.

"Shit! Allen, damn you!"

"That was not the reaction I was hoping for."

She threw her arms around him, shaking.

"What's wrong?"

"Nothing, I think I am going crazy. That's all."

That afternoon, Jeremy picked up the phone and was thrilled to hear Christian on the other end.

"Jeremy, what are you doing today?"

"Hanging out. Why."

"Come swimming. I am home alone and bored."

"Where is everyone?"

"Chris is working at Dad's garage and my parents took Candice to camp."

"No more camp for you?"

"Too old."

"I'll be right over."

"I'll order pizza."

Jeremy hung up the phone elated. He slipped into his bathing suit and walked down the street. All alone with Christian, swimming shirtless. The thought almost made a mess in his shorts. He smiled as he knocked on the door.

"Come on in."

Jeremy opened the door as Chris was coming out of the laundry room.

"So, Chris, your brother is working in the garage?"

"Yes, and, believe it or not, he likes it. As for me, I need a profession where I don't get dirty every day."

"He will probably make a fortune though. I had to get my brakes redone last month and it cost me a bundle."

"My dad probably only charged you for the parts. Can you imagine if he had added labor?"

"No shit."

The pizza came and the guys took it out to the pool. Chris took off his shirt and went to lay down in the sun. Behind dark glasses, Jeremy took every inch of his body. He was gorgeous. Jeremy got up and dove in the pool. A few minutes later, Chris dove in and the two started wrestling and dunking one another.

A while later the two guys were on the deck drying off. All afternoon, Jeremy kept sensing feelings from Chris. He hoped he was not just imagining things as what he was about to do could change their friendship forever. Looking into his eyes, Jeremy took Chris by the shoulders and kissed him on the mouth. Running his hands along his back, he pressed up against him. Feeling himself stiffen as their most intimate of body parts came into direct contract with each other. Confused and freaked out, Chris pushed him away.

"No!"

He had no idea about his friend, or the fact that he thought he was gay too.

"Jeremy, no. I am not…"

Panicked, Chris ran off the deck and back into his house, shutting himself in his room. Jeremy fought the urge to go after him and went home upset. He needed to talk to him but now was not the time. Christian, almost having to prove himself that he was not gay, took out a porno from under his bed and flipped through it. Letting nature take over, he let his hands go where they may and a few minutes later, he was done, sweating and out of breath. Ashamed and mad at himself, he threw the magazine across the room and collapsed onto his bed.

That night, Hope was preparing dinner when Gretchen dropped off Faith.

"How's everything going?"

Hope shook her head.

"How was she?"

"She was good, as always."

Gretchen could tell something was wrong with her sister-in-law.

"Hope, what's wrong?"

"Nothing."

"Hope, you can tell me."

Hope looked up and turned to Gretchen, hoping she could trust her.

"Gretchen, some weird things have been happening around here."

"Where?"

"In this house."

The words turned Gretchen white as a ghost.

"Like what?"

"Remember the other day when you came over for coffee and I asked you if you could smell something weird?"

"Yes."

"The whole house smelled like death. Except I was the only one to smell it. And I have been hearing a baby cry. It always happens when I am in the bathroom. I heard it once a few months ago and it started again a few days ago. I heard it again today"

Gretchen nodded.

"I think I am going crazy."

"I'm sure it's nothing."

"No, do not do that. Allen did that. He dismissed my feelings and I know something is going on here."

"I don't know what to tell you, darling. Did you want to talk to someone, professionally?"

"I do not think I have gotten to the therapy stage of this yet. If this does keep up, I don't know."

Allen came in before the ladies could finish their conversation.

"Gretchen, do you and Ben want to come over for dinner?"

"No, mine is almost ready. Thanks, though. Hope, call me later okay?"

"Sure."

Gretchen left. Allen turned to his wife.

"What was all that about?"

"Nothing, just girl talk."

Chapter 31

Jeremy knocked on Mayhelm's door. He heard someone call from inside and walked through the front door. He had decided against calling and wanted to talk to Christian face to face. He went into the kitchen and started to talk to Chris.

"Listen I really want to talk to you about what happened today."

No response.

"Look, could you at least put down the paper and look at me when I am spilling my guts?"

"Jeremy!"

Christian came running in from the bathroom. Christopher put down the magazine.

"What? What's up?"

"Nothing. Jeremy, I have those movies you wanted. They are in my room."

Jeremy followed Christian into the bedroom and began to panic.

"I almost apologized to you brother for the whole kissing thing."

"Keep your voice down!"

Christian shut the door.

"Chris, I need to talk to you about what happened today."

"No, I don't want to talk about it ever again."

"Chris I am sorry. I just thought, I mean…"

"You thought I was gay?"

"You know being gay is not the worst thing in the world. Shit, it does not make me the Antichrist!"

Chris realized he had hurt Jeremy's feelings. He had no idea about Jeremy being gay but he was still his friend and he had to know that.

"I didn't mean that, Jeremy, I had no idea about you. When did you find out? How old were you?"

"I admitted it to myself last year."

"So the whole thing with Donna?"

"A farce. We went out, but we were never going to go all the way."

"Did she know?"

"Nobody knows but you now."

"I don't want that responsibility."

"Well, you got it today when I stuck my tongue down your throat."

Jeremy sat down on his bed.

"Is this going to make things awkward between us?"

"Awkward? Jeremy, you kissed me! Are you attracted to me? If you are, yeah, things will be awkward for a while."

"I can get over you. I don't want to screw up our friendship."

"Don't worry about that. I can keep my mouth shut."

"I'm glad to hear that."

Jeremy got up and went to the door.

"Listen, I have got to go. My mom will be home soon."

"Are you sure everything is okay with us?"

"Yeah."

Jeremy went home and Christian went to the kitchen. Christopher looked over his paper.

"What was that all about?"

"Nothing. Jeremy is just having some issues."

"Is it the whole gay thing?"

Christian turned to his brother, stunned.

"Is it?"

"How did you know?"

"I could tell. Anyway, there were rumors going around school about it. You were just too nice a person to pay attention to them."

"Look, you can not tell him you know."

"Who cares? He is still my friend."

"I'm surprised at you attitude. You are not exactly the more open minded of the two of us."

"It is not like he wants me."

Christopher started to put things together.

"Unless, what did he want to talk to you about? What did he have to explain? Did something happen between the two of you?"

Christian turned away.

"Oh my god!"

"Chris, the only reason I am telling you this is because you are my twin. Despite the fact that we have nothing in common, there is nobody in the world I feel closer to. I know I can tell you anything."

"Oh my god!"

"Would you stop saying that? Yes, Jeremy got mixed up. He had feelings for me and he thought I was gay too. So yes, he did kiss me."

Christopher sat there, stunned into silence.

"What did you do?"

"I pushed him off and told him I was not into that. I freaked out and ran into the house.

I told him the same thing you just said. We have been friends all our lives. I am not going to judge him."

"So you two are cool now?"

"Yes."

"Well, that will teach me to go into work early."

Christian smiled and resumed his hunt for dinner.

Gretchen climbed into bed with Ben and woke him up.

"Gret, not tonight. I am not feeling good. That is why I went to bed early."

"Wake up sport, we need to talk."

"I hate sentences that start like that."

"Relax, it's not about that. It's about your sister."

Ben shook himself awake and sat up, relieved that the headache he has earlier had subsided.

"What about her?"

"Something strange is going on in her house."

"What?"

"She's hearing things and sensing things."

"And?"

"Coincidence? After what happened in that house, knowing the history the house has, how can you just shrug it off? Ben, we should have told her before she moved in."

"No way."

"What if she finds out we knew all along and never told her? She'll hate us. What if the same thing happens again? You know the story."

"You're not going to tell her anything. Understand? Nothing!"

"But..."

"Case closed, Gretchen. Go to sleep."

Ben turned over and went back to sleep. Gretchen pulled up the covers around her neck and closed her eyes, praying for sleep to come quickly, praying for the young family next door.

The next morning, Miranda splashed water on her face. She had just thrown up everything she had eaten in the last twelve hours. She wiped her mouth off and sat on the edge of the bathtub. She couldn't be. There was no way. She went to the phone and dialed the restaurant.

"Mariner's."

"This is Miranda. Please tell Mr. Moore that I'm not coming in today. I've got the fish out for today's special thawed out in freezer number two. Zack knows what to do with it."

"I'll let him know. Hope you feel better, Miranda."

"No kidding."

She hung up the phone feeling guilty. She had no reason to be; she hadn't called in sick once the whole time she had worked there. Mentally calculating the last month, she got in the car and drove to the store. When she got home, she saw Oren was still in bed. She snuck into the bathroom and locked the door. Three minutes later, she held the positive pregnancy test in her hand. How could this have happened? They had been trying like crazy for two years, tearing apart their marriage in the process. They hadn't made love in months, save for the day she attacked Oren after watching the Mayhelm boys cut her grass. She had to be sure. She went back to the phone and made an appointment with her doctor for that day.

She sat in the doctor's office after peeing in a cup. Dr. Hunter sent the urine to the in office lab and returned a few minutes later.

"Miranda, the results are positive. You are pregnant."

She hung her head low, fighting back tears.

"Is this unplanned? Unexpected?"

"Dr. Hunter, you know I've been trying to get pregnant for years. We stopped trying a year ago. Oren and I stopped having sex altogether a few months after that. Now, we hardly talk. This baby wasn't exactly conceived in love. I doubt it will be the joyous occasion it should be."

"Then make it be. Let the baby bring the two of you back together. You're in a very delicate state right now. You weren't able to get pregnant before, but now, through some miracle of nature or science, you are. I want to be sure you can carry the baby to term. You're going to need all the help and support you can get."

Miranda hadn't even thought of that. What if, after all this time, she couldn't carry the baby to term? The thought devastated her. Dr. Hunter was right though, she would need Oren now more than ever. She gathered her things and headed to the door.

"When do I need to come back?"

"Make an appointment for next month. Call the office if you need anything."

"Thank you doctor."

Miranda walked to her car, wondering what to do. She wanted to be happy, elated, but wasn't sure how Oren would react. She wanted to wait until she was a few months along, but wasn't sure she could wait that long. On the way home, she decided to do something she hadn't done in years.

"Parker, I am not buying a lotto ticket."

"Come on, Genie, Nova is going to buy the tickets and the jackpot is over two hundred million dollars."

"What a waste of money."

"A dollar? I know for a fact you got more than that from your last table."

"I'd better have or I won't be paying my bills!"

"Come on."

Genie rolled her eyes and pulled five dollars out of her pocket.

"When we win, we can all quit."

He handed the money to Nova and Genie laughed as she left.

"She's probably taking the money and hitting the road."

"She won't get far."

Genie rolled her eyes again and went to clean her tables.

Miranda walked quietly into Mary, Mother of God and went to the back where the candles were. She put five dollars in the slot and lit a candle, kneeling down in front of it. She hadn't been to church in years because of her work schedule. She always had to work on Saturday evenings and Sunday mornings. It was her busiest time of the week and she hoped God understood. She needed his help now. She crossed herself and began to pray. She prayed for the strength to rebuild her marriage and keep her baby safe and strong. She still loved Oren and resolved herself to putting things back together. She only hoped he felt the same way. Feeling better than she had in months, she drove home smiling.

Chapter 32

Hope was home alone when she really started to fall apart. She was standing in the kitchen when she felt a presence behind her. She turned around and screamed when she saw all four dining room chairs stacked on top of the dining room table. They looked like some sort of Chinese acrobat team. She walked slowly around the table, unsure of how they got that way. She turned toward the counter and saw the woman, dripping blood from her wrists. The blood dropped and pooled on the linoleum floors. Hope shook her head and covered her eyes. When she opened her eyes, the woman was gone, but the blood was still on the floor.

"Fuck no."

Hope grabbed her purse and ran out the house. She sped to the library. She needed answers and she needed them now. Something was going on in her house, something that was set to either scare her or drive her out of her mind.

She ran to the computers in the back and logged on. She went to the St. Bernard Daily and went back ten years, using her address as the search point. A front page headline dated July 15, 1994 told the story. Hope shrieked when she read it. Zooming in on the picture that accompanied the story, she felt herself go pale. She printed the story and drove to Allen's office, scared to death. She stormed into his office and threw the article on his desk.

"Read this."

"Hope, I was in the middle of a call."

"Someone died in our house, Allen."

"Hope, I'm sure you're overreacting."

"Someone murdered her children and then killed herself in our house Allen!"

Allen picked up the article and began reading.

"They contributed it to post partum depression. Are you reading? The boy that lived there before that got put in a mental institution after they found him torturing pets in our backyard, the same yard our daughter plays in!"

The picture in the paper showed the paramedics taking out the body of the woman Hope had seen in the kitchen earlier that afternoon.

"She drowned her daughter and smothered her baby. Did you read how old her daughter was Allen?"

"Four."

Allen couldn't believe what he was hearing. Something sinister was in their house and now it was trying to get to his wife, the way it got to the other woman and the little boy.

"Did you look closely at the picture?"

Allen looked closer and, in the background, saw his sister-in-law and brother-in-law being questioned by the police.

"They knew, Allen. My brother knew what happened in the house and he never told us. They all knew."

Allen got up and went around to try to calm his wife. She shook away from him.

"We've got to get out of there."

She ran away from him before he had the chance to stop her. He ran to the garage, not wanting to get too far behind her. He got to his car and shook his head when he saw four flat tires.

"Fuck no."

He ran back into his office to find his boss.

Doris picked up the phone on the third ring. It was Kevin Ryan.

"Doris, it's Kevin."

"Kevin, how is she?"

Doris had been waiting for weeks, hoping that the information she had given him about Herb's health history could help save his little girl.

"She's better. She isn't out of the woods yet but they used the information you gave me to narrow it down to one thing. Apparently, Herb was sicker than they thought and it wasn't just lung cancer that killed him."

"What happens to her now?"

"They're doing surgery tomorrow to repair some of the damage, but the outlook is one hundred percent better than it was when I came to see you."

Doris felt tears well up in her eyes.

"Kevin, I'm so glad to hear that. I'll keep praying."

"Doris, here come the doctors. I need to go. Thank you for everything."

"Keep me updated."

Doris hung up the phone and peeked out the windows when she heard screeching tires across the street.

Hope ran into Gretchen's house and got Faith. She took her home and went to the bedroom. She sat Faith down and pulled out a suitcase from the closet. She turned to start filling it and Faith got up and went to her room to play, closing the door behind her. She pulled out her dolls and started playing, wondering why her mommy had taken her away from her cousins. She was having a good time. Hope walked into the bathroom to get some stuff and walked into a flood. The tub was full and overflowing onto the floor, flooding the hall. Hope shook her head, trying to dismiss what she was seeing. She walked out into the hall and stood in front of the hall mirror. Standing behind her was the woman she had seen earlier, the same woman from the paper, the same woman that killed herself and her children.

"Leave me alone, god damn you!"

Hope smashed the mirror to bits with her bare hands, slicing them to shreds. Faith, hearing her mother scream, tried to get out of her room, but the shut door would not budge. She started crying for her mommy. Unfortunately for her, Hope Boudreaux had slipped away from reality. She couldn't hear her daughter's screams, just the cries of the baby that had been taunting her for months. She put her hands over her ears and screamed. She had to do something; she had to stop it all. She ran to the garage and got the gasoline can from next to the lawnmower and started pouring. She covered the kitchen, the living room, and the bathroom. She had to stop the cries. She had to stop that brat from crying. She emptied the gasoline can between the three bedrooms and got a match from the bathroom. She struck the match and threw it on the bed, the bed she had shared with her husband, the bed they were using to try to have another baby. She went to the kitchen and set fire to the tower of chairs, still stacked on top of the table. The fire spread quickly, engulfing the living room and hall. Hope started to choke on the smoke and went outside. Seeing the bloody mess her hands had become, she fainted on the front lawn.

Doris had just turned on *Gulf States International* when she first smelled the smoke. If someone was burning trash, she was calling the cops. She looked out her window and was horrified when she saw the house across the street in flames. She was about to turn to the phone when she saw Faith through the window, banging to get out. She had been trapped in her room and couldn't get out. Doris began to panic. Someone had to know. Someone had to know she was trapped inside. That's when she saw Hope lying in the grass. She had to do something. Doris's only thought was to save the child and, despite being a prisoner in her own home for over fifteen years, she ran out her front door and grabbed two of the bricks that lined her walkway. She ran across the street and went to the window, hoping she was strong enough to break the glass. She threw one of the bricks and shattered one of the panes. As smoke came billowing out of the window, she could hear Faith screaming. She used the other brick to break the rest of the window and called out to the little girl, whose name she didn't even know. Doris leaned in and grabbed Faith, ripping her housecoat and cutting her arm in the process. She pulled her out of the window and collapsed in a fit of coughing. She heard the fire trucks coming and pulled Faith away from the fire. By this time, Mary had come out of the house.

"Doris, are you alright?"

"Mary, is she dead?"

Mary went to check on Hope who was unconscious but still alive. The paramedics took Hope into the ambulance as the fire fighters tried to control the blaze. Faith had since passed out and as Allen sped into the circle in his boss's car, he saw his daughter being loaded into an ambulance in front of his burning house. What had happened? What the hell had happened and where was Hope? He pulled into Ben and Gretchen's driveway and ran to his house. He was stopped by the firemen.

"I live here. Where's my wife?"

"She's been taken to Gulf States Memorial."

"My daughter?"

"They're with her now. You can go to the hospital with her."

"Is she alright?"

"That lady pulled her out."

He pointed at Doris and Allen couldn't believe his eyes. The paramedics had Doris wrapped in a blanked while they bandaged her arm. Mary tried to lighten the mood.

"You know Doris, this was a hell of away to decide to leave your house."

Doris smiled. Her smile faded when the paramedics tried to take her to the hospital.

"No. No. I just want to go back to my house. Can't I just go back to my house?"

"Ma'am, we need to bring you to the hospital and have you checked out."

"Is that necessary? Can't you do it from here?"

The EMT looked at Mary like she was crazy. Mary took him aside.

"She's agoraphobic. She hasn't left her house in fifteen years . She's scared to leave. Can't you do it here?"

"She had never left her house until..."

"She went to save the little girl."

"I guess we can make an exception."

The men followed Doris across the street where, once inside, she checked all the closets. She didn't want anyone sneaking in to hurt her while she left the door open. Satisfied that her house was safe, she was examined.

At the hospital, Allen sat as Faith woke up. Her lungs had been cleared and she was fine. She had minor burns on her arms and cuts on her legs where Doris, unable to get her through the window, pulled her across the broken glass. The fire had been put out, the entire home destroyed. The fire inspector came up to Allen.

"Mr. Boudreaux?"

"Yes?"

"I'm Mitchell Young, fire inspector. I know this is a bad time, but we're charging your wife with suspicion of arson."

"What?"

"You're not charging her with anything yet."

The doctor in charge walked up to Allen and Mitchell.

"Doctor, an accelerant was used to start the fire, probably gasoline. We found the can in the bedroom."

Allen couldn't believe what he was hearing. Had Hope tried to kill herself and Faith? The news didn't get better.

"Mr. Young, we're holding Mrs. Boudreaux for psychiatric evaluation."

"Psychiatric?"

"We don't believe she was in her right mind. She woke up screaming about how the house was trying to make her crazy and how she had to stop it. We had to restrain her."

"Well, we won't do anything until we get the report from your people."

Allen snapped back into reality when he heard his in-laws calling his name. Gretchen had gotten home and found out what happened from the babysitter. She and Ben had gone to tell Malcolm and Muriel. All four of them were there. All Allen could think about was the fact that probably all of them had known about the house before he and Hope had moved in, and said nothing.

"How's Faith? How's Hope?"

"Faith is fine, you can see her in a minute. Hope is in the psychiatric ward, sedated and restrained."

"Whatever for?"

Allen looked straight at his mother-in-law.

"She thinks the house tried to drive her crazy. It almost worked. She set fire to it with Faith still inside. Both of them could have died. If she isn't full blown crazy, they're going to arrest her for arson."

"I can't believe that."

"Can't you, Benjamin? You knew, you all knew what went on in that house and none of you said a damn thing. You knew about the woman killing her kids and about the boy before that."

"You're talking crazy, Allen."

"Go to hell, Malcolm! You never said anything and now all Hope and I worked to build is destroyed, my daughter was almost killed and my wife is crazy. Go to hell, all of you!"

Allen walked away, furious. He couldn't stop them from seeing Faith but he was sure as hell going to try.

"Jo Ann, you are missing all the drama."

Miranda was on the phone with Jo Ann while Oren made dinner.

"The girl at number six, you know Mary Sunshine's sister-in-law, burned her house down."

"I know. My mother called me earlier this afternoon."

"Did she tell you that her daughter was trapped inside and almost died?"

"Did she tell you that your friend, Doris, is the one that pulled her out?"

"What?"

"Yes. Doris ran out of her house, broke a window and saved Faith."

"I never heard that."

"Ask Doris. She's the big hero."

"I will."

"Can you talk right now?"

Miranda took the phone into the bedroom.

"I can now."

"How are things with you and Oren?"

Miranda smiled.

"I think they're going to get better. We talked a little today and went out for breakfast."

"What brought this on?"

"I'm pregnant."

Jo Ann couldn't believe her ears.

"What did you say?"

"You heard me."

"Is it..."

"Oren's? Of course it is."

"But you said you didn't..."

"Yea, well one day we got horny and rolled around like dogs in heat. Lo and behold, I got knocked up."

"What does he say?"

"He doesn't know yet."

"What?"

"I'm waiting for a few weeks to pass. I want to be sure nothing goes wrong."

"I understand that honey, but he has to know."

"Don't worry. He will. How's everything on your end? Any more kids? Any girls this time?"

"Not yet."

"Well, keep me posted. Oren's calling me. I have to go."

Miranda hung up the phone and went to have dinner. To her surprise, Oren had taken out the good china.

"I recall saying we were going to use these more often."

"Special occasion?"

"Actually, it is. I got a raise and a promotion at the motel the other day."

He didn't tell her it had been months or that he was saving money behind her back.

"What to?"

"General Manager."

"Oren, that's fantastic."

"Thank you."

She went and kissed him on the lips, lovingly.

"What was that for?"

"Nothing. New beginnings."

"I think we should toast to that."

Oren got two wine glasses off the shelf and poured wine for each of them. He handed her a glass and she hesitated.

"I guess I have news for you too. I was going to wait, but this toast is totally perfect timing."

"What is it?"

"I'm pregnant. I went to Dr. Hunter's and got it confirmed the other day."

"Pregnant?"

"After four years. Yes."

"Wow."

"I wasn't going to tell you just yet. I was going to be sure everything stayed okay. Dr. Hunter is worried I won't be able to carry the baby to term."

The news hit Oren like a ton of bricks. That would explain a lot. If there were problems with Miranda's reproductive system, that would explain why it was so hard for them to get pregnant.

"How do you feel about it?"

"The baby?"

Miranda nodded and Oren smiled broadly.

"I can't believe it. I'm thrilled."

"Really? I know that you and I..."

Oren kissed her lips softly.

"We have some things to work through."

Miranda nodded.

"A baby. All right!"

Oren picked up Miranda and swung her around before setting her down and holding her close. She closed her eyes and melted into her husband's strong arms, feeling safe in the fact that they could work through anything.

Genie was getting ready for bed when the phone rang. She sighed and picked it up, wondering who would be calling her this late.

"Hello?"

"Genie, it's Park. Are you watching the news?"

"Park, I've got enough news in my own neighborhood. Do you know the house next door to mine burned down?"

"No."

"Anyway, no I am not watching the news. I have to work early tomorrow."

"Fuck work! We won!"

"Won what?"

"The lotto. Genie, me, you and Nova hit the jackpot."

"Are you screwing around with me?"

"No. Nova and I were both watching the drawing. We're coming over."

"What?"

"Shut up, we're on our way!"

Before Genie could say anything, Park hung up the phone.

Chapter 33

The next morning, the three of them were in the city at the lotto office, waiting for it to open. The office opened and they went in.

"Can I help you?"

"Yes, ma'am, we have the winning numbers from last night."

Nova handed the lady the ticket as the three of them held their breaths as the numbers were verified.

"Congratulations. We have a match."

Genie couldn't believe her ears. Parker spoke up.

"How many other winners were there?"

The woman punched something into the computer, looked up and smiled.

"Just one, just your ticket."

"Holy shit."

"Let me go in the back and get the papers you have to sign."

The woman left them alone. Genie smiled.

"This is a lot more fun then the food stamp office."

"Ma'am what was the final jackpot?"

"Two hundred seven million. After taxed, you'll be getting one hundred eighty million. You need to decide if you're going to take the lump sum or the annual draft. If you take the check today, I can write each of you a separate check. I need to see your driver's licenses."

They handed their things over, practically jumping for joy.

"I can't believe we get sixty million each."

"We are definitely going to need a lawyer."

"I'll call Patrick."

Genie took out her cell phone as the others were finishing the paperwork.

"Pat, are you working today?"

"Yes."

"Well, clear your schedule. I'm coming over with some friends for some very important business."

The woman verified their information and handed each one of them a check.

"We need to get to Pat's office. I don't like having all this money on me at all."

The three of them drove to Pat's office and went straight in.

"Patrick, we all need lawyers."

"Did you three hit someone?"

"Better, we all won the lottery."

Pat couldn't believe what he was seeing as they all put their checks on his desk. He couldn't believe his mother was a millionaire.

"Sit down and I'll explain what we need to do."

All three of them sat down, wide eyes and anxious. They couldn't believe what was happening to them.

"Look at this."

Cameron passed a picture to Cora. He had just opened a letter from Colleen. The picture was of Colleen in her habit. Cora filled with pride as she looked at her daughter.

"What does she say?"

"She says she's getting along fine. It's not like summer camp. She says it's a lot of work and, of course, praying. She picked her name."

"I didn't think she did that till she took her final vows."

"Well, here it is. Mary Christopher."

Cameron laughed.

"Mary Chris for short. I guess that way, she doesn't offend either brother."

"What about her sister?"

"Well, there is no Saint Candice."

"Cameron, I am so happy for her, and so proud."

"Me too."

He leaned over and kissed Cora.

"Me, too."

"I'll act as the executor of your estates."

Pat was finishing up with his mother and her friends.

"Free of charge, of course."

He winked at Genie.

"I've got the bank accounts set up and everything else is taken care of."

Nova and Parker left the office. Genie stayed behind with her son.

"Mother, I can't believe you're a millionaire."

"Multi-millionaire, darling."

"What are you going to do with all that money?"

"Well, for one thing, little Geoff and any other child you and Melissa may have will never have to worry about college tuition. I'll take care of that."

"And Jeremy's kids."

Genie hesitated. She had inadvertently found out the truth about Jeremy a few months back, but was afraid to confront him with it. She had to confide in someone though.

"Actually, and I tell you this in the strictest of confidence, I don't think Jeremy is going to be having any kids."

"Why not?"

"Well…"

"You can confide in me, Mom."

"I found something a few months ago that suggest that Jeremy isn't interested…in women."

"Oh. Did he tell you anything?"

"No. He had my bank card in his desk and I went looking for it and I found what I found. He doesn't know that I know."

"Do you want me to talk to him?"

"Not about that, but…I doubt your father got around to talk to him about sex. I worry about that so much. Just talk to him about being…safe. He's eighteen years old and I'm sure he's no virgin, but…"

"I understand."

Patrick went around to his desk and sat down.

"That said, what are you going to do about your house?"

"Well, I'm not moving. I am in the mood for a little extreme makeover."

"You're not moving? After what happened to the house next door?"

"No, but I have something in mind that'll ensure nothing like that ever happens again. Can you help me?"

"I'm listening."

Pat listened to his mother's plans, a smile spreading across his face.

Allen walked down the halls of St. Matthew's Psychiatric Hospital with a pit in his stomach. Hope had been deemed unstable by the doctors and cleared of all arson charges. She had been moved to Saint Matthew's earlier that afternoon and had just met with the head doctor. Allen was meeting with Fr. West to outline her treatment plan. He and Faith had moved in with his parents, not having talked to Ben, Gretchen or his in-laws since the scene at the hospital. The events of the other day were still fresh in his mind and he wondered how Hope could have put herself and their daughter in such danger. He had read up on the history of the house and was horrified by it's past. He knocked on Fr. West's door and went inside.

"Allen, good to see you."

"You, too, Father. I haven't seen you since you left Mary's."

"Has it been that long?"

"Yes."

Allen sat down as David sat.

"I must say, I was shocked to see we admitted Hope."

"Has she said anything?"

"I talked to her earlier today. She still thinks the house tried to drive her crazy."

"Father, I'm not sure it didn't. I know the Catholic Church doesn't endorse supernatural or paranormal phenomenon, but I do think there was something evil in that house."

David nodded.

"We are a Catholic run facility, but we don't shut our eyes to any possibility. The hospital has already run all the medical tests and there's no sign of brain damage or any other medical contributing factor. I'm afraid this was purely psychological."

"So she is crazy?"

"She's not well."

Allen sat silent.

"How are you holding up? How's Faith?"

"She doesn't remember anything. She has a few cuts and burns, but that's all. I'm not doing well. I brushed Hope off numerous times. If I had just paid attention to her…"

"Would you like to talk to someone?"

"I don't think so."

"It might help."

"I'll let you know."

Allen got up. He wanted out of there.

"How long do you think Hope's treatment will last?"

"Weeks. Months. We'll be able to tell more once she starts to open up."

"Can I see her?"

"She's sleeping in her room, but you can go in for a moment."

David led Allen down a corridor that looked more like a hotel than a hospital. He opened the locked door from the outside and let Allen in to see his wife. Hope slept like an angel. David didn't tell him the staff had to sedate her again. David sat next to the bed and lovingly stroked her hair. He held her hand and lowered his head as tears ran down his face.

Chapter 34

Nine months later, the May sun shone down on Sherwood Circle for the dedication of the Geoffrey van Matthews Memorial Playground, located at number six Sherwood Circle. Genie had the house torn down and the ground leveled. Her first major purchase was the building of a professionally built playground. It was a place where all the neighborhood children could come and play. Right now, everyone on the circle had come out as the mayor dedicated it in front of three or four news crews. The story was a big one, a happy ending to the tragedy that had befallen the small community. Doris peeked out her window in time to see Kevin Ryan walking up her walkway. She opened the door and smiled.

"I had no idea you were in town."

"Well, I have someone for you to meet."

Kevin ushered his daughter to Doris's doorstep.

"Crissy, this is Mrs. Doris."

"Nice to meet you, Crissy."

"You, too, ma'am."

"Crissy, you go over and play in the park."

The little girl skipped across the street. Doris shook her head.

"Doris, she's all better. It took two surgeries and a lot of medication but she's one hundred percent cured."

"I'm so happy."

Doris hugged Kevin with tears in her eyes.

"Look at her over there playing."

"She may never have been able to if you hadn't helped me like you did."

"Well, whatever the relationship between Herb and your mother, I'm glad something good came of it."

Doris looked around.

"Is your wife here?"

"She's across the street. I heard about what happened at that house."

"It was horrible."

"I heard what you did."

"It was nothing."

"Bull."

Kevin held his hand out.

"Doris, I'd like you to meet my wife."

"Bring her here."

"Doris, all your neighbors are having a good time. Come with me and the moment you start to feel uncomfortable, I promise, I'll walk you back inside."

Doris hesitated, then waved to Miranda, nine months pregnant and waddling over to the park. She took a deep breath and tried to calm her stomach. She took Kevin's arm and the two of them walked across the street.

"I don't believe it."

"What?"

Mary pointed to Doris. Jo Ann's jaw dropped.

"Doris has a hot man and she's out of her house. I'll be damned."

Peter had little Pete on the merry go round. Chad was hanging around, trying to look as cool as a twelve year old can, talking to some girl. Jo Ann shook her head.

"Chad talking to girls. I am not ready for that."

"Speaking of girls, any process on the baby making? It's been a while now."

"No. Peter and I talked about it and we're fine with what we've got. Yours, mine and ours."

"Are you okay with that?"

"Yes ma'am. I am truly happy, just me and my boys."

Jo Ann took Mary by the arm and they went to talk to Doris who was talking to Miranda and Oren.

"She has one more year and then she'll take her final vows."

Cameron was showing everyone the latest picture of Colleen and filling everyone in on well she was doing. Genie smiled as she watched Geoff out the corner of her eye. She was happy for Cora and Cameron. All of their children were turning out to be something to be really proud of.

"Genie, I can't believe you haven't bought some big mansion by the lake?"

"Why not? I'm happy here. I do have the cabin in Maine and the condo in Palm Beach."

Genie laughed. She had done a bit of splurging and hadn't even scratched the surface of the sixty million.

"And you have this."

Cora motioned to the playground.

"Genie, I still think this is a remarkable thing that you did."

"Well, I wish I hadn't had the opportunity to do it. I wish Allen, Hope, and the baby were still living here."

"I know. I'm glad it's over though. Do you believe those stories about the house being haunted?"

"I'm not sure what I believe."

Jeremy walked up to Genie smiling. He had come out to her over Christmas and she had taken the news surprisingly well. She had never told him she already knew. She noticed someone in tow and, no matter how much she psyched herself up for this, she didn't know if she was ready.

"Mom, this is a friend of mine, Bradley."

Genie smiled.

"Nice to meet you, Bradley."

Genie shook hands with her son's gay lover.

"Jeremy, I have to get something out of the car. Will you excuse me? It was nice meeting you Mrs. Van Matthews."

"Same here, Bradley."

After he was gone, Genie spoke to her son.

"He seems nice. Where did you meet him?"

"Do you really want to know?"

"Not some sex club?"

"No, gross. Actually, I went to a club to see Parker do his drag show."

"I can't imagine."

"It's pretty crazy."

"I'll bet."

Genie had only seen Parker a few times since they won the lottery. The three of them had quit The Breakers. Parker was trying to take his act on the road. Nova was in L.A. going to stunt woman school.

"He's really nice."

"Honey, if he makes you happy, then I'm happy for you. Just don't take him for granted and be sure he knows how important he is to you. I think that's where your daddy and I messed up."

"God, Mom, we're not getting married."

"It's just sex, right?"

Genie's jaw dropped at the comment made by her older son. Patrick snuck up behind her, dressed in a suit.

"I like a man who dresses for the playground."

"Sorry, I'm late. Court ran longer than I expected. Is he ready to go home yet?"

Pat looked at Geoffrey, playing in the sandbox.

"Hardly."

"Well, I guess we can stay a bit longer. I need to get out of this suit."

"Go in the house and put something on of your brother's. Be careful when you dig through the drawers, though."

Patrick laughed and went next door inside his mother's house.

Ben and Tim York were busy playing on the see saw when their cousin Faith came running up to them.

"Faith, do you want to play in the sandbox?"

"Okay."

Gretchen couldn't believe her eyes. Across the street, a good distance from the crowd, sat Allen and Hope. Hope looked like she was hanging onto her husband for dear life.

"What are they doing here?"

"It's a public playground, Ben."

"I don't think it's good for Hope to be here."

Hope hadn't spoken to her brother since she had been released from St. Matthew's that winter.

"Should we talk to them and say hello?"

"No."

"Ben, she's your sister?"

"I want to talk to her, but she has to be ready."

"The problem is honey, she may never be ready."

Gretchen squeezed Ben's hand. She looked up at him and noticed tears in his eyes. Across the yard, Hope called out to Faith and the three of them left the playground without even acknowledging Gretchen or Benjamin.

The spring day was winding down and Sherwood Circle was returning to normal. Families ate, couples slept, peace came over the circle. One thing was for sure though; they had all better stay on guard. Because for the residents in the city of New Orleans, in the suburb of St. Bernard, in a subdivision called Nottingham, on a cul-de-sac called Sherwood Circle, peacefulness never lasts long.

Epilogue

Two weeks after the dedication, Miranda gave birth to a beautiful baby boy, Oren James Grant Jr. Oren flourished as General Manager of The Breakers Inn and, a few years later, went on to run the Hotel Bentley. He and Miranda stayed married. She was never able to get pregnant again, but they lived happily as a family with their little miracle.

Gretchen and Ben eventually moved out of St. Bernard for a promotion at Ben's company. They never talked to Allen or Hope again, a fact that tore Ben apart. He tried to remain in contact, but every letter was returned, unopened.

Doris began to venture out more and more. Her failing eyesight led her to ask Miranda to drive her to the doctor's. It was the first step in winning back her independence. She stayed in touch with Kevin and his family. She died peacefully in her sleep years later.

Jo Ann and Peter never had any more children. Chad became a teacher of all things, getting back all he gave out as a child. Mary stayed on Sherwood Circle until she died there, the subject of a nursing home never being brought up again. Jo Ann became active in St. Augustine's PTA and nobody ever called her white trash again.

Genie also stayed on Sherwood Circle, never having to work again in her life and never having to worry about the electricity being turned off. Jeremy eventually moved out and, although the relationship with Bradley didn't work out in the long run, moved in with a nice guy and built a lasting relationship with him. Melissa turned into a baby machine, having three more babies and filling Genie's house with grandchildren.

As for the Mayhelms, Cora and Cameron stayed happily married. Cora never did regain the use of her legs. Christopher took over his father's garage and continued the tradition of honest work at a fair price. One year after the dedication ceremony, Colleen took her final vows as Sister Mary Christopher and went to work as a staff psychologists at Saint Matthew's, working closely again with Father West. Among all of Cora and Cameron's children, Christian's future seemed to surprise everyone the most…

…the last passenger exited the Airbus A321 as the crew gathered their belongings. They were overnighting in the hotel before leaving for Chicago first thing in the morning.

"Chris, we'll meet you at the hotel."

"I'll be at the shuttle bus in a minute. Wait for me."

Chris walked into the cockpit, stepping aside for the first officer. He was alone with the captain when he finally spoke up.

"Do you want to have dinner tonight, in my room?"

"I thought we went through this."

"So that's it? We're finished because you say we are?"

"Look, we had a good time, but…"

"Damn Ted, why can't you be honest about who you are?"

Ted turned around with tears in his eyes.

"Chris, I have a wife and a family. And they can never know about us, about what went on between us."

"I cared for you."

"I cared for you too, but it's over."

Chris fought back the tears welling up in his own eyes.

"Well then, this is as good a time as ever to tell you. I took the trainers job. I'm moving to Dallas next month."

Ted shook his head slowly. He didn't realize how hard the news would hit him.

"I wish you wouldn't do that."

"You gave me no choice."

Chris walked off the plane, tears stinging his eyes. He wiped them away as the screen went blank. The audience in the Grand Ballroom of the Hotel Bentley Los Angeles erupted into applause as the presenters took the stage again, envelope in hand.

"And the winner for Best Actor in a Daytime Drama goes to…"

She opened the envelope as Christian waited with baited breath.

"…Christian Mayhem, *Gulf States International*."

Chris couldn't believe his ears. He had gone out to L.A. to try acting and had done several commercials and television pilots before landing a big part on the number one rated soap opera on television. He had played Chris Montgomery for four years and this was the first time he had even been nominated. He never expected to win. He got up, kissed his wife sitting next to him and went on stage. His family was cheering from the audience. His friends on Sherwood Circle were cheering him on from their living rooms, never having been prouder of one of their own.

The end!

Printed in the United States
72718LV00004BA/1-48

9 781424 148165